Under an African Sky

Under an African Sky

A NOVEL

ELENE CATRAKILIS

Under an African Sky: A Novel
Copyright © 2026 by Elene Catrakilis. All rights reserved.
Published by Belvedere House, Marietta, Georgia

Learn more at EleneCatrakilis.com.

Cover artwork by Chrysoula Argyros and Abe Mathabe.

Publisher's Cataloging-in-Publication
(Provided by Cassidy Cataloguing Services, Inc.)
Names: Catrakilis, Elene, author.
Title: Under an African sky : a novel / Elene Catrakilis.
Description: Marietta, Georgia : Belvedere House, [2026]
Identifiers: LCCN: 2025922840 | ISBN: 9798999173713 (paperback) | 9798999173720 (hardcover) | 9798999173706 (ebook) | 9798999173737 (audiobook)
Subjects: LCSH: Female friendship--South Africa--Fiction. | Greeks--South Africa--Fiction. | Housekeepers--South Africa--Fiction. | Mothers--South Africa--Fiction. | Forgiveness--Fiction. | South Africa--History--1961-1994--Fiction. | BISAC: FICTION / Historical / 20th Century / Post-World War II. | FICTION / World Literature / Africa / Southern Africa. | FICTION / Literary.
Classification: LCC: PS3603.A8977 U54 2026 | DDC: 813/.6--dc23

Without limiting the rights under copyright reserved above, no part of this publication may be reproduced, stored in or introduced into a retrieval system, or transmitted in any form or by any means (electronic, mechanical, photocopying, recording, or otherwise, whether now or hereafter known), without the prior written permission of both the copyright owner and the above publisher of this book, except by a reviewer who wishes to quote brief passages in connection with a review written for insertion in a magazine, newspaper, broadcast, website, blog, or other outlet in conformity with United States and International Fair Use or comparable guidelines to such copyright exceptions.

This is a work of fiction. While this novel includes references to actual historical events and public figures, these are mentioned only in passing and in a factual context. All characters and events depicted in the story are fictional, and any resemblance to actual persons, living or dead, is purely coincidental or used fictitiously.

Publication managed by AuthorImprints.com

To my parents who are always with me,
and to my husband and children who walk beside me
—this book is for you.

Of old You created me from nothing
and honored me with Your divine image.
But when I disobeyed Your commandment, O Lord,
You cast me down to the earth from where I was taken.
Lead me back again to Your likeness,
and renew my original beauty.
Grant me the homeland for which I long
and once again make me a citizen of Paradise.

—*Idiomelon* from the Orthodox Funeral Service,
translated from the Greek liturgical text

You won't find a new country, won't find another shore.
This city will always pursue you.

—C.P. Cavafy, "The City"

Contents

1. City of Gold 1
2. Room at the Back 18
3. The Morning After 43
4. A Blue Shawl 59
5. Not of the World 74
6. The African Clock 92
7. Two Steps Forward and One Back 115
8. The Wedding Day 129
9. The Sewing Basket 151
10. The Fafi Runner 178
11. A Small Gathering 191
12. The Uninvited 201
13. Holy Water 211
14. A Weeping Icon 227
15. The Hand of God 241
16. The Beloved Country 246
17. The Greek Birthday Song 253
18. A Time to Heal 263
19. A Second Chance 275
20. The Dance of Isaiah 282

    Epilogue 294

ONE
City of Gold
Sofia

Johannesburg, December 1989

Far away, at the southernmost end of Africa, lay a country where mountains graced coastal cities, where lions and elephants roamed free across savannah plains, where the soil was rich with diamonds and gold, and where immigrants had taken a chance on the hope of a better life. Yet many tears had fallen in this place. Back in the forties, the ruling party had passed laws that separated people by the color of their skin. This system had caused much suffering and now, even at the tail end of its life, apartheid lingered in the air, exhausting everyone.

Sofia Levantis lived in this divided country in a city built on a reef of gold. Two days before New Year's Eve, a time meant for celebration, Sofia sat in her car watching mourners gather for a funeral. Johannesburg's Greek community packed the courtyard of Saints Constantine and Helen. They had come to bury yet another victim of the rising crime. Even as Sofia stared at the bowed heads, the black clothes, she was certain of one thing: She would never allow her children to emigrate from South Africa like all the others who were leaving.

Despite this certainty, when she got out of the car, she admitted to herself: This is not normal. Three funerals in three months. She slammed the door harder than she'd intended. Heads turned in the nearby courtyard and she sensed the familiar scrutiny. She had never grown accustomed to those stares, admiration from men and envy from women. Quickly, she slipped on sunglasses, hiding her large eyes and the fine lines that deepened each time she thought about losing her children. Not ready to join the others, she lingered in the parking area. Hushed whispers floated across the street: "This should never have happened...," "Crime is out of hand...," "We must leave this country before it's too late." Stop, she wanted to shout and began pacing up and down. She'd left a country once. And once was enough. There was no need for the children to uproot themselves. Things would settle down.

Her gaze moved past the church and past the trees to the urban skyline. From a distance, Johannesburg looked like any other city with its concrete towers of steel and glass. But up close, it was a different sort of place, from the pyramids of golden dust circling the gold mines to the mauve light bathing the mansions and tree-lined streets during jacaranda season.

In the parking lot, a bored-looking guard directed cars to open spots. The sun glinted off a gun strapped to his holster. The gun wasn't unusual in a country on the brink of change. But armed guards at funerals—what next? Before she could consider this further, her feet slammed into something on the ground, the force of which nearly catapulted her into the air. She caught herself and stared down at a man curled up on a cardboard square stuck between two vehicles. One foot had slipped out of his temporary shelter. He looked small, but when he leaped up with a crazed look on his dark face, he seemed to double in size, and she sprang back. He shoved a can of coins under her nose, rattling it loudly. Breathing deeply, she dug into her purse. No loose coins. She pulled out a fifty and pressed the note into his skeletal hands.

"Are you sure?" he said.

She nodded.

"You're not from here," he declared, waving his windfall in the air as he sauntered away.

The security guard rushed over. "You're crazy," he said, face flushed and panting. "He'll waste that money on drink." He grabbed the makeshift bed and flung it after the homeless man. "Next time I catch you, I'll shoot!"

The man didn't look back.

"Leave him alone," she said.

"Wait till he returns to steal your car." His blue eyes bore into her. She held his stare until he walked away cursing, loud enough for her to hear.

"He's harmless," she shouted and walked away in the opposite direction. It was not worth getting into arguments with the likes of him. Back at her car, she unlocked the trunk. A fragrance of roses and lilies filtered upwards. The flower-studded cross had barely fit into the trunk. Could this really be for her son's best friend? In spite of the heat, she shivered. It could so easily have been one of her children. Over six feet tall, Alex had been at her house just last Saturday after the soccer match he and Dimitri had coached. Childhood friends. At one time she had even suggested Alex as a husband for Natalie. "Mom, he's like a brother," Natalie had insisted. Then that phone call in the middle of the night. A few minutes later, Dimitri had stood at their bedroom door: "Mom, Dad. Alex has been shot.

Armed robbery. He's gone. We've lost him." A brilliant young doctor, taken down before he'd even reached his prime.

Something made her look up. It may have been the way the sun's rays bounced off the golden cross crowning the church. Its brilliance was too much. She let her eyes rest on the dome. It seemed to her the familiar shape had been there forever, shimmering white and serene in a city trembling with fear and uncertainty. "There is more to this world than what the eye can see." Her father's words. She had spent many a Sunday listening to him chant, tilting her head upwards during the liturgy, staring at the sky-blue cupola of their village church. But Cyprus was a lifetime ago.

Her gaze moved back to the courtyard, overflowing with mourners. Grace's slim, dark figure towered above the others. Tall and regal, her maid was easy to spot. Years under apartheid had not robbed her of that quiet dignity. What would she ever do without her faithful companion and housekeeper?

She had sent Grace ahead to see if the church side door was open. Grace's full lips were pressed into a thin line and a frown creased her normally smooth brow as she made her way back.

"What happened?" Sofia asked.

"It's locked," Grace said. "I couldn't find the old man who looks after the church. I found Mr. Pappas. He refused to open the door. For security reasons." She rolled her eyes, and that was all Sofia needed.

"Typical Mike Pappas," Sofia scoffed "He'll never change, even if the rest of the country does." She had hoped they could slip inside quietly. But in a country where Blacks and whites were forced to live apart, Grace's presence would not go unnoticed at a white funeral. "No problem," Sofia decided. "You'll come with me through the narthex. You must say goodbye to Alex. Of all the friends who came to the house, he was your favorite."

"I don't want to cause trouble. I'll just wait outside," Grace said.

"No, you'll come with me," Sofia said. Grace's stubborn streak drove her crazy. She turned back to the trunk and tugged hard at the cross. It refused to budge.

"Let me help." Grace nudged her out of the way and Sofia ignored the arched eyebrows as Grace stared pointedly at her black stilettos. With a quick thrust, Grace lifted the cross and stood firm and steady in flat-soled shoes. "I'll carry this. It's not that heavy."

"Fine," Sofia said. There was no point in arguing with Grace when she assumed that tone. From the corner of her eye, a flicker of movement caught her attention. A small, stooped figure burrowed his way through the crowd.

"It's Michalis," Sofia said. Her heart swelled with affection. He would help them. Years ago, this man who never spoke a word turned up on the church steps and took it upon himself to care for the property. No one knew where he had come from nor how old he was. Over the years, priests had come and gone. But Michalis had served and survived them all, becoming as much a fixture of the church as the holy altar.

As he drew closer, Michalis circled his arms in the air. Guttural sounds came from his throat.

"He wants to open the side door," Sofia said, always able to understand him. "Thank you, Michalis. Don't worry. Grace will come with me. Through the front." She was itching to have a word with Mike Pappas. She'd had enough of that man and his attitude. "But if you could carry the cross for us, that would be a big help."

Michalis shrugged. He lifted the cross that was almost as big as himself from Grace's hands. His wiry arms were strong, and he took off like a man on a mission.

"We should also get moving," Sofia said.

"I'm ready," Grace said, with just a hint of hesitation.

Between the parking lot and the church entrance, the jacaranda tree poured a great purple cloud of blossoms over both sides of the fence. When Grace stopped near the tree and looked at her, Sofia said, "Good idea. Wait in the shade till it's time to go inside."

Sofia paused by the gates. So many people. Dark designer suits and black couture dresses everywhere. Like her, these immigrants had left Greece and Cyprus with very little except tons of ambition and determination. They'd succeeded beyond their wildest dreams in a foreign land, competing to own the most expensive cars and the biggest homes. Now, in the face of death, they all looked pale and stunned.

As she entered the courtyard, heads turned again. Once more, she adjusted her sunglasses and wove her way through the crowd without lingering in conversations. She'd learned not to trust people too easily. As they greeted her with "*Zoi se mas*," Life to us, she accepted their hugs, responded with quick kisses on their cheeks, and moved on, until she reached the edge of the square. From there, she scanned the courtyard in search of her husband's silver-gray hair. Nowhere to be seen. As usual, he would be late. In thirty years of marriage, she didn't think Nick had ever been on time for anything.

But she was more concerned about Natalie and Dimitri. Where were they? At any moment, the hearse would pass through the gate. A headache throbbed behind her eyes as she glanced at her watch. Could she really go ahead with Natalie's wedding in the aftermath of this funeral? The forty-day mourning period would barely have passed.

She became aware of a finger tapping her shoulder and turned to find Penny Apostolou's round face beaming at her. Sofia could not respond even with a forced smile. The two of them never agreed on anything at committee meetings.

"I'm sorry about last week," Penny said. "It was a misunderstanding. The board members explained everything to me afterwards."

She nodded grudgingly, not quite convinced of Penny's sincerity. As president of the philanthropic and education committees, she often received opposition for the charities she chose. Her choices were not always the same as those of the other board members. Not that their resistance influenced her decisions. "Those scholarship funds had always been earmarked for underprivileged Black children," Sofia said, trying to drill the point into Penny's skull. The sneaky attempt to steer the scholarship funds elsewhere had failed, but Sofia did not easily forget.

"I know. My mistake," Penny said.

"Right," Sofia said.

"I guess you'll have to postpone Natalie and Peter's wedding?" Penny continued. "Is the wedding before or after the forty-day mourning period?"

What? For a moment, Sofia was caught off guard. It was one thing to wrestle privately with a dilemma but quite another to have a busybody offering unwanted advice. Preparations for Natalie's wedding had consumed her for over a year.

After a long pause, she said, "Postponing would be a logistical nightmare." She wondered if Nick's secretary had mailed all the invitations. If so, she prayed that Penny's invitation would get lost.

"I hear you're not going to the cemetery?" Penny said.

Unbelievable. How did this woman know *everything*? Sofia glanced around, wondering how to escape from her.

"They say you're going straight to Maria's house to organize the food. Should I come? I'm sure you could use a helping hand."

The knot in Sofia's shoulder tightened. With Penny, there was always an ulterior motive.

"I can't go to the cemetery," Penny insisted. "My feet are already swollen from the heat." She raised her skirt. Plump legs strained against compression stockings. Her puffy feet spilled over the edges of pointy-toed shoes at least a size too small.

"Grace is helping me, but you're welcome to join us," Sofia said, unable to inject politeness or enthusiasm into her voice.

"You're so lucky, Sofia," Penny continued. "Your daughter found such a good Greek boy. All the mothers wanted Peter for a son-in-law. I heard he was given the award for Outstanding Achievement in Medicine at the Hellenic Banquet?"

Dear God, Sofia thought. The woman was back to Peter and Natalie again. A small blue eye, a *mati*, meant to deflect envious glances from others, glinted on a chain around Penny's neck. Of course it wouldn't occur to Penny that the blue eye was ineffective against envy lurking in the eyes of the person who wore the *mati*. Considering the way Penny was staring, all but burning holes through her, Penny could jinx the whole wedding.

Just ignore her, Sofia decided, scanning the horizon in desperation. She wished she'd gone with Natalie to the dress fitting, but the timing with the funeral was tight. Natalie had a hundred things on her mind. One distracted moment and a person could look up to find a gun pointed at their head. Like Alex.

At that moment Sofia saw Natalie's mane of dark hair. *Thank God.* Gosh, Natalie looked so thin. It had to be the wedding nerves. Her beautiful girl. Her easy child. She loved her so much. A much better daughter than she had ever been.

"Mom, are you alright?" Natalie said as she came up to Sofia and hugged her. "You look pale."

"I'm fine." She made big eyes at Natalie and inclined her head in Penny's direction. "Don't say anything about the bridal fitting," she whispered, straightening Natalie's collar and tucking a stray hair behind her ear. In the fullness of Natalie's mouth, the slanting cheekbones, and hazel-colored eyes, Sofia saw a mirror image of her younger self. She wanted this girl's life to be perfect.

"*Koukla mou*, my darling." Penny thrust her body between them and kissed Natalie on both cheeks. "This is such a sad day. Are you alone? Where's that good-looking fiancé of yours?"

"Peter is still at the hospital. Working. He'll come by the Dukas's house later to give his condolences," Natalie said.

"At least you're here," Penny said. "Such a lovely dress. You're so beautiful, even black looks good on you."

Sofia cringed as Penny's gaze drifted to Natalie's engagement ring and fixed on the diamond. She's probably assessing the carat size, Sofia thought.

"Dad's waiting for us," Natalie said, and pointed toward a circle of men standing with Nick.

"See you later, Penny," Sofia said. Relieved to escape, she linked her arm through Natalie's and quickly steered her away.

Nick must have been there the whole time. How had she not seen him? Nick's hands sliced through the air as he talked and the men listened, appearing enthralled by his every word. Restless energy spilled out of him. He could never be still, constantly driven by the tug for more. No one would guess from listening to Nick speak that he held no degrees. Only she knew that beneath the polished veneer and beautifully cut suits, a persistent fear that he was not good enough weighed on him—an anxiety that he would reveal himself to be an immigrant undeserving of his good fortune.

Nick looked up and met her gaze. His face lit up, and her irritation with Penny melted away. Nick was her safe haven. In the beginning, he had loved her first. But with time, she had caught up and loved him back.

As they drew closer to the men, Dr. Botoulas's voice could be heard. "We uprooted ourselves. We left fathers, mothers, brothers, and sisters to come here for a better life. Now we're burying our children. For what? Nothing is worth the lives of the children. Something must be done."

Here we go again. The never-ending discussion, Sofia thought. The group widened the circle as she and Natalie joined. They exchanged greetings and commiserations. Nick squeezed her hand and kissed Natalie before the men turned back to the political situation.

"Nick, can't *you* place pressure on the government to do something about this violence? You've hosted enough fundraisers for the new president," Johnny Poulos said.

"I wish I could," Nick said. "But De Klerk doesn't consult with me. He's in a tough spot. It's a case of damned if he does, damned if he doesn't. If he abolishes apartheid, the conservative Afrikaners will revolt and brand him a traitor. If he preserves apartheid, he won't be acting in the best interests of the Black majority, and again, the country will explode into a civil war."

"What do *you* think, Sofia?" someone else asked.

She wished the government had abolished those horrible laws a long time ago. The country would have been reconciled by now. But she wasn't going to get into that at a funeral. "Nick's right. It's a difficult situation," she said. Deep down, she was afraid. What if the country could not outrun its racist past?

"The children must get out while they can," Dr. Botoulas insisted.

No, for heaven's sake. She felt a rising panic. The doctor was old and worn down. It was not in the Greek DNA to give up.

"We'll become like gypsies," she said, trying to keep the defiance out of her voice. "We'll wander from one place to another, with no roots."

"No, the Greek never loses his roots," he insisted. "He takes his traditions and his faith with him, wherever he goes." Maybe the old man saw something she failed to see or didn't want to see. But the sad gleam in his eyes worried her, and she had no answers, so she turned to Natalie. "Let's go inside the church."

"Good idea," Nick said, waving them off with a flurry of his hand.

As Sofia and Natalie reached the steps by the exonarthex, Grace was already waiting for them. At the same time, Mike Pappas squeezed past the other mourners.

"Sofia, I'm so sorry," he said. "I didn't recognize Grace earlier. You know how I love Grace."

"Why not apologize to Grace? She's standing behind you."

Mike turned. "Grace, I'm so sorry. I always see you dressed in your pink uniform at Sofia's house. You look so different today."

"Maybe you've never really seen me," Grace said. Her defeated expression stole a little more hope from Sofia's heart. Mike's face flushed a deep shade of red. At least he had the decency to feel bad, Sofia thought, but she wasn't going to let him get away with it.

"Grace has served you at least thirty times at my home, Mike." She let that dangle in the air for a few seconds. "So I don't know what to say, except that we need to find seats." With that, she swept past him and ushered Grace and Natalie into the church.

As she stepped into the narthex, she breathed in the fragrance of incense, burnt rose petals, and melting beeswax, the familiar scents of her childhood, a time when her home was just a stone's throw from the village church, and the hymns and the incense from the early morning liturgies floated across the square and into the house, where she lay curled up in bed. Around her now, the church walls of Saints Constantine and Helen brimmed with the same iconography she had known back then, solemn faces and stories in shades of red, blue, and gold.

At the candle stand, she lit three candles. One for the boy who had died. One for Natalie. One for Dimitri. Please God, look after the children. An unexpected gust of wind blew through a side window. The flames jumped up and down and bent backwards. Quickly, she cupped a hand over the candles and watched the tiny flames rise again. She crossed herself and made space for Natalie.

Grace waited a few feet away, apart from everyone, beneath a row of icons lining the wall. Her eyes were large and somber, matching those of the saints above her head. She stood quietly, clutching the handle of a black purse Sofia had given her last Christmas.

"Let's go," Sofia whispered. Looking reluctant, Grace followed Natalie, then stopped as they entered the packed nave.

"Madam, I'm going to stand at the back of the church. It's better," Grace said, a determined tone in her voice. She then stepped away and pressed herself into a recessed nook against the back wall.

"Stubborn," Sofia muttered. Grace gave a small, painful smile that said I know what I'm doing. And Sofia knew there was nothing she could do except move along with Natalie.

The rows of gleaming mahogany pews had already filled with mourners. "Peter's parents are over there," Natalie whispered and pointed to her future in-laws.

Mark and Anna Economou sat on either end of the pew, guarding the empty space between them. Sofia liked Mark well enough, but Anna was a handful. Such a diva. Why on earth was she wearing that voluminous black skirt and ruffled blouse with wide sleeves? Always looking for attention. Even at a funeral.

Sofia slid into their pew, gave Anna a quick hug, and motioned to Natalie that she sit next to her future mother-in-law. The thing about in-laws was that you had to take the whole package, Sofia reminded herself. And Anna had raised an excellent son. She had to give credit where credit was due.

A sudden hush fell over the church as undertakers in dark, stiff suits positioned themselves at the nave entrance. Nick snuck into the pew behind them at the very last minute. "Keep the space next to you for Dimitri," he whispered over her shoulder, as if that would not have occurred to her.

A rustle of skirts and shoes broke the stillness as people stood, twisted, and turned. Sofia craned her neck above the crowded pews till her eyes found Dimitri's. Grim and somber, he stood at the head of the casket, clenching and unclenching his fists. A groan rose in her throat and she choked it back. He was too young to be escorting the body of a friend. His black suit made him look even more pale, and his contorted face struggled to control an expression she would never forget.

Father Christopher, swinging the censer back and forth on its golden rope chain, led the pallbearers into the church. The hand of the old priest trembled, and he looked shaky on his feet. Where did he find the strength, Sofia wondered, to keep doing this?

Steve and Maria Dukas followed their son's casket. They stumbled down the aisle, holding on to each other. The living dead, Sofia thought. It wasn't normal for parents to bury their children. What was the point of their lives now? All their dreams and hopes would be buried with their son. She crossed herself furiously. Please, God, protect everyone's sons and daughters.

The pallbearers reached the white, marbled solea spilling over with flowers. The white cross she had brought dominated the space. As Sofia watched six pairs of black shoes edge carefully up a single step, she bit her bottom lip. Strong, young hands heaved their friend's casket and lowered it onto a steel stand. Alex's mother let out an agonizing howl that ripped through the church, tearing at Sofia's heart. She tightened her grip on the front pew.

Trembling, Dimitri staggered back to the pews and slipped in beside her. A sheen of perspiration and tears glistened on his cheeks. Nick squeezed his shoulder from behind.

And then. "I'm leaving this country," Dimitri whispered, staring straight ahead, as if he were addressing an invisible person rather than her or Nick.

"What?"

"You heard me. I'm finished with this place."

Sofia collapsed onto the bench. Her worst nightmare. Another wail tore through the church, and she realized it was not coming from Alex's mother. It had come from *her* mouth.

"Are you alright?" Nick leaned over.

"I have to sit." There was always one child who drove a parent crazy. She felt curious eyes on her. She sat up straight and pulled her body to the edge of the bench, focusing on the icon stand that stretched across the width of the solea. She let her eyes rest on the Sweet-Kissing icon, depicting the Mother of God holding the Christ Child on her lap. A small baby Jesus stretched a tiny hand toward His Mother's cheek. Sofia blinked back a few tears. Even the Mother of God had cried for her Son at one point in history.

She felt herself trembling and looked up at Dimitri. When he tightened his jaw like that, she knew there was no going back. Dear God. She had left a widowed mother once. Was this her punishment? Her son would leave her, too?

She thought about his clever jokes that made her cry tears of laughter, his speeding fines that made her cringe, his mismatched socks that drove her crazy, and the unsuitable women who chased him. And she knew without a doubt that she could not live without seeing him every day. She looked up into the mosaic eyes of Christ staring down from the heavenly blue dome just as Maria Dukas's cries filled the church again, floating upwards, touching Christ, before echoing down, full of emptiness.

Natalie nudged her. "Mom, are you okay?" Everyone else was standing. She stood up too quickly and the dome spun in a blur of angels around Christ's face. Again, she clutched the front pew as the ancient words of the chanter's funeral hymn filtered through the church:

Of old you created me from nothing and honored me with Your divine image. But when I disobeyed your commandment, O Lord, you cast me down to the earth from where I was taken. Lead me back again to your likeness, and renew my original beauty. Grant me the homeland for which I long and once again make me a citizen of Paradise.

Where was this homeland? She had learnt this hymn at her father's side all those Sundays when she'd clutched his hand as they'd walked to church, so proud to be the chanter's daughter. And the words rose easily from her heart to her lips. Every time she heard this hymn, distant memories of something familiar stirred within her, like a dream slipping away just before waking, leaving her desperate with longing. For what, she didn't know. There were moments when she who had everything, who should have been content, felt a stab of loneliness so deep and excruciating that it left her breathless.

The undertakers carried the flowers, the wreaths, and the cross down the aisle again. Thankfully, there were no eulogies. No one was in a state to speak or listen. She made her way out but kept looking back at Dimitri. He stood beside his friend's casket, unmoving, avoiding her eyes. *Look at me. I cannot live without you.* He continued to stare straight ahead.

Natalie and Nick had also disappeared into the crowd. But she could see Grace standing beneath the shade of the jacaranda's great purple cloud of blossoms. Grace stood on the other side of the fence, her round face pressed against the iron bars. Sofia pushed her arm through the rails and squeezed her hand. Grace squeezed back.

The bell tolled and Father Christopher escorted the coffin and the pallbearers to the waiting hearse. He continued to cense while Dimitri and the others pushed their friend's casket into the black limousine for one last ride.

Feathery wisps of gray smoke spiraled from Father Christopher's censer, hovering in the air for a few seconds before vanishing upwards with his prayers, *"Kirie Eleison, Kirie Eleison,"* Lord, have mercy. Above, the vast presence of the African sky screamed of God's glory, and in the courtyard below, Alex's mother whispered, "Why?"

A breeze rustled through the trees, scattering blossoms over Sofia's head. She bent to cup a handful of petals from the purple carpet at her feet, but when she stood up, the petals slipped through her fingers. Sofia was no longer certain of anything.

TWO

Room at the Back

Grace

As Grace brushed away the jacaranda blossoms from her jacket and eased into the back seat of Sofia's car, Sofia whispered from the front. "Grace, don't say anything when Mrs. Penny gets into the car, but Dimitri told me he wants to leave South Africa."

"What?" Grace let out a long sigh. This was not good. "Don't worry, Madam. You know how Dimitri overreacts. He doesn't mean it."

Sofia looked unconvinced but nodded toward Mrs. Penny, who came waddling down the path. "Not a word in front of her."

Mrs. Penny clambered into the front seat. "Grace, you don't mind sitting in the back?" she asked.

"No, I'm fine, Madam." She fastened her seatbelt and was relieved to be in the back seat. At best, Sofia was a terrible driver. She hammered the gears and accelerated way too fast on sharp corners. Now with Dimitri's plans to emigrate and the unwelcome passenger, Grace knew it was going to be a rough ride.

Her body swung left, then right, as Sofia veered onto the highway, swerving to dodge a huge truck. Worse than usual, Grace thought. Why couldn't Dimitri have waited till after the funeral to tell his mother something like that?

She clutched the seat edge and peered at the dashboard clock in front. Almost two o'clock. Isaac would begin writing his exam at any minute. If he failed one more time, she didn't know what she would do with him. All she wanted was for her son to get a degree. Was that too much to ask? She'd sacrificed so much for him. And she could not have done it without Sofia. If Master Nick ever found out that Sofia had secretly paid for Isaac's private tutor, he'd hit the roof.

Sofia slammed the brake pedal again to avoid a car in front and Grace lurched forward, clutching the seatbelt that dug into her chest. If only Mrs. Penny would shut up, then Sofia could focus. She leaned forward and tried to hear what they were saying. Of course, Mrs. Penny was speaking in Greek, thinking that she would not be able to understand. But after so many years with the Levantis family, Grace had picked up the language and could follow most conversations.

"Dimitri must be devastated. He and Alex were such good friends. The country is going to hell. Everyone's leaving," Mrs. Penny was saying.

Grace watched for Sofia's reaction, but Sofia remained quiet and kept her eyes on the road.

"Only God knows what will happen. Many young people have already left," Mrs. Penny continued.

Sofia's hands tightened on the steering wheel.

"Sofia, is Dimitri seeing anyone?"

"No."

"I have a niece staying with me. I'd love to introduce them." Grace inched forward.

"Do I know her?" Sofia asked.

Grace was intrigued.

"No, she's from Cape Town. She's my brother's daughter. She graduated from the university there but moved to Johannesburg because she got a job at a law firm here."

"Is she pretty?"

"She's gorgeous. When she was eighteen, she took second place in Cape Town's Miss Greece competition."

That can't be right, Grace thought. She had seen Mrs. Penny's brother and his wife. They did not resemble Greek gods. It was not possible that they could produce a goddess. What on earth was Sofia thinking?

"How old is she?" Sofia said.

"Twenty-four. She might come by the Dukas house after work today."

"You should bring her to Natalie's wedding," Sofia said. "Since she's staying at your house, it would be rude not to bring her."

What? Sofia guarded that guest list like a tiger. She had even shouted at Master Nick the other day when he wanted to invite one more guest. This made no sense unless Sofia was thinking a girl might keep Dimitri in the country. That's what this was about! But it was not going to work. She remembered seeing this girl a few years ago. A Christmas party at Sofia's house. Mousy looking. Not Dimitri's type at all.

"Oh, how kind!" Mrs. Penny's voice was ecstatic. "She's beautiful and so intelligent, and of course, she comes from a good family. Dimitri is going to love her."

No, he's not. Grace wanted to warn Sofia and tried to catch her eye in the rearview mirror, but Sofia ignored her, so she gave up and sat back, shaking her head. She had seen Dimitri's girlfriends over the years. Most of them looked like models—tall, blonde, and beautiful. This girl did not match his criteria.

Before long, they pulled up to the driveway of the Dukas's home. Sofia pointed a sensor at the electric gates. The gates remained shut and the walls on either side towered above them.

This was not good. They were parked in the driveway where Alex had been killed. Grace looked around, half-expecting to see thugs loitering in the street. Reluctantly, she offered to get out and see why the gates were not opening.

Before she approached the gates, two large Alsatian dogs sprinted across the lawn. She froze. Dogs frightened her. She watched as they thrust their black noses through the iron bars. Only the gates stood between her and them. Shut up, she wanted to shout. They barked like mad things and she moved backwards. They were almost the size of horses. She was a small child again, back in the Black townships. Police with search dogs had descended on the homes at night, scouring the streets, kicking down flimsy doors, and arresting innocent people for unnamed crimes. Everywhere there was screaming and shouting. And in the chaos, her father's calm voice, "Stay down. Don't move. Be quiet."

Mrs. Penny's angry voice broke through the noise. The woman climbed out of the car. She barely reached Grace's shoulders, but she waved those tiny fists and cursed at the dogs in Greek, using words even she had not heard before. The dogs barked even louder.

And then she surprised herself. "*Voetsak!*" she shouted. The Afrikaans expletive rolled off her tongue. The dogs stopped. In the stunned silence, she wiped tears from her cheeks. Where had that word come from? Then she remembered. There had been times in the past when she'd been cursed with that same word. "Voetsak." Go away.

"Look at that," Mrs. Penny said. "They understand Afrikaans." She also switched to Afrikaans. *"Bliksem and Donder,"* thunder and lightning, she shouted in her thick Greek accent. That's how hard Mrs. Penny threatened to hit the monsters if they didn't shut up. Then Sofia added to the commotion, honking the car horn over and over.

The Dukas maids came running down the path, huffing and puffing. It's about time, Grace thought. She saw that Polina and Fransina also wore black dresses beneath their aprons. Polina grabbed the dog collars, yanked the animals back, and clipped leashes around their necks. Fransina flipped a manual switch by the wall and the gates rolled open for the car.

"I'll wait here till you've locked up the dogs," Grace said.

"Don't be afraid. They always bark at visitors," Polina said, pulling the huge animals back as they lunged forward.

Fransina took the dogs from Polina and led the monsters to another iron gate that separated the backyard from the front. Only then did she feel her heartbeat slow down a little.

She hadn't seen Polina in a while and they hugged. They talked about the tragedy that had befallen the Dukas family, and when Fransina returned, they went through the whole story again, as if repetition might peel away some of the horror.

"We wanted to go to the funeral," Polina said, her voice sorrowful. "But our Madam needed us here, so we had to stay home. How was the funeral service?"

"It was so sad. There were hundreds of people. All the Greeks of Johannesburg had gathered. Everyone was crying." She told them whatever she could remember, trying to connect them to the boy whom they'd minded and played with and taken care of over the years. She told them who had attended, who had carried the casket, and who had cried the most. They dabbed at their eyes with the back of their hands. "How much longer can we suffer the curse of this land?" Polina said.

Sofia's voice interrupted, sharp and impatient, "Grace, ladies, please." She was already inside the house, sleeves rolled up as she leaned through the open kitchen window. "There will be time for socializing later. The people will be arriving at any minute. I need those boxes from the car so I can start warming things in the oven. Now."

Grace cringed. Sofia had a manner that rubbed people the wrong way. And she was even more abrupt when she had her own worries.

Fransina made a scornful clucking sound and Polina muttered something inaudible under her breath.

"She's not the way she sounds," Grace said. "The funeral upset her."

"She *is* like that," Fransina insisted. "I heard the other Greek ladies talking about her one day. She likes things to be done her way. It's because she has a lot of money, they say."

"I've lived with her for thirty years. I know her better than those ladies," Grace said.

Polina and Fransina looked at each other, and then at her as if she were the crazy one.

Enough was enough, Grace decided. She had work to do and opened the trunk. The aroma of freshly baked *spanakopita* pies and leftover flower fragrance drifted upwards. She handed them a few boxes and took the remaining ones.

She didn't care what they thought, she told herself. They trudged up the driveway, arms stacked high with boxes, and then she stopped just before they entered the kitchen. She *did* care what they thought. Against her better judgment, she said, "I want to tell you a short story quickly." The other two looked at her with eager eyes, obviously happy to ignore Sofia.

"One time," she began, "when Isaac was still a baby, he was burning with fever. Sofia called a white doctor in the middle of the night. She pretended Dimitri was sick and insisted that the doctor come to the house. When the doctor arrived, I'll never forget the look on his face as she led him to *my* room at the back and presented him with a Black baby. But he did his job and examined my boy. He gave him good medicine. By morning my Isaac was sleeping peacefully. *That's* the Sofia I know." A cold shiver went down her spine as she finished the story. *She might have lost Isaac that night.*

"Wow," Polina said. "If it were not you telling us the story, Grace, it would be hard to believe." Fransina nodded, looking suitably impressed.

She felt rather pleased with herself until they walked into the kitchen, and Sofia began barking instructions before they had even put down the boxes. "Where have you been? I'm waiting for you." Her voice was sharper this time. "Polina, wipe the inside rims of the glasses on the buffet table. Fransina, unpack the pastry boxes and stack the platters over there."

Grace gritted her teeth. Sofia had gone and undone all her efforts. The softened expressions on Polina and Fransina's faces hardened again.

"Now. Not later," Sofia said, waving her arms in the air. And when she stormed off, they looked at Grace as if to say, *Really*?

She was now tired of mediating. It hadn't worked. "I need to use the bathroom," she said.

Polina pointed to the maids' quarters on the other side of the yard, and she was tempted to tell them that at Sofia's house she did not have to use a separate bathroom. But she kept quiet and marched across the lawn. In the homes of Sofia's friends, she knew her place and would never create an issue. Things were about to change in the country. She had been patient her whole life. She could be patient a little longer.

She used the separate bathroom, washed her hands, and headed back to the main house. Unlike the other maids, she didn't need directions for what she was supposed to do. She and Sofia had been together for so long that they understood one another without the need for words. From the moment Sofia had looked at the tiles, Grace knew. The tiles were not clean enough for Sofia. Or for her.

In the laundry room, tucked behind the kitchen, she put on her apron and sat down for a minute to swap out her good black shoes. She squeezed her swollen feet into the Nikes. The sneakers had a thick sole, and Alex had told her this would help her plantar fasciitis. He would have been such a good doctor. The boy had studied ten years to get that degree. What a waste. She thought of Isaac. He had been studying for five years. She looked up trying to find a wall clock. How far was Isaac into writing his exam? Was he remembering his work? Her eyes spotted a white doctor's coat hanging from a hook. She let out a soft cry and jumped up. Had Alex worn that white coat even once?

She grabbed a bucket and mop and headed to the small scullery, where she filled the bucket with soap and water. She watched the bubbles rise to the surface. All she wanted for Isaac, and Dimitri, and all the children of this country, was a better life in the new South Africa. Instead, they had buried one boy, another one wanted to leave the country, and then there was Isaac. Deep down she feared Isaac might not be able to pull it off. She remembered his pained expression when he was home on study leave. He was not a true learner. He hated studying and hadn't looked well-prepared as he'd pored over his textbooks. Of course, if he worried about his exams half as much as she did, he'd be fine. If only he wanted the degree as badly as she did.

She gave the mophead a tight squeeze before lifting it onto the tiles. The mop squished softly as she slid it back and forth. If Isaac failed again, she might wring his neck. She squeezed the cotton strings tighter, twisting out more and more water.

Just as she finished, a familiar voice trailed down the passage. It was Mrs. Penny. The woman never stopped talking. She wouldn't be surprised if Mrs. Penny talked in her sleep.

"Grace is so intelligent for a maid," Mrs. Penny was saying as she and Sofia rounded the corner. "She knows exactly what to do without anyone telling her."

For a maid, Grace bristled. She felt like shoving the mop into the woman's mouth. In the past, she was more forgiving of unintentional stupidities, but it seemed to her that the older she got, the less she was able to absorb blows.

Sofia caught her eye and tapped her left ear. It was one of their secret codes. *Mou ephage ta aftia*. She is eating my ears. In English, it sounded silly, but in Greek, it was perfect. It almost made her smile and she nodded back at Sofia. It was going to be a long afternoon, for sure.

~

Soon, cars were pulling into the driveway, doors slammed, and the dogs began barking again. Grace watched as Mr. and Mrs. Dukas stood in the doorway of their kitchen looking lost, as if they were in somebody else's house, unsure where to go or what to do next. Their black clothes hung loosely from their shoulders, and their faces were whiter than the tiles she'd just mopped. That was the thing about suffering, she thought.

It looked the same on everyone. Young or old, rich or poor, black or white. Pain was pain. It broke everyone.

Sofia eased off their jackets and handed them to Grace. Grace watched, feeling helpless as Sofia led the two bewildered parents into their own sitting room.

"I'll bring them a cup of tea," she called after Sofia. Yes, Sofia nodded.

When she returned with the tea, Mr. Dukas looked up with a dazed expression. His face looked so old and tired, his voice barely a whisper. She leaned down to catch his words. "Can I have a stiff whiskey, please?"

"Of course." She wasn't sure what a stiff whiskey was. But she went to the bar and poured a double shot into a crystal glass as if she knew exactly what she was doing. She didn't add water or ice. That should keep it stiff. She returned to the grief-stricken father and placed it in his trembling hands. He gulped it down in one swallow. "I'll get you another one," she said and took the glass. She must have done it right.

In a short time, the house began to overflow with people. She watched as mourners trooped in from the cemetery and small clumps of red soil marked the freshly mopped tiles. Too bad. She was not going to mop again.

Instead, she picked up a tray and weaved her way into the dining and living rooms, collecting empty glasses and plates and keeping an eye on the wall clock. For sure, she would not make it home in time to catch Isaac's phone call.

All around her, people were quiet. As they nibbled on fish and sipped cognac and whiskey or tea and coffee, she noticed that the trauma of the burial seemed to fade. The conversation grew louder, and people turned to the topic on everyone's mind: What was going to happen in the new South Africa? In a room full of Greeks, everyone had an opinion. And she knew from experience that all the opinions would be different.

"I'm telling you," Costa Pappas said, "De Klerk had better not make the mistake of releasing Mandela."

Was he being serious? From the corner of her eye, she watched Costa. He was a small man with a protruding stomach and a bald head. Small in every way, especially the mind, she concluded as she listened to his stupid theories with growing irritation.

"De Klerk has already released those other terrorists. If he releases Mandela too, there's going to be a bloodbath. The Blacks will take over the country and it will go to hell. They have no idea how to run a country. And there'll be nowhere for us to run—except the ocean. Or worse, back to Greece and Cyprus."

There was a stunned silence. The others stared at him curiously. Were they embarrassed because she was standing here? Or were they afraid that they would be run into the ocean or back to their homeland? Or maybe they believed that the Blacks would not be able to run the country? Or all of the above?

Costa laughed until he realized nobody else was laughing. He gave a nervous giggle when he noticed her. She held out the tray for him. Her hands shook and the glasses trembled.

"Sorry, Grace," he stammered, placing his glass on the tray. "I didn't see you."

That's the thing about being invisible, she wanted to say. But she kept quiet.

"Obviously, I wasn't talking about you," he continued. "You're not like those other Blacks who riot in the streets. I'm talking about the *tsotsis*, the thugs, causing havoc with their bombings and strikes and killing innocent people."

She gave him the vacant stare she had perfected for people like him, but then something odd happened. It was as if a little wire suddenly snapped inside her head, and she no longer had control over herself. She gripped the tray. "Sir, it's got nothing to do with either *those* Blacks or *this* one standing in front of you. It's not about *Black* or *white*. It doesn't matter if we're Black or white, rich or poor. We're all people and we're all the same on the inside. Everyone deserves to be treated with respect."

"Of course, I didn't mean you, Grace," he tried again.

"So, here's the way it is," she said, ignoring his reasoning. "Mr. de Klerk has no choice in the matter. He has to free Mandela, whether he likes it or not. Any day now, *my* country will become a free nation. And if my son manages to finish his studies and pass his exams and become a lawyer, he will take his place in the new South Africa, the country of his birth. My homeland. And that of my father. And of my father's father."

There was another stunned silence, even louder than the first one. She had no idea what had come over her. Part of her was saying shut up, but the other part raged on.

"It's your homeland, too," she said. "But it's your *second* homeland."

"Grace, why don't you and the other ladies take a short tea break." Sofia's voice interrupted. She hadn't seen Sofia approach from the other side of the room.

"Okay, Madam." She trudged back to the kitchen and slammed down the tray at the kitchen sink. She took a couple of deep breaths and looked out the window. How did people end up becoming like that man?

His words stung. They landed on her heart, pinching into her, hurting more than if someone had taken the barbed wire glinting on the fence outside and pushed it into her.

She felt a soft touch. Sofia squeezed her shoulder and whispered in her ear. "He's a silly old man. Don't listen to him. Take a break. We'll go home soon."

"Yes, thank you, Madam. I don't know what came over me. I'm not usually so sensitive. But no wonder Dimitri wants to leave the country when there are people like him around."

"It's been a rough day."

When Sofia returned to the living room, Polina came up beside her. "What does your boss say now? Does she give us permission to drink tea at our own Madam's house?"

Ugh, she thought, tempted to hurl the tray at Polina since she had missed the opportunity to throw it at Costa. She'd had enough of silly people for one day. She wasn't sure who was worse: Costa or Polina. If they were at her Madam's house, they wouldn't be drinking and eating out of *separate* cups and plates or using *separate* toilets. She wanted to tell this to Polina, but she had no more energy left. And what was the point of making Polina feel as bad as she did? Polina and Fransina had made up their minds about Sofia anyway, and she was wasting her breath to convince them otherwise. Best to let it go. So she piled extra spanakopites, *tiropites*, olives, cheese, and *koulourakia* onto a plate while Fransina poured boiling water into a scratched metal teapot.

She carried the tray with their *separate* crockery and *separate* utensils to the table, away from everyone else, under the trees in the backyard. They spread out the small feast, and she told herself not to mind the steel mugs that most white households reserved for the use of their Black staff. Instead, she heaped lots of sugar and poured plenty of milk into each mug. Sweetness helped the bitterness go down. It was actually true, and she wondered where she'd read that because she felt better as she swallowed the tea. They ate and drank in silence.

Polina was the first to speak. "Do you believe things will change for us, Grace? After De Klerk releases Mandela?" There was an edge of desperation in her voice.

For a long time, she didn't say anything. She thought about the boy they had buried. She thought about Dimitri wanting to leave. She thought about Costa and his dumb theories. But most of all, she thought about Isaac.

"Grace?" Polina prodded.

"Yes," she finally answered. What would be the point of all this without hope? Why would she put up with all the hurtful things if she didn't believe that one day things would improve. "It will take time. Remember, a few years ago we couldn't even walk around Johannesburg without those passbooks." She shivered at the humiliating memory of the identity documents that dictated where Black South Africans could exist after dark. "We had to carry those things everywhere. All the time."

"That *dompas*—the stupid passbook," Fransina said, spitting out the words. "After work hours they made us become foreigners in the white cities. One time I forgot mine and I was out after curfew. A policeman refused to believe I had one at my Madam's home. He threw me into the back of a police van with a bunch of criminals. Can you believe that? Me, in the back of a truck with criminals? My Madam's husband had to bail me out at the police station. I will never forget this. I was so ashamed."

"Our children will have better lives," Grace said. "If we don't believe this, then there's no point in carrying on."

"*Your* son will be okay. We heard that the Levantis family is paying for his tuition," Polina said. "Is this true?"

She sat bolt upright. How did they know everything? Somehow, between the maids and the madams, nothing stayed a secret.

"He is studying very hard to pass his exams," she said. "My Madam and her family help with the fees." She hoped this last bit sounded vague.

"Soon, Isaac is going to be a somebody in the new South Africa, mixing with lawyers and judges," Polina said, not without a tinge of envy in her voice. "He'll set up a law practice with Sofia's son while my son is still running wild in the streets."

If only she knew that Sofia's son was thinking of fleeing the country, Grace thought.

"I think it's a waste of time and money," Fransina chimed in. "All that studying. They should just give him the money."

"If they give him money, at some point it will run out. Then what?" Grace said, although she suspected that Isaac would agree with Fransina, which irritated her even more. "We have spent our lives cleaning other people's houses, scrubbing other people's toilets, and washing other people's clothes. Surely, we want something better for our children."

"At least the Levantis family pays you well," Polina said. "How did you get a job with *them*?"

Grace ignored the subtle inquiry about her salary. It was none of their business. "I was lucky," she said. "My father was a chauffeur for an old Jewish man, Mr. Goldberg. This man was a friend of Mr. Levantis. One day my father overheard the two men talking about Mrs. Sofia needing help with a newborn baby. My father asked Mr. Goldberg if he would put in a good word for me. And he did that favor for my father."

"And they took you just like that?" Polina said.

"Yes, Mr. Goldberg was a lawyer who did a lot of work for Mr. Levantis. They trusted each other. I turned up on the doorstep of the biggest house I'd ever seen. I rang the doorbell, and the most beautiful woman I'd ever seen came to the door. Mrs. Sofia was even more beautiful when she was younger."

"Yes," Polina said. "That is true. The Greek ladies always talked about this."

"Anyway, Isaac was screaming his head off," Grace said. "Mrs. Sofia unknotted the blanket holding the baby on my back and pulled him out. I'll never forget the way she held him. I'd never seen a white woman hold a Black baby like that before. And the minute she took him, he stopped crying. I couldn't believe it."

"Maybe she's not that bad," Polina said.

"No, she's not bad. She took me to the cot where Dimitri was also crying. The minute I picked him up, *he* stopped. Mrs. Sofia and I stood there laughing and crying, holding our babies. That's when she asked if I'd like to work for her."

"You're lucky with her, Grace. But I agree with Fransina. All that book learning is a waste. I mean, it's white people's books and white people's ideas."

"That's the only way you can get inside another person's head. By reading what they write," Grace said. Even she could hear that her voice was a little loud, so she toned it down. "How are we going to understand them if we don't get inside their heads?"

"You always liked reading," Polina said. "How did you learn to read? You don't have a higher education than me. Standard three?"

"Again, my father," Grace said. "Not that he knew much, but he insisted I try. He'd bring me books from Mr. Goldberg's children. And he tried to teach me from the little he knew."

The other two looked at her in silence, and Grace was not sure she had convinced them.

"It's the only way out," she said, more to herself than her companions. "Reading and understanding is the only way out."

As they sat outside a little longer, the wind rustled the long, thin branches of the weeping willow, making a soft swishing sound as it passed through the trees. Across the lawn, the verandah of the main house was visible. She saw that the men and women had separated, the way the Greeks usually did at such gatherings. Most of the men had moved outside while the women remained inside. The men spoke in low voices, but she could feel their anxious fear and terrible sadness stretch across the lawn. It made her heart sore.

Everyone had their sorrows and their worries, she thought and stood up. She began collecting the mugs and plates and placed them back onto the tray. "We should go inside," she said. Her friends did not seem to be in a hurry to get back to work, but they also stood and gathered the remaining utensils.

Back inside the kitchen, she rinsed, stacked, and piled plates into the dishwasher. The rhythm of mindless tasks always soothed her. She listened to snippets of conversation from the ladies sipping their tea at the kitchen island.

Again, the voice of Mrs. Penny filtered through. "Sofia, I want to introduce you to my niece, Thalia Georgiou, my brother's daughter."

She put down the dishes and wiped her hands on her apron. *This was interesting.* The girl had to be the one Mrs. Penny had talked about in the car.

No, this is not going to work, she decided as she assessed the situation. For one thing, the girl was dark-haired with curly hair pulled back in a bun. For another, she wasn't the skinny type that Dimitri normally chased. She saw the disappointment in Sofia's eyes. They were both thinking the same thing. This girl would not be able to keep Dimitri in South Africa.

He will find the right person himself, she thought and turned back to her dishes. She'd barely stacked another two platters when she sensed a collective wave of attention flutter towards the doorway. Now what? Ah, of course. It could only be Dimitri. He had a way with the ladies. He looked so much better than he'd looked at the church. He had some color back in his cheeks now. But why was the rascal terrorizing his mother, telling her he was going to leave the country on a day like this? Later, she would give him a piece of her mind.

"Dimitri, when are you coming for dinner?" One of the ladies had cornered him. "My daughter will be home for Christmas."

Hah, Grace thought. Get in line. Plenty of girls were chasing this boy.

Before he could answer, a different voice, softer and with a different accent, interrupted. "Dimitri, where shall I put this baklava?"

And now? Grace thought. What's going on? It was Annelize. The Afrikaans girl. She had seen her once or twice in Dimitri's car and never given her a second thought. Sofia was so adamant her children would marry Greeks. And Dimitri had so many friends anyway. The girl must also have known Alex. It didn't make sense that Dimitri would bring her to this gathering.

The girl stood quietly with her pale skin and long blonde hair amongst all the dark-haired Greeks. This girl could keep Dimitri interested, Grace thought. She threw a quick sidelong glance at Sofia, who appeared quite stunned.

It was Annelize who broke the hushed silence. "Hello, Mrs. Levantis. I made some baklava and brought it to serve with the tea and coffee."

Another awkward silence.

Oh no. The Greeks never served sweets after a funeral. But how would the poor girl know what they served at a *makaria*? "I'll take it," Grace said. "Give it to me and I'll put it with the other things."

Dimitri shot her a grateful glance, and the two retreated from the curious stares.

When she returned from the refreshment table, there was still an awkward silence in the kitchen. Mrs. Penny was fiddling with a thick gold chain around her neck, as if she wanted to strangle someone with it. The dark-haired niece was pouring numerous cups of tea that no one drank. Sofia still looked shocked, staring into space.

Not even five minutes passed before Mrs. Penny began to stir. "Tsk, tsk... Of all the women this boy could have. So handsome. So clever. And a lawyer. It's unbelievable that he should fall into the clutches of a *xeni* who is not one of our people. We have so many beautiful Greek girls in the community. Why on earth would he even think of looking elsewhere?" And then she answered her own question. "Of course, these girls know how to trap them. They have their ways. Do you think he'll marry her, Sofia?"

Argh, Grace thought. Why does this woman never keep her mouth shut?

"No, of course not," Sofia replied in a quiet voice. "You know how these young men are. They date different girls until they're ready to settle down."

Two minutes, Grace guessed, and then they would be leaving. Maybe sooner. She watched Sofia wipe her hands on a kitchen towel and walk out, head high. Then, a backward glance. The Look. *We are leaving.* Good, Grace thought, feeling a little guilty for thinking this. She might be able to catch Isaac's call after all. Mrs. Penny had done her a favor.

She hurried to the scullery and untied her apron before gathering Sofia's platters and their personal belongings.

"Grace." A thin, frail voice followed her down the hallway. It was Mrs. Dukas, who hadn't budged from her chair the whole afternoon. "I need to pay you for today." She pushed a shaking hand with a fistful of notes toward her.

"No, please, Mrs. Dukas. I don't want money. I can't accept this."

"But you must, please. You've been working the whole afternoon."

"I didn't come as a maid today. I came as a mother. To help another mother."

Mrs. Dukas began to cry, and she wanted to hug her. She lifted her arms and then dropped them, unsure if that was an appropriate gesture. Mrs. Dukas put the money down on the entrance table and hugged Grace.

"Thank you, Grace. Thank you."

Grace hugged her back awkwardly.

"My son is gone, Grace. What will I do now?"

She had no answer and tried not to cry as Polina and Fransina led Mrs. Dukas away, supporting her arms, one on either side.

"Thank you, Grace," they said and waved her off as she walked to the car with Sofia's things. Sofia was already in the car.

———

They drove in silence. Sofia seemed far away, wrapped in her own thoughts. Grace waited. Sofia would talk when she was ready.

After about ten minutes, Sofia said, "I'm sorry about what happened with Costa Pappas."

"Don't worry about it, Madam."

And then.

"Did you see the girl Dimitri brought to the house?"

"Yes."

"What do you think?"

"She's very beautiful."

"Never mind the beauty. She's not Greek."

"Well, most people in South Africa are not Greek."

"You know what I mean. She's a *xeni*."

"Ahh, Madam. Everybody is a *xenos* somewhere. I'm a foreigner in my own country, thanks to the laws of apartheid. Even you were a foreigner when you first arrived from Cyprus."

"You're right. As much as I love this country, I'm still a foreigner in so many ways. There's always a part of me that belongs somewhere else. Once an immigrant, always an immigrant," Sofia said and fell silent again.

"But I still want my children to marry Greeks. It's the only way they'll be able to hold onto their Greek roots."

Grace kept quiet. It always amazed her how someone as intelligent as Sofia, broadminded in so many ways, who had studied literature through a correspondence course, became as stubborn as an ox when it came to her wish that Dimitri and Natalie should marry Greeks.

"I'm sure it will blow over," Sofia said, sounding anything but sure.

"Maybe," Grace said. "He has so many other girlfriends." But she had a hunch it would not blow over. The fact that he had brought her to a Greek gathering was unusual. The way he looked at her. She had never seen such adoration on his face before.

"Never mind the girl," Sofia said. "What worries me more is that he wants to leave the country."

"He's never said such a thing before. It's just the shock of Alex's death."

"He has no idea how hard it is to leave your family and your country," Sofia said.

She cried as she said this, and Grace's heart hurt for her. In all the years she'd worked for Sofia, she'd only seen her cry once, during those three weeks when Dimitri was a baby, and she'd suffered from that terrible depression. Otherwise, she'd never seen her cry. Sofia was tough. But if Dimitri left the country, she would come apart. Dimitri had a special way about him. When he entered a room, he lit up the whole place. Everybody felt better when he was around.

"Ahh, Madam," she said finally. "He's just talking. Don't you remember? Even when he was a small boy, Dimitri would tell us he was going to find a better home when he got cross with you or me. He would pack that small brown suitcase and his sleeping bag and get as far as the gate. In the end, he never left."

"I hope you're right," Sofia said. "I don't know what I'd do without my boy."

"I don't know what I'd do without him either. Or Isaac." And she also fought back tears.

They pulled into the driveway and Johannes waved at them from the guardhouse. She waved back, glad for his presence. The gates rumbled open. They crossed over the grids and into the safety of the mansion's grounds. The gates rolled shut behind them.

When they pulled into the garage, Sofia said, "Grace, I won't need you for anything else today. Why don't you go to your room and rest. It's been a long day."

"Yes, thank you, Madam." She wasn't sure who was more exhausted, her or Sofia. It was only five-thirty, and the summer sun was still high in the sky, but it felt much later. Maybe she could still catch Isaac's call?

She hurried across the footpath that joined the front house to the back where her room was located. As soon as she opened the door, she went straight to the La-Z-Boy recliner and dropped into it. It was one of Sofia's castoffs, but she loved it. Although the brown leather was a little battered, it had adapted to the shape of her body and was so comfortable. Sometimes she fell asleep in the chair instead of her bed. She tugged at the side lever. The footrest elevated her feet. She eased off her shoes and circled her sore ankles in the air. She marveled at how she ached in expected places like the ankles, but now also in unexpected places like her left hip. Later, she would rub ointment on the sore parts.

Isaac's face stared at her from the top of the mini fridge near her chair. She reached for the photo frame and stroked his cheek. "You never smile," she whispered. From early boyhood, a shadow of fear lurked in his eyes. No matter how hard she had tried to coax it out of him, it was always there. She was sure it came from not having a father. "I'm sorry," she said.

"I had other plans for our small family, but fate decided otherwise when the gold mines swallowed up your father." She kissed his cheek before putting the photo frame back in its place.

She let her eyes glide across the titles of her favorite books crammed on the bookshelf rescued from one of Sofia's cleaning frenzies. *Cry, the Beloved Country.* She reached for that one. She had read it so many times and never tired of it. Long ago, she'd realized that her passion for books surprised white people and irritated her Black friends. Only Sofia seemed to delight in this passion and kept her well stocked with books from the courses she had taken. She was convinced she had also earned an honorary degree alongside Sofia. Today, even though she was too tired to read, she kept the book on her knees. Like an old friend, she thought, as she stroked the cover and closed her eyes. Books were easier than people.

At the Dukas house she had walked back and forth between the maids in the kitchen and the guests in the living room, not quite belonging to either group. The same old problem. Too black for the white world, and too white for the black world. In the past, she had tried to cultivate two personalities, one for each group. She had stopped doing that because it was tiring, and because they were all people, as she'd told Costa Pappas. At fifty, she was getting too old to play games anyway. A person could forget who they were in an effort to please others. Isaac was the only one who mattered. And Sofia.

When the phone rang, she bolted from her chair and grabbed the receiver.

"Isaac?"

"Yes, Mom, it's me," he laughed.

And she also laughed.

"How was it, son?"

"Uh, I'm not sure."

"What? You failed again?"

He began to laugh. "No, I'm only teasing you. It was hard, harder than I expected, but I think I did okay. I only left out one question, and it didn't count for a lot of marks. We'll know in a few weeks."

"A few weeks? How long do they take to grade one paper?"

"I'm not the only one who failed. Quite a lot of us were rewriting. And now the professors are going on vacation before the new academic year begins."

"So you're sure you did okay?"

"As sure as I can be," he said. "Mom, I have to go now. My friends are waiting. We're going to celebrate."

"Okay, son." She didn't understand what they were going to celebrate if they didn't know their results, but they were young and didn't need much reason to celebrate. One more year. If she could just get him through this final year, then everything would be okay. She picked up *Cry, the Beloved Country*, which had dropped to the floor, and sat back in her chair. She triangled the book over her chest and closed her eyes again.

It sounded like he'd passed the exam. And if Dimitri changed his mind about the emigration thing, then Sofia would also be happy. These boys. They wore down their mothers. But everything would be okay in the end. She had to believe this. She folded her arms over the book and felt her eyelids growing heavy.

THREE

The Morning After

Sofia

Sofia had barely slept all night. She lay in bed listening to the sound of rain dripping against the window panes and turned on her side. A light snore escaped from Nick's slightly open mouth. She threw back the covers and flung her legs over the side before pulling on a silk robe. She stood there a moment longer, half tempted to throw a pillow at him. How did he sleep so easily?

"Is there any reason why you're standing in the dark, staring at me while I'm sleeping?" Nick mumbled, his eyes still closed.

"I'm trying to understand how you can sleep when the world is unraveling around us."

"What's unraveling?"

"Our family! Your son wants to leave the country. But how would you know? That's my job, right?"

There was no response and her voice grew louder. "He doesn't understand that it's not easy to have two homelands. In his case, it would be three, and he'd be twice removed from his roots. He'll be like a gypsy, wandering from one place to the next, with no ties to anything or anyone."

"Where does he want to go?"

"America."

"Let him go."

"What? Are you crazy? Who's going to look after everything you've built up here?"

"Let him go. He'll see that the grass is not greener on the other side. He'll come running back—and be more appreciative of what he has here."

"What if he doesn't come back? Did you see that girl who came with him to the *makaria* yesterday?"

"Oh, you mean the blonde? Yes, she's very pretty."

"You're not worried? What if it's serious? Maybe she's the one who's gotten into his head about emigrating."

"More likely into his pants," Nick said.

"My point exactly. Maybe that's why he's not thinking straight. It's all about the physical attraction. Nothing else matters for him."

"Nothing wrong with physical attraction. Why don't you get back into bed. It's still early."

"I'm talking about serious matters and you don't seem to care," she said.

"I'll speak to him. I've told you a hundred times. The more you nag, the more stubborn he becomes." He offered this sleepy explanation as if he were providing a scientific observation. Rex poked his nose around their bedroom door and gazed at her with eyes full of sympathy. She knelt down and stroked the Alsatian's face. His wet nose nuzzled her hand. At least Rex understood her pain.

Within minutes, as if on cue, little Lola came tapping into the room on her dainty poodle legs. Funny how things turn out, Sofia thought. She hadn't wanted a guard dog. The alarm system was more than enough, and Grace didn't like large dogs. But Nick had insisted, so she and Grace conceded on the condition that they also got a poodle. He'd agreed, even though he thought poodles were silly animals. Now Lola ran straight past her and scrambled onto the bed where she snuggled under Nick's arm. She stared at the two, unsure who looked more content, Nick or Lola. "Come, Rex, let's go," she called and headed to the kitchen.

The aroma of freshly brewed coffee and sizzling bacon filtered through the air. Grace's voice and the clang of a spatula against a frying pan rang through the house. "Your mother will die of a broken heart if you leave."

Her heart quickened at the sound of these words. She walked slowly into the kitchen. From the back, Dimitri's head looked the same as that of the ten-year-old boy who had sat at the same table waiting for pancakes.

"Why should Dimitri care if his mother dies?" she said, injecting a pitiful tone into her voice.

Dimitri looked up.

"Mom, please..."

He shoved the Sunday papers towards her and pointed to the gruesome headlines with ink-stained fingertips. Necklace killings, murders, rapes, and robberies.

"Don't believe everything. They exaggerate stories to sell papers," she said.

"I don't need newspapers to tell me what I know, Mom. I carried my friend's body yesterday."

There was nothing she could say to that.

A slight pause, and then: "I'm definitely going to America. After Natalie's wedding."

"You're what?" He hadn't given a time frame yesterday.

"I'm leaving. At the end of March."

She stared hard at him. He was dead serious. An emptiness expanded inside her, threatening to shatter her from the inside out.

"Why?" she finally said. "What will you do there? What about your articles here? Mr. Rubenstein will be so disappointed if you don't clerk for him."

"They offered me a scholarship at Columbia. I'm going to do a master's in international taxation. It's a fantastic opportunity."

"You already have two degrees. And now you want to get another one in New York?"

"I didn't say I'm going forever, but things won't settle down here. I just want to explore other options. Too many expectations are being pinned on Mandela. He's just a man."

"Grace, help me with this boy." Grace stopped scrambling the eggs and held the spatula midair as if she might whack Dimitri with it.

"Mandela is not an ordinary man," Grace said. "You can't leave. The country needs you."

Only his bowed head revealed any emotion on Dimitri's part. Sofia watched as Grace piled his plate high with more bacon and eggs. She knew exactly what Grace was thinking. *Who was going to serve him breakfast in America?*

"Besides," Grace continued, "Isaac needs your help when he graduates from law school. Your mother and I have all these plans for the two of you to go into politics together. If you run away, who's going to help Isaac?"

"He'll be fine, Grace. I'm the one with the wrong skin color."

"I can't believe you just said that. If I hadn't helped raise you, I'd think you were a racist," Grace said, pretending to box his ears.

"You know me better than that," he said. "Yesterday, we buried Alex. It could easily have been me. One bullet was all it took."

"It's a terrible tragedy, but that doesn't mean the same thing will happen to you. We just have to be extra careful when we're out." Even as she said this, Sofia knew she was clutching at straws.

"That's nonsense, and you know it, Mom. No one can be vigilant 24/7. We can't walk around with eyes in the back of our heads all the time. Nor can we stay locked up inside the house," Dimitri said.

Sofia sighed and looked outside. It had begun to rain again. The boughs of the trees hung low, almost touching the ground from the weight of the water. A good day can be predicted from the morning, her mother used to say, and so far, it had not begun well.

"It's the last day of the year," she said. "Whatever you're doing on the last day of the year, that's what you'll be doing in the new year, too. So we shouldn't be arguing. Let's try to put everything behind us. We must move forward now."

"Exactly. That's why I'm moving to a new place."

She felt that familiar tightening in her neck muscles and moved her head left, then right, trying to stretch away the pain. She exhaled slowly. Dimitri could never just accept advice. He always had to try his way first.

"Just for a while," he added when she said nothing. And then. "You also left a country once. And a widowed mother. To find a husband." He added the last part with a tone suggesting her reason was frivolous compared to his.

She cringed. "It was different back in my day. My mother and I were very poor. Your father has built an empire. You and your sister will never have to worry about money like I once did. This is our home now, and I could never leave a country again."

"I'm not asking *you* to leave," he said. "I'm the one who wants to try a different place."

"And what will I do here without my children? One day, when you have your own children, you'll understand what I'm talking about." She could hear her voice becoming shrill but could not help herself. "You have no idea what you're saying. Nor what I went through. Nor what it's like to be a foreigner."

She watched him pick at the bowl of strawberries, paw-paw, mango, and pineapple, all washed, peeled, and cubed by Grace. She clutched the edge of the table. She wanted to throw her arms around him and beg him not to leave.

"This isn't a normal life," he said. He pushed the fruit away, and a flush of emotion colored his cheeks. "We live in this huge mansion, but our world is so limited. Iron bars and gates, locks and keys. It's like a jail."

God help me, she silently begged, just as Natalie strolled into the kitchen, her hair tousled from sleep.

"Maybe you can talk sense into your brother's head?"

"I just want to live in a normal society," Dimitri continued. "In a place where a person looks at someone and sees another human being. Not the color of their skin."

"And you think you're going to find that in America? They may no longer have laws promoting segregation, but they have problems too. Maybe worse than ours," Sofia said.

"I don't know if a perfect place exists," Natalie said. "Besides, you can't leave me here alone with Mom. She'll drive me crazy. And you'll be lonely over there."

"You're getting married. You'll have Peter by your side. And I won't be alone. Annelize is coming with me," Dimitri said.

Even Natalie looked stunned and Sofia caught her breath. She watched her fingers splay out over the tabletop as she pressed down to steady herself. She knew it. The Afrikaans girl had rattled his brains so much that he couldn't think straight.

"What exactly do you mean? And what are your intentions with this *xeni*?" she said.

"Her name is Annelize. She's coming with me to America. And I have no intention of breaking up with her, if that's what you're hoping."

There was a long pause as she glared at him. He clasped his hands behind his head, shifted his weight backwards on the chair, tilting its front legs midair, daring her to stop him.

"Are you thinking of marrying this girl?" she whispered in a hoarse voice. Penny's voice rang in her ears. *Of all the women he could have.*

"Would that be such a terrible thing?" he said.

"Yes!"

"Why?"

"*Why?*" She stormed out of the kitchen. Rex and Lola sat on their haunches, ears pricked, eyes large.

In the entrance hall, she took a deep breath and came back. "I've spent my whole life making sure you and Natalie don't lose your Greek roots. I never wanted to leave my country and risk losing everything that I am. When you were little, I pretended not to hear when you spoke to me in English, forcing you to speak Greek, making you fluent in both languages."

"Mom, we can't disregard a person because they don't speak Greek."

She ignored him. "Every summer we went to Greece and Cyprus, often alone, without your father, while he worked to provide for you. We went so that you could absorb the Greek culture into the depths of your heart. So that you would have roots, something to hold onto, our faith, our culture, our language. And now you're going to throw all that away?"

The pained expression on his face made her want to slap him.

"Do you expect me to sit across the table from a girl who doesn't understand a word of Greek and force us all to speak English? She doesn't know our church, our family values. Are those enough reasons for you?" she said.

"What is going on here?" Nick stormed into the kitchen, eyes blazing. "I'm on the phone in the study, and your screaming is drowning out the other person's voice. Dial it down, please." And he marched out again.

"See how you're upsetting your father who works so hard for you to have everything."

"Notice how we're speaking English right now," Dimitri said.

"That's not the point. We could change to Greek in a second."

"She could learn Greek in a second."

"It's not that difficult if a person wants to learn," Grace chimed in. "I learned Greek."

Sofia glared at her. Grace was supposed to be on *her* side. "We know nothing about this girl or her family. They could be crazy for all we know. And how well do you know her? Is she the type of person who will stand by you when life throws you some surprises?"

"Would you listen to yourself? I should record you. It's all wild speculation with no proof whatsoever," he said.

"Don't you play lawyer with me. I'm your mother. I didn't send you to law school so that you could be clever with me." She could hear her voice rising again as she boiled with anger.

"I'm sorry you're upset. But you should get to know her, and her family. You'll see they're very nice people."

"I don't have to do anything. Maybe they are nice. But they are not Greek."

"I can't change that fact. She loves our faith and our culture, and I know she could learn Greek," he said. And then, more desperately. "She's a really nice person. And she's so clever. She finished her law degree in two years while I took three."

"Oh, for heaven's sake." Sofia crossed herself. If she got this wrong and her children lost their roots, then all her efforts in a foreign country would have been for nothing. "The girl will say anything and do anything to get a ring on her finger. Once your father and I are dead, your children will never hear or speak a word of Greek again."

"Mom, would you listen to yourself? You sound like the Afrikaners who created a political system to protect their culture."

"Are you saying *I'm* a racist?" she said, stung to the core. "I can't believe you just said that. You have no idea what you're talking about." Desperately, she turned to Grace, who shook her head as if she, too, thought Dimitri had lost his mind.

"Maybe that's the wrong word," he backtracked. "Tribal or clannish? Maybe a bigot? You have this superiority complex about being Greek."

"See, Grace. That's why we have children. To bring them up so they can call us names. That's our thank you."

"He doesn't mean what he's saying, Madam. Dimitri, you're still upset from the funeral, and you're being disrespectful to your mother," Grace said.

"I respect my mother, Grace. Does she respect me and my choices?"

"The young people must respect the old people," Grace said.

"Respect, what's that? Forget it, Grace. Dimitri is on his own mission," she said, and turned away from his cold stare. "Do whatever you want, Dimitri. Marry whoever the hell you want. I don't care."

"I'm the one who's going to live with her. Not you."

She stood up and reached for Natalie's wedding folder on the bureau. Enough of Dimitri. She skimmed through Natalie's guest list. Anastasiades, Bakis, Christoforou—all good Greek families—with lovely daughters.

"There are so many nice Greek girls at our church," she said, realizing how desperate she sounded.

"I'm not in love with any of them."

"But you might still meet a nice Greek girl and fall in love. You never know. There's no need to rush into anything."

"So, you're saying I should give up the woman I love for some unidentifiable woman whom I may or may not meet at some point in the future?"

"The woman you love! What do you know about love?"

"Enough to know that when I'm with her she makes me a better version of myself. And I'm bringing her to Natalie's wedding," he said.

"Okay, great. Hopefully she'll create a better version of you than I did. And fine, bring her to the wedding. We'll seat her at the main table and announce to the Greek community that you're officially off the market."

"Mom, leave him alone. Maybe he loves her." Natalie's quiet voice interrupted.

Sofia stared at her. She had forgotten that Natalie had been standing there. "Love. Please! Give me a break. It's called lust and that fizzles out quickly," she said.

"Mom, Dimitri is not stupid. Let him make his own decisions."

"Yes, but he must make *good* decisions. Listen to me, both of you: There's always more than one person we can love in this world. The point is to choose the one who is the most suitable because we have to live with that person for the rest of our lives."

"Mom, have you ever been crazy head over heels in love?" Natalie said.

"This is not about me. I've been married for thirty years."

"But have you?" Natalie insisted.

"It's not my personality to be crazy head over heels in love, but everyone makes mistakes when they're young," she said. "In our day, we were more practical when it came to marriage. The kind of love you're talking about is an illusion. The books, the fairytales, and the songs make it into something it's not. Only naïve people believe all that rubbish."

Their puzzled expressions annoyed her even more.

"Enough already." She was sick and tired of this conversation. "Are you going to help me with these seating arrangements for your wedding? Or am I going to do everything myself as usual. It's your wedding, not mine."

"Sometimes I wonder," Natalie muttered.

"What?"

"Nothing."

She stared at Natalie. What was wrong with *her*? Both her children were on a mission to drive her crazy on the last day of the year? Before she could have a go at Natalie, Nick came into the kitchen.

"Well, it looks like Dimitri isn't the only one who wants to leave the country," Nick said.

"What do you mean?" she said, as they all turned to look at him.

"Father Christopher was held up at gunpoint last night after he left the Dukas's home," Nick said.

She felt a strange lightheaded sensation in her head and crossed herself. This would give Dimitri more ammunition.

"*Kyrie eleison.* Lord have mercy. Is he okay?"

"Yes, just very shaken up."

"Well, Mom, another reason to leave. I rest my case," Dimitri said.

She cringed and closed her eyes.

"But what happened to Father Christopher?" she continued. She liked the old priest. He was a sweet, gentle soul who radiated holiness even when he wasn't in church.

"Apparently the robbers had second thoughts about killing him when they spotted the priest's collar. They took his car and left him standing on a street corner."

"Poor thing."

"The bad news is that he called me this morning to say that he's resigned from his position at the cathedral, effective immediately. This morning's liturgy will be his last. Now we don't have a priest."

"Can he just do that?" Sofia asked.

"He booked his flight. He's going back to Greece."

"But what about the wedding?"

"Maybe we'll have to postpone it," Natalie said.

She turned to Natalie and stared hard at her. "Are you and your brother intentionally pushing my limits this morning? The invitations have gone out."

"Be quiet. All of you. As long as I'm around, everything will be fine," Nick interrupted. "We don't have to postpone the wedding. I was expecting this. The old guy has been grumbling for a while that he's buried more people who have died from unnatural causes than any other priest. I'd already arranged for a backup priest. The replacement priest has agreed. It's all confirmed."

"How did you manage that?" Sofia said, half relieved, half anxious. "I don't want someone we don't know officiating at Natalie's wedding. I want everything to be perfect."

"He's one of the best," Nick said.

She wracked her brains trying to think which priest ranked in the category of "best."

"We're waiting for some administrative issues to be cleared up with the archdiocese and the bishops. If all goes well, he'll be here next weekend," he said.

"Oh, so he's not from Johannesburg? Where's he from? Cape Town? Who is it?"

"You know him very well."

"I do?" She hated it when he dragged things out for maximum effect.

"It's Father Theo," Nick said, looking pleased with himself.

She felt her heart thud against her chest and watched the coffee mug drop from her fingers, shattering on the ground. Coffee splattered and spread all over the white tiles.

"I'll get the mop," Grace said, running for the laundry room.

"What's the matter with you?" Nick said.

"Nothing, it just slipped from my hand." She felt the blood drain from her face and her knees wobbled.

"I thought he said he would never set foot in South Africa while apartheid existed." The words stumbled from her mouth as the room closed in on her.

"The apartheid government is over," Nick said. "Everybody knows that. Even monk priests who spend half their time secluded in monasteries."

"I don't know why you would ask him of all people," she said. "It's not like we don't have other priests here. Why didn't you discuss this with me first?"

"You have enough on your plate. And you know we're short of priests. The ones we have are tied up with other weddings that same weekend."

"But it's such a long way for Theo to come—"

"If Theo can't do a favor for an old friend, then what kind of a friend is he? Let him come and see how we live in the real world instead of hiding away in monasteries and churches, praying all the time."

"Well, he can't stay with us," she said. "I'm busy with the wedding and having him here will be a huge distraction. You know how these priests are. They don't eat this or that and they're always fasting. I don't have time to worry about him now."

"Fine," he said, holding up his hands in mock surrender. "But that's so inhospitable and rude. Let him stay here for a couple of nights to settle in, and I'll arrange for the house on the church property to be prepared for him. He can stay there the rest of the time. Problem solved."

She shook her head. No, the problem was not solved. She had woken up with the intention of talking sense into Dimitri's head, and now she was being confronted with a time in her life when she had been anything but sensible.

"Come now, Sofia. I know he was a little in love with you when we were growing up, but so was everyone. I'm sure he's over his crush by now."

Sofia stared hard at Nick. She could hardly believe what he had just said. Dimitri and Natalie fixed their eyes on her, faces beaming with amusement and curiosity.

"Tell us more, Mom," Natalie teased.

"Yes, Mom, please tell us more," Dimitri added.

"All the men were in love with your mother, Natalie. When she walked down the street, heads turned," Nick said.

"Heads still turn," Natalie said. "For a fifty-year-old, Mom's in pretty good shape. But Mom, how come I never knew this story?"

"Because your dad is just making up stories to defend his actions." She could feel her cheeks flaming as she walked out of the kitchen, desperate to be alone as a hundred painful memories flooded to the surface.

"Don't listen to them, Madam. They're full of nonsense this morning," Grace said, as she mopped away all evidence of the spill.

Upstairs, in her dressing room, Sofia leaned against the marble vanity and stared at herself in the gilt-framed mirror. White as a ghost, she thought, and dabbed French moisturizer on the fine lines that seemed to multiply every time she looked at her reflection. Natalie's question still rang in her ears. *Mom, have you ever been crazy head over heels in love?*

From the corner of her eye she could see the light reflecting off the crystal knob on the end drawer. She hadn't opened it in a long time, but she knew it was there. Slowly, she pulled open the drawer and reached inside. There it was. Her fingers touched it. A small powder compact. She pulled it out and held the gold container in the palm of her hand. A remnant from another time.

It had been a gift from Theo on her seventeenth birthday. She had been so happy about this small token—in her naiveté, believing it was proof of his love for her. Her fingers traced the outline of Cyprus embossed on the small lid. On one side of the island, a miniature Aphrodite emerged from the waves washing the shores. On the other side, a Byzantine church sanctified the waters. She opened the lid. Tiny particles of powder and fragments of dry gardenia petals still clung to the corners, releasing a faint fragrance from a night long ago. She had left a mother and a country because of him. Even after she closed the compact and put it back in the drawer, the scent of the past lingered in the air.

FOUR

A Blue Shawl

Sofia

Cyprus, 1959

The blue waters of the Mediterranean turned gray as the sky darkened, and on the southern shores of the island, a sleepy village flared into brightness to celebrate the feast day of its church, St. Fanourios. The liturgy had just ended, and the main square pulsed with people pouring out of the church. In the village square, singers, *bouzouki* and *klarino* players had already struck up the music. A feverish excitement filled the air as men, women, and children jostled each other for front row tables on the square. A beautiful young woman led a circle of dancers, their hands joined as they moved in rhythm with the music. Everyone's eyes were on her. She set the pace and carved the way forward with a smile. With her free arm outstretched, she waved a white handkerchief to the beat of the music. Her feet and pleated skirt moved back and forth in perfect unison. Anyone paying careful attention might have noticed that her eyes were scanning the sea of faces. She was looking for one face.

"*Yeia sou*, long life and good health, Sofia," the band members called out as she circled the square. Nick, the dancer to her left, squeezed her hand tighter and encouraged her pace. "Let's go," he said with a playful smile on his lips. She caught his eyes lingering on her waist, where the blue dress clung to her hips. A pang of guilt washed over her. She was fond of Nick, but she was not in love with him.

"Have you thought about what I asked you?" he whispered as she led them around the square. Yes, she had. For weeks, Nick had regaled her with stories about the gold and diamonds buried in the soil of a faraway country at the southern end of the African continent, begging her to join him once he was settled in that new country. But she had no intention of leaving Cyprus. Or the man whom she loved. At the same time, she didn't want to hurt Nick's feelings. Once he left, he'd forget all about her. Or at least, that's what she hoped would happen.

"I can't give you an answer yet," she said, wanting to let him down gently. She wove their group around widening concentric circles of other dancers, and again, her eyes skimmed over the crowd. Where was he, the one who had stolen her heart?

When she spotted Marianna watching from one of the tables, her heart ached for her mother's loneliness. The other women leaned in together, laughing and talking. Marianna, although on the same table, sat apart, rigid and detached. They always kept her at a distance on account of her beauty and husbandless state. Why did her father have to die so young and leave her mother alone, Sofia wondered for the hundredth time. Only the expression on Marianna's face as they made eye contact hinted at a sliver of joy. Her mother's whole life revolved around her child, Sofia thought, feeling the weight of this responsibility even as she danced to the carefree songs of the island.

Earlier that day, they had argued once again. Marianna's words still rang in her ears. "Cyprus is a small island. People talk, especially in this village. Gossip is like money here. They pass it back and forth hoping it will grow. *It's better to lose an eye than your reputation.* Don't spend too much time with either Nick or Theo at the dance."

Sofia steered the dancers to the other side of the square and shot another glance at her mother, who didn't appear too concerned about Nick at her side. It was Theo who raised her mother's hackles. Marianna's biggest concern seemed to be his calling to the priesthood. And for the life of her, Sofia could not understand this resistance. The Greek Orthodox faith allowed its priests to marry, as long as this happened *before* ordination. But her mother would ignore this valid defense whenever she brought it up, and turn away, sighing loudly.

As she circled the square again, she saw Theo. Her heart and feet skipped a beat. He stood alone, near the church, under an old oak tree lit up with string lights for the festivities. He gave her a longing look and touched the top of his head, their secret signal. She loved the way that lock of hair fell over his forehead and the intensity of his dark eyes. Then he turned and walked away. She barely restrained herself from dropping Nick's hand and running after Theo.

Two more songs. She forced herself to dance, waiting for the crowd to thicken and the right moment to escape her mother's eagle eyes. If her mother guessed what she had decided, she'd be as good as dead. But she had made up her mind. It was now or never. Tomorrow, Theo would be leaving. And it would be a long time before she could see him once he enrolled at the theological school in Athens.

"I need a break," she whispered to Nick, hating herself for lying. A shadow flickered over his face.

"Suit yourself," he said, and continued without her.

Flushed and perspiring, she broke away, almost forgetting to grab the blue shawl she'd borrowed from her mother. It lay tossed across one of the chairs and she quickly grabbed it. Her mother would be furious if she lost it. She draped the shawl over her shoulders, enjoying the silky softness against her bare skin.

As she made her way through the crowd, she looked back one more time. Her mother was still with the women. Theo's parents sat with all the other priests at the clergy table. The food had yet to be served. It would be a while before any of them left the celebration.

The church bell tower stood white against the dark sky as she made her way along a footpath that joined the neighboring village to hers. Theo had already disappeared, and she followed the well-worn footpath he would have taken. A full moon lit the narrow track. She breathed in the crisp evening air that carried the fragrance of mountain herbs mingled with unexpected bursts of wild jasmine. The branches of the fig trees hung low, heavy with ripened fruit, and brushed against her skin as she sped past. And from the surrounding pine trees, the mating calls of night birds and the hum of cicadas blended, charging her with fear and excitement.

When she reached the deserted square of her village, she stopped to catch her breath. Empty chairs stooped forward, leaning against bare tables. She could see a light in Theo's house next to the church. She looked around once more, hoping there were no eyes peeping at her from behind closed curtains.

She put the thought out of her mind and walked up to the front door of his house. She lifted her hand, then dropped it without knocking. A gardenia bush glowed under the porch light. Its white flowers and soft, velvety buds were unfurling, releasing an intoxicating fragrance into the warm evening air. She bent down and plucked one of its flowers, tucking it between her breasts. She took another deep breath, and again her hand hovered at the brass door knocker before she tapped softly, and waited. One minute. Two minutes. Where was he? Had he changed his mind? And then she heard his voice through the keyhole: "Sofia, go around to the back."

Of course, she should have thought of that herself. A light breeze tugged at her shawl as she hurried to the back. For a split second, it crossed her mind to keep on walking, but when the kitchen door swung open, Theo stood there, looking even more nervous than she felt. On his face, a strange expression, both eager and reluctant.

"I knew you would come," he said and pulled her close. She clung to him as the blue shawl slipped from her shoulders, but she didn't care. Let it fall.

"How am I going to live without you?" he whispered into the nape of her neck.

"You have God," she teased.

He gave her a wry smile. "Come," he said, as he took her hand and led her into his bedroom. She had never seen it before and tried not to look at his bed but couldn't help noticing how large it was in such a small space. The somber faces of the saints stared sternly from the icons filling the one wall. They made her nervous and she turned away.

On the floor, multiple bookstacks caught her attention. "So many books," she said, making exaggerated steps around the stacks.

"I can't make up my mind which ones to take and which ones to leave behind. I still have to decide."

"Take me," she said.

"I wish," he said.

"And what about clothes?"

"There on the bed." He pointed at two pairs of long black pants, two short-sleeved white shirts, and two long-sleeved white shirts.

"That's it?" She threw herself on top of his meager belongings. "That would never be enough for me. I think you'll need a few more things."

"Like what?"

"A few kisses to keep you motivated?" She lay backwards, holding out her hands to him.

He bent over her and she wrapped her arms around his neck, pulling him closer. A worried look appeared on his face.

"What's the matter?" she said.

"Nick."

She wanted to shake him. This was so typical of Theo, worrying about his friend at a moment like this. "He's going to be fine," she whispered, brushing her lips against his. "Once he's in South Africa, he'll forget all about me. I heard that his uncle has a list of eligible women lined up for him."

This seemed to appease him, and he began to slide the thin spaghetti straps off her shoulders, the ones her mother had said were too provocative and had wanted to replace with bell sleeves. He stopped again. *Now what?*

"Do you really want this?" he said.

"I've never done it before," she said.

"I should hope not." His serious eyes softened. She was intensely aware of his gold cross dangling over her face, the breadth of his shoulders as he leaned over her, and the terror that his parents could walk in at any moment. But mainly she felt a warmth spreading upwards through her body, even as her ears listened for a creaking door or gate.

"I want you," she said.

He hesitated only for a second before his lips locked hungrily onto hers. His hands were clumsy, faltering on her buttons and straps. Desire and embarrassment flushed over her. They had so little time. She stood up, astonished at her brazenness, and began to undress. He gasped, unbuttoning his shirt, dropping his pants, and then there was no turning back. Their fumbling and shyness transformed into a frantic urgency that took her past that initial thrust of pain to unspeakable heights she had never known before. And in those moments she didn't care if anyone walked in on them. It would be worth it, she told herself.

Afterwards, she lay with her head on his chest, still reeling from the pain and the pleasure, and listened to his beating heart. "If anyone were ever to find out about this..." she whispered as the wind banged the shutters outside.

"No one will find out. I promise," he said. "We're going to get married as soon as I finish my studies, and no one will ever know about this except you and me."

As he stroked her arm, she spotted the blue dress, a crumpled mess on the floor, and thought of her mother. She untangled herself from his arms and legs and climbed out of the bed. Filled with disbelief at what she had just done, she slipped back into her dress and ran her fingers over the skirt, trying to smooth out the wrinkles.

"What are you thinking?" he asked, pulling up her zipper and spinning her around to face him.

"I'm going to miss you," she said.

"I'll write often, I promise," he said.

She traced her finger around the edge of his gold cross. He unclasped it and handed it to her with the chain. "I want you to have it."

"No, I can't," she said. "My mother will know it's yours."

"Then don't wear it. I can't always be with you, but God is always with you. I need you to remember this."

"I'm not sure if God will want to know me after what I've just done," she said, feeling the shame settle into her. "Keep it for me, Theo. I'll take it another time."

He cupped her chin in his hand. "You're so stubborn, but too beautiful for God to be angry with. I, on the other hand, future servant of God, will have to offer some explanation for taking the virginity of an innocent young girl."

"Not so innocent anymore," she said.

Suddenly, the creak of the front gate made them both jump. He looked at her, and his eyes reminded her of a startled deer. He scrambled into his shirt and pants and peered through the window.

"I'm sure it's nothing," he said, sounding anything but sure. "Here, take the gardenia flower." It had fallen into the rumpled sheets. She took it and helped him straighten the bedcovers before they rushed to the kitchen, where he let her out the side door. She began to run into the night, then stopped and went back. She clung to him a moment longer. *What if he had loved her only for that short time?* "You won't forget me?" she asked. He kissed her lightly on the lips. "Go, *agape mou*. I love you." His voice was tender, and his smile made her believe that she would be the center of his world forever.

She hurried across the small stony pebbles of the deserted square, past the dark silhouettes of the shopfronts, and stumbled just as she reached the shadow of the church towering over her. Breathless, she lay on the ground in the outline of its ancient shape. The enormity of what she had done began to sink in, and she started to tremble. Discarded napkins from the restaurant fluttered around her. She picked herself up.

Her heart was pounding by the time she entered her mother's house and slammed the door behind her. She leaned against the wall and let out a sigh of relief. The front hall and kitchen were still dark. Thank goodness, she thought. Her mother was not yet home.

A ray of moonlight slanted through the open window, touching the icon of St. Fanourios on the mantelpiece. The saint's face glowed in the dark. He was one of her favorites. Unlike the stern faces of the older saints, this youthful-looking saint wore an expression of exasperated tolerance, edged with a tinge of sympathy. Through his prayers, lost objects or even a perfect husband or wife could be revealed. *Oh no!* She gripped her bare shoulders. Her mother's shawl. She'd forgotten it at Theo's house. Should she run back and get it? No, that was a crazy idea. Please, St. Fanourios, she begged, let Theo find it and hide it. How could she have been so stupid? Exhausted, she crept up the stairs.

In her bedroom, she tossed the gardenia onto the side table and slipped out of the blue dress for a second time that night. She remembered the way Theo's eyes had looked when she stood naked in front of him. She climbed under the bedcovers and fell into a restless sleep, tossing and turning, dreaming about Theo's eyes, his lips, his hands, and a rippling blue wave that floated toward her, rising and falling.

It seemed she had barely closed her eyes before the rooster from next door began to crow. She got up and splashed her face with cold water, dreading the interrogation that surely awaited her downstairs.

When she walked into the kitchen, her mother kept her back turned. She was brewing Greek coffee in a small copper *briki* and the room was filled with its strong aroma. And a sullen silence.

"What time did you get in last night?" her mother asked, still with her back turned.

"Before you."

"Usually, I can't get you inside the house when there's a *panagyri* celebration."

"I was tired."

"From what? It's not as if I have you working in the fields all day."

Her mother swung around and looked her in the eye for what seemed like an eternity.

"Where did you disappear to last night?"

"What do you mean? I was at the festival like you. There were so many people—"

"Don't lie to me, Sofia. I hope you weren't with the priest's son."

"Why do you hate him so much?"

"I don't hate him," her mother said. "You could compete with any woman in the world, and you would win, but you cannot compete with God for this man's heart. It's already taken. *This man belongs to God*. From before he was born. He comes from a long line of priests."

"Can he not love both God and me?"

"Yes, but God will always come first. You're not the type to be satisfied with second place. And he's too much like you anyway. He lives inside his head most of the time. He'll never make any money, and in the long run you won't be happy with him. Trust me. I know what's best for you."

"But I love him, and maybe I know what's best for me," Sofia said.

"Pah!" Her mother wiped her hands furiously on her apron and exhaled a loud huff, as if to emphasize her martyrdom in bringing up a stubborn daughter all alone in a gossipy village. "When you're stuck in a village with two roads that lead to nowhere, and he's tending to his flock in some mountaintop village while you're surrounded by small-minded people who gossip all day long, then we'll see how far love will take you."

A sharp rap at the courtyard door interrupted her tirade, and they both turned and stared at the door. The latch creaked as someone unhinged it from the other side. The door opened and she felt her jaw drop. Theo's father stood on the doorstep, looking even more intimidating than usual.

The cheeks of the old priest were flushed and even his bristly, white beard seemed to tremble with rage. He clutched a plastic package and shoved it into her mother's hands: "This is yours, I believe." An expression of horror spread across her mother's face as she looked inside the package. Sofia peered over her mother's shoulder and died a hundred tiny deaths. If only the earth could open up and swallow her. The blue shawl lay at the bottom of the package.

The priest focused his venom on her mother.

"It used to be a beautiful piece of silk, but it fell into some dirt along the way. The owner did not look after it. Now it's torn and ruined. Maybe you can piece it together since you're such a good seamstress."

"Thank you, *Pater*." Her mother's voice and hands were shaking.

The old man turned to leave, and then stopped as if something had just occurred to him. He fixed his piercing eyes on her.

"My son sends his best wishes. He left for the monastery early this morning. He won't be back for a *long* time." The priest emphasized the word *long*. "He's going to explore the monastic path. Then he'll decide about the priesthood and theological school."

A cold chill ran over her, freezing her arms and legs, and she was aware of trying to say something but only a soft cry came out.

Her mother put an end to the agony. "God has always been your son's chosen path, *Pater*. He belongs to the church. We wish him well."

He turned and finally left. Across the road, which separated their house from the neighbor's, *Kiria* Tasoulla did not even pretend to be minding her own business. She had stopped pegging her freshly washed sheets on the clothesline and simply stared at them.

Her mother slammed the courtyard door and bolted the latch with a loud clang. They walked back into the house without a word.

Still not talking, her mother ripped the blue shawl from the package. It billowed out like a veil. There was a long thin split down the middle and she tossed it onto the floor.

As she stared at it, the open palm of her mother's hand struck her hard across the cheek, catching her by surprise. Tears sprang to her eyes. Her mother had never hit her before.

"What were you thinking? That he would leave God for you?"

"I love him."

"See what love got you? Nothing but shame. On top of that, you've lost your name, and once you lose your name, it's gone. You can never get it back again."

There was nothing she could say to that. The clock ticking on the mantelpiece sounded loud. In the bitter silence that followed, she wished she could undo what she had done. She stared at the icon of St. Fanourios next to the clock. He stared back at her. The sympathy in his eyes seemed to have vanished.

"Not even the saint can help you now," her mother said and began to cry. "I had so many dreams for you. I tried so hard. My fingers are dented with holes from the needles I've pushed in and out of silks and satins over the years in order to give you the best. And still, I failed. If your father were alive, this would never have happened."

The memory of her father made her heart ache even more.

"If I were you, I'd go after Nick Levantis. Follow him to South Africa. Before the end of this day, everyone will know you were alone with the priest's son last night. Your reputation is in tatters now, just like the shawl. They'll never let you find a husband here. You have to leave this place, Sofia. There's no other way."

Horrified, she stared at her mother. *Leave her home? Leave Theo?* She wasn't sure what terrified her more.

"Give me one month, please. If I don't hear anything from Theo, then I promise I'll do as you say."

"It's a little late *now* to do as I say."

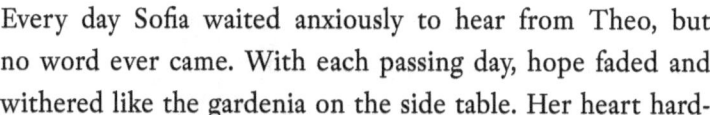

Every day Sofia waited anxiously to hear from Theo, but no word ever came. With each passing day, hope faded and withered like the gardenia on the side table. Her heart hardened. How could she have been so stupid? She would never trust anyone again. Her friend Katina visited sometimes and updated them on the latest rumors. The scandal had not died down. Her mother had ventured out once or twice, but the whispers and smirks on the neighbors' faces lingered, and she was forced to stay home, unable to show her face in the village.

After a month, Sofia woke up early one morning, before the rooster began to crow. She rummaged in the bedside drawer for a piece of paper. She knew she still had it. There it was, beneath pins and pens and elastic hair bands. Nick had given it to her just before he left Cyprus in case she ever needed anything. He had scribbled down a telephone number belonging to an uncle he would be staying with in South Africa. Clutching the scrappy piece of paper, she went downstairs. She knew her mother would be there, sitting in the darkness, waiting for the sun to rise. She placed it in her mother's hands and said, "Please call Nick's uncle and make arrangements for my ticket to South Africa."

Her mother sat back and studied her face thoughtfully, as if she didn't quite believe her daughter had finally come to her senses. "It's better that you go," her mother said. "There is nothing here for you. And with the Turkish threat always hanging over our heads, we never know what will happen on the island from one day to the next. In South Africa, with Nick Levantis by your side, the world will be yours." Her mother crossed herself and stood up straighter than Sofia had seen in a long time. "I'm going to the call box on the square," she said, holding the piece of paper as if it were gold.

Sofia climbed the stairs to her room. Again, she opened the side drawer next to her bed and dug around till she found a small powder compact. Theo had given it to her the year before. When he was still in love with her. Cyprus was embossed on the gold lid. On one side, Aphrodite emerged from the waves. On the other side, a Byzantine church graced the waters. She opened the lid and placed a few fragments of dry gardenia petals into the compact before closing it and tossing it back in the drawer. Theo had made his choice. And she had made hers.

She sat down in the small window seat where she'd sat so many times before. Outside, the sky began to change from black to gray, and she watched as the dawn painted the village in a soft haze of purples, pinks, and reds. The colors softened the rough edges of the cobbled paths and rocky outcrops. Sadness filled her heart, but she smiled at the small world she loved so much. She had never wanted to leave this place. Beyond the whitewashed homes, the road forked. To the left, the fields were scarlet with poppies. To the right, across the square, bells chimed for the early morning liturgy as women in black scarves hurried into the church.

FIVE

Not of the World

Sofia

The new year rolled in without celebration or fanfare. The Greek community decided there would be no hats or streamers, no dancing or music out of respect for Steve and Maria's son. But one day at church, Maria pulled Sofia aside. "I want you to go ahead with Natalie's wedding. Life is short. Look what happened to my Alex. Don't delay joy. You never know what might happen from one minute to the next." Deeply touched, Sofia hugged her tightly and forged ahead with Natalie's wedding preparations.

She was up early one morning before the sun had risen. She sat alone in her study checking the to-do and guest lists. Her finger ran down the page as she skimmed through items: tuxedos, gifts, flowers, bonbonnières, food tasting. Lots of checkmarks. This made her happy. Then her eyes found Theo's name with a question mark next to it. She punched her pen into the paperwork, marking it with spots and tiny holes. If only the old priest hadn't left.

In the morning coolness, she shivered and reached for the beige shawl draped on the chairback. She threw it over her shoulders and walked to the bay window. Dawn peeped over the terraced lawns and perfectly manicured flower beds. "If you choose Nick Levantis," her mother had said, "the world will be yours." In a way, her mother had been right. And yet, there were times when Nick drove her crazy. Like now. Why had he gone and invited Theo into their home? She had never forgiven Theo. It was so unnecessary to have him in her home now, during a time of joy.

A soft voice interrupted her thoughts.

"Mom?"

She spun around to see Dimitri. Dark circles framed the bottom of his eyes.

"You look like hell. What happened to you?" she said. Please, God, she silently begged, don't let him start again with his obsession about leaving the country.

"I'm fine. I wanted to tell you that I invited Annelize for dinner this evening."

"What?"

"Since we have the priest arriving, and Grace is preparing a special dinner, I thought it might be a good time."

"Why would you invite *her* to meet the priest for heaven's sake? She's not even Orthodox."

"Not just the priest, but you and Dad, too. The wedding is two weeks away, and I thought it would be nice for her to meet everyone beforehand. It'll be less awkward on the day."

Dear God. There are two weeks left till the wedding. Please give me a break somewhere. She tried to listen and understand what Dimitri was saying. Instead, all she could hear was her mother's voice. *I had so many dreams for you. I tried so hard. And still, I failed.* That's how she felt right now.

"Mom, are you listening?"

"Yes, but I still don't understand why you want to bring her here this evening."

He shook his head as if he didn't understand. "Why do you hate her so much? You don't even know her."

"I don't hate her! But why *her*? You could have any girl you want. All you'd have to do is snap your fingers and a hundred Greek girls would come running." But when she saw the color drain from his face, she stopped. *I don't hate him,* her mother had insisted when they used to argue about Theo. She was becoming her mother!

"Fine," she said, never able to refuse her firstborn anything. At least he wasn't talking about leaving the country. She could deal with the girl later. "I'll tell Grace we have an extra person this evening. I need to get dressed now."

He turned to leave. And then. "Mom, I don't think a person can choose who they fall in love with. It just happens."

"I don't agree. You *can* choose. It all depends on whether you choose with your head or your heart. *That* makes a big difference. Believe me. But let's leave this discussion till after Natalie's wedding."

"Okay," he said, and hung his head like a martyr. She knew that tactic. He'd perfected it as a young boy, and she tried to ignore it now. As he turned to leave, he stopped again. "What if a person chooses with his head *and* his heart?"

She rolled her eyes and shooed him away. He knew how to work her. Could she possibly be wrong about the girl? Only time would tell.

She headed back to her bedroom where Nick was walking out of their dressing room, fresh and smiling, ready to face the day. He buttoned his shirt sleeves and gave her a peck on the cheek.

"I have a huge favor to ask of you."

"No."

"You haven't even heard what I want to say?"

"Whatever it is, the answer is no." She recognized that wheedling tone. She had been married to him long enough to know his clever manipulations. "I have a busy day ahead, and your son just informed me that he's bringing Annelize to dinner this evening."

Nick stopped buttoning his shirt and gave a long low whistle. "I wasn't expecting that," he admitted. "At least he's not talking about emigrating. Well, maybe having a priest here will be a good thing for the whole family. Speaking of priests, that's the favor. Can you please pick up Theo from the airport."

"You've got to be kidding me? Absolutely no. I'm busy today. Why can't you go?"

"I know. I promised I'd take care of him. But the unions are acting up today because President de Klerk is repealing the apartheid legislation. They're striking everywhere. It's chaos out there. I have to help a tenant who needs extra security at one of my shopping malls."

"What does that have to do with me?"

"I can't go to the airport. Please."

"Why can't the driver go?"

"Because it's rude and inhospitable. Come now, Sofia, how can I send a stranger to pick up a friend? It's not the Greek way, and you know it. The man is flying five thousand miles for our daughter's wedding. Someone from the family must pick him up. I don't understand what your problem is."

"I'm not going," she repeated and stormed out of their bedroom.

In the kitchen, she grabbed the cup of coffee Grace had already poured and paced up and down.

"Everything okay, Madam?" Grace said.

"Ugh, no, not really, Grace. Have you sorted out the guest room for our visitor this evening? Towels, linens, all that stuff?"

"Yes, Madam. Everything was ready from yesterday. Master Nick reminded me ten times. Later today I'll put fresh flowers in the room."

"You see," Nick said, as he walked into the kitchen, a defiant expression on his face. "You have staff doing everything and yet you kick up such a fuss about the poor man coming to stay here for a few days. And then you refuse to help with one small favor as if I ask for your help every day."

If only you knew what you were asking, Sofia thought. She had laid to rest a million memories that she had no intention of digging up ever again. Seething, she tried to think of an alternative plan.

"Maybe Natalie can go?" she said.

"Sorry, Mom, I can't." Natalie breezed into the kitchen sounding anything but sorry. "I'm meeting the bridesmaids this morning to discuss the final arrangements." She grabbed her bag and jacket and dashed out before anyone could say a word.

Nick sighed heavily and looked at his watch. "I have to go. I'm late. This will take a maximum of two hours from your day. His plane lands at ten."

Grace poured another cup of coffee. "Madam, it's fine. Your meeting with the banquet coordinator is at one o' clock today. You'll be back from the airport long before then."

"There you go! Thank you, Grace," Nick said triumphantly. "At least one person in this household feels sorry for me." He blew them a kiss and rushed out of the kitchen.

"Grace, sometimes I wish you'd keep quiet," she said.

"Madam, I don't understand." Grace looked at her with a puzzled expression.

"No, you certainly don't."

"Try me," Grace said. Grace witnessed her life at such close quarters that it was impossible to hide anything from her.

"A long time ago, I used to know this priest. Very well. When he was still just a man."

"Ah, I see," Grace said, raising an eyebrow. "Well, he's still just a man, I assume."

"I'd rather not have to deal with him right now."

"It's only for a few days. Then he's going to stay at the old priest's house. Johannes and Freddy cleaned it, and we've made it comfortable. Before you know it, he'll be out from under our feet."

"Right," Sofia said.

"Besides, we can't have a wedding without a priest," Grace added in her matter-of-fact way.

Sofia finished her coffee in silence and got up to leave. Not even Grace was on her side for this one. As she walked away, she could feel Grace's eyes on her.

―

At the airport, Sofia paced up and down in the arrivals hall, fidgeting with a long strand of pearls around her neck. What was she supposed to say to this man who had dumped her without a backward glance? The shame she'd brought on her family came back to her. Her mother's solemn face at the airport when she'd put her only child on a plane all those years ago.

Pull yourself together, she told herself. All she had to do was pick him up, be polite, and then drop him off at the house. The others could take care of him after that, and she could go on with her day.

Around her, happy faces waited for loved ones. She hadn't thought about Theo in years, although, if she had to be honest with herself, there had been a few times when his absence had sprung at her from nowhere, surprising her with its intensity. But she pushed those thoughts away.

She glanced again at the flight monitor. Flight OA 266 from Athens had landed early. The automatic doors swished open and shut, disgorging passengers every few minutes. She saw his long black *rason* and gold cross before she saw him. *In the world but not of the world.* She stared at this man of the cloth, and somewhere beneath the beard and vestments, she found the face of the young man she had loved so much. He had barely changed, except for a beard and a sprinkling of gray hair. She had promised herself she would not think about the last time they were together; but that scene was exactly what popped into her head as she stared at his tall imposing figure.

He must have sensed her scrutiny because he looked up and met her gaze with a hesitant smile. She took a deep breath as he strode towards her.

"Look at you. You haven't changed one bit." He opened his arms wide, engulfing her in a huge bear hug, and she soaked up the melodic sound of his voice. She'd forgotten how beautiful it was. His Cypriot accent had softened, replaced by a more neutral Greek tone. She brushed her lips against his cheeks and stepped back, an awkward intimacy already separating them.

A thousand questions sprang to her lips, but she held them back. "How was your flight?"

"Very nice, thank you. I'm not used to first class. That was very generous of Nick. Where is that friend of mine? He hounded me to come, and now he's not even at the airport?"

"Well, you know Nick. When something comes up for work, then everything else takes second place." She bit her lip, not wanting him to think that sometimes she took second place. "But he's looking forward to catching up with you."

He only had one suitcase, battered and worn. She led him quickly across the gleaming floors until she realized he was no longer at her side. She turned and saw him set down his suitcase in the middle of the arrivals area. He stood there, rooted to the spot, looking left and right, amazement all over his face. A pride of African lions sauntered towards him from an eye-catching mural. The beat of African drums rolled out from a multicolored kiosk overflowing with wooden tribal souvenirs, brightly colored bead bracelets, coasters shaped like the African continent, and tiny animals—lions, giraffes, and elephants—carved in wood. One or two people turned to stare at him, and for a second she felt a flash of sympathy for his disorientation. When he saw that she was watching him, he gave an embarrassed smile, picked up the suitcase, and quickly caught up with her.

"Everything is so different here," he said.

"Yes, but we need to get going." She had no intention of playing tour guide, even if he did look like a fish out of water.

Outside, as they crossed from the terminal into the parking garage, newspaper vendors sang and shuffled their feet from side to side. They clapped their hands high above their heads, flaunting brightly colored posters strapped to their chests. Green and yellow letters boldly proclaimed *One man, One*

Vote, in anticipation of Mandela's imminent release and the upcoming elections.

"I picked the right time to come," he said, pointing to the posters.

"A lot of change is going on in the country. It's a very different place from where you've just come. Nick said you were at Mt. Athos?"

"Yes, I left the two younger priests in charge of my parish in Cyprus and flew to Greece so I could go to Mt. Athos before coming here. And you're right. Nothing has changed on Mt. Athos in over a thousand years. That place moves to its own rhythm."

At her car, she watched him place his suitcase in the trunk. "What's it like on Mt. Athos?" she said. Had he really found what he needed? she wondered.

"It's the closest place to heaven on earth. When you wake up at midnight to attend the liturgies and look up at the sky filled with stars, you feel the prayers of thousands of monks before you."

Waking up at midnight to pray? She didn't think she could do that. He made it sound as natural as breathing.

"As long as you're happy," she said, trying not to feel resentful. They climbed into the car.

"That's where you went, after that night?" She backed the car slowly out of the parking space.

"What night? Oh. You mean *that* night? Yes. It was the only place I could go." And there was a sadness in his voice as he said this.

"I just want to know one thing," she said, unable to stop herself. "Why did you leave without a word? No explanation, nothing. And not once did you ever try to contact me."

"What do you mean without a word? I wrote ten letters. Not one or two. Ten. *You* were the one who never replied."

"What?" She barely missed hitting a vehicle that appeared from nowhere and veered into another parking bay, bringing the car to a screeching halt.

A nerve twitched in his neck and he gripped the car seat.

"Are you lying to me? I never received any letters. Not even one."

"I don't lie," he said, looking her straight in the eye. "And I don't know what happened." His voice grew quiet. "It's a very isolated place up there on the mountain, deliberately cut off from the world. But I had a friend there, another monk, who promised to help me. He knew how important it was that you receive those letters. I trusted him."

"Well, your friend let you down. I never received anything," she repeated. "Not one single letter." She imagined one of the monks tossing Theo's envelopes into the sea and hoped that man was rotting in hell, if this was the case.

Theo sat very still, looking as bewildered as she felt. And then.

"You didn't waste much time waiting for me. I heard that you left for South Africa soon afterwards to marry Nick."

His voice was accusatory, as if *she* had wronged *him*.

With a sharp intake of breath, she turned to face him. "Do you know what I went through after you left? My mother couldn't show her face anywhere because of the scandal. People turned their backs on her. Her sewing orders stopped completely at one stage. And that was our livelihood. Within two years after I left, she passed away. I'm convinced she died of a broken heart and loneliness."

She felt her insides constricting with the anger that churned up inside her.

"I'm so very sorry. I've never forgiven myself."

Someone beeped loudly, making them both jump, and a driver waved his hands impatiently. "Are you leaving or not?" the person shouted. "You're half in, half out. Commit. Make up your mind!"

She waved to apologize and they left, the air between them thick with emotion and confusion as she entered the highway. Every now and then he checked his seatbelt buckle when she accelerated and overtook other cars. They drove in silence for a while.

"Are you happy? With Nick, I mean."

"Of course, I'm happy," she snapped. What did he think? That she was still pining for him? "Nick is a good man who loves me, and I live a wonderful life in South Africa. What about you? Are you happy with the life you chose?"

"With God, one is always happy. Unlike people, God never lets you down."

Well, good for you, she thought.

"In the end you didn't stay on Mt. Athos with the other monks though. Since you didn't follow the monastic route, you might as well have married before becoming a parish priest."

"Yes, my spiritual father told me I wasn't suited for the rigors of Mt. Athos. Nor for the monastic route. He had also urged me to marry before my ordination."

"But you didn't."

"There was only one woman I could have married." He said this as if he were speaking about a woman they both used to know.

She swallowed hard and blinked back tears, desperately trying to think of something less sad.

"Tell me about the children," he said, as if reading her mind.

"Dimitri and Natalie are my greatest joy. You'll meet them this evening. The only problem I have right now is with Dimitri. He's gotten it into his head that he must leave South Africa. He'll do to me what I did to my mother."

"No, don't say that. Sometimes God works in mysterious ways. He may still change his mind."

"From your mouth to God's ears," she said. "Maybe God listens to priests."

"Not always," he said, as they pulled up to the brick-paved driveway leading to the estate.

He looked astonished as he gazed up at the wrought-iron gates protecting the entrance. She realized that the towering wall topped with layers of electrical wires, cameras, security lights, and motion sensors must have looked strange to him.

"You've probably never locked up anything," Sofia said.

"I've never seen so many grand properties that are gated and walled like prisons," he said. "Is this your home or a resort?"

"It's the way we live," she said.

"The walls are very high," he said.

She tried, and failed, to activate the gate sensors from the car. It drove her crazy when the sensors did this. She beeped impatiently and Johannes rushed over from the guardhouse.

Theo's eyes grew large as he stared at the AK-47 assault rifle in Johannes' hands. She rolled down the window and Johannes lowered the rifle, peering into the car, his face full of friendly curiosity.

"*Kalos Irthes*, Father. Welcome." Johannes grinned and switched back to English, having used up the full extent of his Greek vocabulary. "Hello, Madam. Grace told me we were expecting a special visitor today. Welcome to South Africa, Father."

Of all her staff members, Johannes reminded Sofia most of the villagers back home. He made it his business to know everything about everyone.

"*Efcharisto*, thank you," Theo said, switching easily from Greek to English. "Is this normal in South Africa? To welcome a person with a rifle in your hands?"

Johannes roared with laughter. Even his shoulders shook with amusement as he interacted with his new best friend. "No, don't worry, Father. As long as I'm here, nothing will happen to you. I noticed some suspicious people around here today, so I'm not taking any chances, that's all. But you don't have to worry about anything."

"Really? Why is that?" Theo threw a sideways glance at her, and she could tell that he was beginning to relax. It was impossible not to be charmed by Johannes, although she would have preferred less charisma and more vigilance.

Johannes leaned closer to the window. "The *tsotsis*, thugs, are afraid of priests. They know priests have big connections up there," he said, pointing his rifle at the sky while flashing a conspiratorial smile at Theo.

"If that's the case, I'll give you a few of my white-collared shirts," Theo said, clearly enjoying himself. "Might be better than waving that thing around as if it's a toy."

Another roar of laughter. "No one will believe I'm a priest, Father. I drink too much beer on my weekends off."

She began to grow impatient. Johannes would drag this out for another twenty minutes if she allowed it. She accelerated and the wheels of the Mercedes made a squealing sound over the iron grid. Johannes stepped back with a reluctant smile.

When she brought the car to a halt at the end of the tree-lined driveway, Theo said, "Wow! What does Nick do again? Does he own the gold mines or the diamond mines? We could fit our whole village into your garden!"

"He works hard in numerous business enterprises. I hardly ever see him. That's the only bad part."

As they stepped out of the car, Freddy came rushing over. He had been washing and polishing the silver rims of Nick's BMW. All the cars were lined up in a row. On Fridays he washed each one, but now he left the bucket of water and sponges to take Theo's suitcase. She could tell he was also curious by the way he kept glancing at Theo's long black cassock.

Theo looked embarrassed and held onto his suitcase. "No, thank you. Where I come from, we carry our own things."

"And this?" he said, pointing to a bright red Porsche in Freddy's lineup.

"Oh, another one of Nick's toys."

"Another? How many does he have?" Theo began counting the lineup of cars and stopped at eight, dissolving into laughter.

"A few. I've forgotten how many." The lifestyle she took for granted suddenly looked over the top, even to her eyes.

"Sofia, before we go inside, please listen to me for a minute." He took her hands in his, and she was surprised by how warm they felt. "There are so many things we left unsaid. Whatever happened in the past, happened. I don't want it to spoil our friendship. My world is different from yours. But you made a good choice, and I don't want you to have any regrets."

"No regrets," she whispered. "That's difficult, though. It's not easy to forget."

He took a deep breath and cupped his hand under her chin, "What I think you really mean is that it's not that easy to forgive."

"Do you blame me?"

"No, I blame myself. But I beg your forgiveness for the hurt I caused. Somewhere in your heart, I hope and pray you can find a way to forgive me. For your own sake, not for mine, you have to make peace with the past. Otherwise, it's impossible to move forward."

Before she could reply, the door burst open, and Nick charged outside, reminding her of an excited schoolboy eager to see a playmate.

"Finally, we got you here!" Nick rushed over, and they greeted each other with a hug and much backslapping. "My friend, the priest. Look at you, a man of the cloth, wearing the black rasa and a beard. All respectable and proper. Just don't expect me to kiss your hand."

"You haven't changed at all. Except that you dress better than when I last saw you," Theo said. Immediately, they fell into the familiar pattern of ribbing each other.

"You haven't changed either. That's what happens when you hide in churches and monasteries. You stay young and fresh. Unlike the rest of us fighting in the trenches. Luckily, we have Natalie's wedding, otherwise we would never have managed to get you here."

"I'm very excited about the wedding. I can't wait to meet the family."

"We're glad to have you with us. It's going to be a fantastic wedding," Nick said.

"Although you were too busy to meet me at the airport," Theo pointed out.

"I'm sorry. I had a work crisis. But I sent my better half. Doesn't she look well? I've taken good care of her, don't you think?" Nick placed a possessive arm around her waist and kissed her cheek.

"She's even more beautiful now," Theo said. "You're a lucky man."

The old rivalry, Sofia thought. Thirty years later and they're still at it. She followed them up the stone steps, planning her escape as soon as possible.

"Well, what do you think?" Nick said as they walked through the front door and into the main entryway of the house. "Not too shabby for a boy who couldn't afford a pair of shoes, right?" Proudly, he waved his hands towards the opposite end of the room where Grace had opened the concertina sliding doors and tucked them into hidden wall slots on either side. The outside greenness merged into one continuous expanse with the inside.

Sofia rolled her eyes. There it was again, his constant need to show off, as if people couldn't see for themselves how well he'd done.

"Bravo," Theo said. "Everyone in our village knew you were the boy who would go most far in life." In the banquet-sized entrance hall, surrounded by artwork worthy of museum walls, she saw that Theo's eyes went straight to the icons she had collected over the years.

"I like the icons," he said, and smiled at her as if he knew without a doubt that she was the collector of these pieces.

"Ah, you're just like Sofia. Your eye is always on the religious objects," Nick said, quickly adding, "Mind you, those icons are priceless."

"I can tell," Theo said. "Well, I'm excited to be in this beautiful country and in your beautiful home. I can't wait to meet Dimitri and Natalie."

A soft voice interrupted them. "Madam."

They all turned.

"Master, I'm sorry to interrupt, but there's an urgent call for you," Grace said.

"Please excuse me—" Nick began.

"But—"

She could not believe he was doing it again. Leaving her to take care of Theo.

"Sofia, we have strikes going on. To be expected with all the new announcements by the government. But I have to deal with it. Unless you want to take over."

"I'm sure I could handle it," she called out after his retreating figure. *If I didn't have fifty other things to take care of. Including this priest.*

"That's fine," Theo said, a reassuring look on his face. "I need to rest and freshen up after my flight anyway, and I'm sure you have a lot of things to take care of for the wedding."

"Yes," she grabbed the lifeline. "Grace will show you to your room, and I know she's prepared the Greek appetizers, *mezedes*, for you. We'll all meet in the evening." She knew she was handing him over like a baton, but at this point, she didn't care.

"Come, Father, please follow me," Grace said, and led him away.

Thank God for Grace, Sofia thought, as she headed upstairs to her bedroom. No regrets, she repeated aloud and stood on the balcony watching Freddy skim a few floating leaves from the top of the pool. In the distance, metal spikes and glass shards glinted on top of the wall protecting their property. She had to get moving for her appointments, but she remained rooted to the spot, unable to move. In this enormous house where she had always been content, cocooned by walls and wealth, a sadness descended upon her. After so many years, the sight of Theo had sparked a million buried memories.

A movement near the olive trees caught her eye. Theo was walking in the garden. His lips seemed to move in a silent prayer, and in his hands, a prayer rope. He was only a few meters away, but in a different world, oblivious to her presence. He had been gone long enough to be forgotten, but the sight of him had dislodged something in the depths of her heart, and she could feel this drop of pain moving through her body. Dimitri's words from the morning came to mind: Mom, I don't think a person can choose who they're going to fall in love with.

SIX

The African Clock

Grace

When Grace knocked and pushed open the guestroom door, she saw Father Theo praying and backed out. But she stayed in the doorway, unable to stop staring at the kneeling man. He had his back to the door and kept his head and shoulders bowed over the coffee table. Since his arrival, there was a sense of peace and calmness in the house. When she stood next to him, it felt as if she were stepping out of the cold and into a warm pocket of air. Only Sofia seemed rattled by his presence. He was a handsome man with thick hair and a face that was only slightly wrinkled. She could imagine a young Sofia hopelessly in love with him. But that was so long ago. Why would she still be so angry with him? He looked like a saint, not that she knew what saints looked like. All he'd asked for was a glass of water and she placed it on a table near the door. She left without a word, leaving the man to pray in peace. That was the job of priests. To pray. Not that she knew much about God. But she liked the idea. And she liked that those who did believe were praying for others. If she found the right moment, she would ask him to include Isaac in his prayers. It couldn't do any harm. The boy needed all the help he could get.

She made her way down the staircase and spotted more packages piled at the front door. Gifts for Natalie's wedding arrived every day, just as Johannes seemed to be growing more slack. He knew very well that deliveries were his responsibility. Not hers.

Huffing and puffing, she picked up the parcels and carried them to the kitchen. Sometimes Johannes reminded her of Isaac's good-for-nothing lecturers. Lazy. Just plain lazy. It had been almost six weeks since Isaac had written that exam. And still, no final results had been released. How long did it take to grade a few papers?

She could hear the phone ringing in the passage and ignored it. It had to be Mrs. Penny again. The woman had already called twice that morning to ask about seating arrangements as if she, Grace, would know where Sofia had seated the niece. Of course, she knew. And unfortunately for the niece, it wasn't anywhere near Dimitri, but she certainly wasn't telling. She had perfected the art of playing dumb. Her job was to keep Sofia calm as the wedding date approached. She wished the day had already arrived so it could be over and done with, and everyone could return to normal. Even she was feeling the strain. There was constant tension and busyness in the house.

She turned to her cooking, which always relaxed her. She opened the top oven and a blast of heat threw an aroma of oregano and lemon into the air as she peered inside. Good, her potatoes were baking to a crisp perfection. In the bottom oven, she admired the *pastitsio's* bechamel sauce bubbling into a golden brown. Everyone loved her potatoes and *pastitsio*, the Greek lasagna. She couldn't blame them.

Through the open window she saw the lamb skewers turning slowly on the rotating spit. At least Johannes paid attention to this duty, although in fairness, he had been hired as the security guard at the front, not a cook.

Anyway, they were ready for the evening gathering. She wiped her hands on a dish towel and glanced at the television that flickered in the corner. Images rolled across the screen: People packed in cars and taxis cruising the streets of Johannesburg, blaring hooters, and flying the African National Congress flags. Everywhere, they sang, danced, and clapped, ecstatic about De Klerk abolishing the apartheid laws. Her father had predicted that she would live to see this day. Of course, she was happy, but for her it was too late. It was all about Isaac now. What would *he* do with this opportunity to live in a free and democratic South Africa.

"Mom?"

She swung around and dropped the dish towel from her hands. "Isaac! Where did you come from? What are you doing here? I was just thinking about you!" She ran over and hugged him. "Maybe the prayers of this priest are already creating miracles."

"What priest?"

"Never mind. How did you get here? What about your classes?"

"I caught a ride with friends. Everyone is celebrating. It's just for a few days."

"Yes, but will you miss class? And what about that exam? Did you pass?"

"There are no classes for a few days."

"Why didn't you tell me you were coming home?"

"I thought I'd surprise you."

"You certainly surprised me. But you didn't answer my question. Did you pass that exam?"

"Of course, I passed."

"Why didn't you let me know, you idiot? You know how worried I've been." A feeling of relief washed over her.

"I'm telling you now."

"This is such good news. What did you get? An A?"

He kept quiet.

"Maybe a B? Or a C?"

"What does it matter what grade I got? As long as I passed."

"Fair enough. How long will you stay?"

"We're going back soon." He sounded a bit vague, but she was too happy to care. "Let me get you something to eat. We have a small dinner party here tonight, but we have a lot of food. Mrs. Sofia won't mind if I make a plate for you. They're going to be so happy and surprised to see you."

She pulled out the Cypriot *meze* platter from the warming drawer: grilled *halloumi* cheese, *sheftalia* and *loukanika* sausages, fried baby squid, and octopus. She'd even made *dolmades*, stuffing the vine leaves with rice and pine nuts in case the priest was fasting from meat.

"I'm going to give you sausages," she said. "You won't like the other stuff."

"Agreed," he said, wrinkling his nose at the squid and octopus. "But I can't stay to greet everyone. I'm meeting my friends in half an hour to celebrate."

She turned sharply and looked at him again. His T-shirt slogan read, *One Man, One Vote*. "I wish you'd stay a little. Dimitri wants to leave the country. Mrs. Sofia is very upset about this. Maybe you can talk to him?"

"Me? Why would he listen to me?"

"Because you're friends."

"Mom, he's a privileged white boy. He has his own group of friends and I have mine. If he wants to emigrate, let him. Good riddance."

"I can't believe you just said that." Who was he hanging out with? she wondered. "He's your friend. The two of you grew up together."

"He's my friend, but he's not really my friend. We come from two different backgrounds."

"I'm sorry you feel like that. I think you're wrong. Anyway, the streets are dangerous tonight. You'd be better off staying here."

"I'll be fine," he said, wolfing down the food on the plate. "I'm not a kid anymore. Don't wait up for me." He wiped his lips with the napkin she thrust into his hands and began walking out the door.

"Isaac," she said, and he stopped. "Your grandfather predicted that apartheid would be overturned in our lifetime. He would have been very proud of you. You are living the dream that he and I were denied. Please be careful out there tonight."

"I will. Don't worry about me. My friends are waiting. My real friends. I have to go." And with that, he gave her a hug and hurried out before she could say another word.

She stared at the empty plate and wiped the back of her hand across her cheeks. Where did these tears come from? She scolded herself and turned back to the television screen.

"This is a Damascus moment for De Klerk," the reporter said. "Oh sure, De Klerk has become a saint overnight," she muttered to herself. Had it not been for the pressure of the resistance movement and Mandela, there would never have been a change. Although she had to admit that De Klerk was giving up power, a difficult thing for any leader to do. She could at least give credit where credit was due.

She topped off the *meze* platter, and then stopped. Her mind replayed the conversation with Isaac. His voice. Something was off. When she'd asked if he'd passed the exam, he answered a little too quickly. And his eyes. They shifted left and right when she'd asked how long he was staying. A feeling of unease crept over her.

As she ran through all the nuances, wondering if she'd missed something, an antiseptic smell filled the air. Peter. She knew it was him without even turning around. He always brought the hospital smell home with him.

"Hi, Grace. I thought you'd be out celebrating," Peter said, attacking the platter as Isaac had done a few minutes before. "I love these dolmades. You make them better than my mother."

Grace laughed as she looked at Natalie's fiancé, still dressed in his hospital overalls. She loved this boy, too, and didn't want to tell him that his mother couldn't cook to save her life.

"Don't worry, Peter. We have Isaac celebrating for all of us today. He was here five minutes ago. He surprised me. He didn't come to see me, of course. He came to celebrate with his friends."

"I don't blame him. It's a big deal. And I'd be worried about him if he wanted to sit home with his mother," Peter said. He washed his hands at the kitchen sink and used her apron as a towel.

"I'm just worried about him out on the streets tonight."

"You're a mother. That's your job. But I'm the one you need to worry about tonight. I must meet the priest who's going to marry me and Natalie, and I didn't have time to change. What's he like?"

"He's very nice. He's also in his work clothes. And he prays a lot."

"Well, we need prayers," he said.

"Here, take this outside before you eat everything," she said, and handed him the platter of appetizers.

While she had been distracted with Isaac, they had all gathered outside, and she peered through the open window that overlooked the covered patio. She loved this window. From here, she could see and hear everything and still feel like she was part of the family, even when she was in the kitchen, apart from them.

Sofia sat as far away as possible from Father Theo, and Grace could tell that she was keeping an eye on Dimitri and Annelize. The poor girl was fiddling with a napkin on her lap while Dimitri sat with an arm slung across the back of her chair. Every now and then he squeezed her shoulder. He's in love with her, Grace decided. And Sofia had better get used to the idea.

She turned back to her work and listened as snippets of conversation floated through the air.

"Tell us about the mother of all welcomes," Master Nick urged Father Theo.

This sounded interesting, and since her work was done for now, she didn't feel guilty about seating herself on a high stool to see and listen better. The priest looked like a normal man now, a glass of red wine in his hand and a playful expression on his face. He spoke in Greek, but she had no problem following him. He began to tell a story about how Johannes had greeted him with an AK-47 rifle.

"Never in my life has anyone welcomed me like *that*," he said, shaking his head. Master Nick wiped tears of laughter from his eyes, but Grace didn't know whether to laugh or cry. This was her country through the eyes of a visitor.

For sure, Annelize was missing some of the jokes. She didn't laugh like the others and only smiled awkwardly every now and then. Poor girl. She wished she could translate for her. It didn't take long for Father Theo to notice the problem too. He switched to English with a Greek accent, and soon the others followed his example. *Good*, she thought. She liked this man. It was rude to speak Greek when the girl didn't understand a word.

"The Greek word *xenos* has a double meaning," Father Theo was saying. Grace pricked up her ears. He was looking straight at Annelize. "It means not only a stranger but also a guest. So a stranger is always welcome in a Greek home because they're automatically a guest too."

Annelize shot him a shy smile.

Wow, Grace thought, and turned back to her pots and pans. She hadn't realized that herself. Maybe the priest would soften up Sofia on this issue.

Or not, Grace thought, as Sofia stormed into the kitchen with a stack of heavy plates and banged them down on the table with a clatter. If only she wouldn't act like that. Grace closed her eyes. For a second, she was tempted to scold Sofia the way she scolded Isaac or Dimitri when they were little and couldn't have their own way. But she quickly reminded herself that she was an employee, and kept quiet.

"I don't know why Dimitri invited that girl to a private family dinner," Sofia said.

"She seems like a nice girl—"

"Don't you start with me, too," Sofia said, cutting her off and turning to the television. "What's happening with the celebrations? Still wild parties in the streets?"

"Isaac came home. He surprised me just a while ago."

"Oh! Why didn't you say so? Where is he? Tell him to join us."

"He's gone out to celebrate with his friends. I'm not happy about that."

"Well, there's no use worrying. These boys will do what they want whether we like it or not. Why don't you take a break and we'll clean up together later. Take some food for yourself and for Isaac. He'll be hungry when he comes home."

"Thank you, Madam." She needed a break. Her uneasiness about Isaac was growing by the minute as wild mob scenes flashed across the television screen. She couldn't bear to watch anymore.

―

In her room, she covered the food with foil and placed it into the small refrigerator. The last thing she needed was food. She ought to be ecstatic with everything that was happening in the world around her. And with Isaac passing his exam. But something gnawed at her, and she couldn't put her finger on it.

She dropped heavily into the recliner and reached for her father's transistor radio on Isaac's desk. Maybe she could catch the tail end of the news on Springbok Radio. She fiddled with the knobs to get a clear signal and remembered the day her father had come home with this treasure, a gadget from the white world, something she had never seen in the Black townships.

"What do you have for me?" she demanded, dancing up and down.

Her father pulled out a small black box and she stopped clapping.

"*This*?" Her excitement vanished.

He pushed a small lever on the box, and suddenly the room filled with a crackling sound, followed by English-speaking voices.

"Where are the people?" she shrieked, jumping up and looking around their one-room shack. "The box is too small to fit people inside it!"

He laughed so hard that tears streamed down his face.

"The box is filled with special electrical pieces that catch invisible waves sailing through the air," he explained. "The box changes the waves into sound, and we hear the voices of white people as if they are standing in our house."

"Oh..." she said. "What am I supposed to do with it?"

"I want you to listen carefully to the way these people speak," he said.

"Why?"

"I don't want people laughing at you for not pronouncing words properly." His voice was agitated and serious. "My whole life, people have laughed at me for the way I speak English. Even though I'm teaching you to read, I don't know if I'm saying these words properly. You read all day by yourself. There's no one to help you."

"I don't need any help."

"It's important to master the art of reading. That way they will never be able to fool you. I don't want you ever to feel that you aren't good enough. You're every bit as good as anyone else, Black or white. Promise me you'll learn to read and speak English properly."

"I promise."

She missed her father more than ever now. Isaac had one more year left. If only her father were alive to see him. Once the newscast ended, she switched off the radio and turned to her bookshelf.

Her eyes settled on *Gone with the Wind*. She had struggled to finish that book. Most of the Blacks in the story were depicted as stupid and uneducated, which annoyed her. But she liked Mammy, who was defined by loyalty rather than color. Overall, she liked the book. It gave her hope. The struggle in South Africa was not unique. Even a country as great as America had experienced a civil war because of race.

As she skimmed through it, the phone rang. She sat bolt upright and reached for the receiver.

"Hello?"

"Mother, it's me."

"Isaac? What's the matter? Why are you calling me?" He sounded like a small child.

"I'm in jail. Can you please come get me?" Isaac's frightened voice crackled over a bad line.

The room seemed to close in on her. She could barely breathe.

"What do you mean you're in jail?"

"They arrested me—"

"For what?"

"Some of the people in my group damaged storefronts when we were dancing in the streets."

"I told you! Didn't I tell you to be careful? But you never listen to me. How are you going to be a lawyer if you're in jail?" she screamed. "Which jail are you in?"

"I'm at John Vorster Square. The police station. I can't talk long. Can you bring bail money?"

John Vorster Square. Terrible thoughts raced through her mind, each one worse than the previous; detainees mysteriously falling from ninth-floor windows, detainees slipping in the shower, cracking their heads open, bleeding to death.

"Mother? Are you there?"

"Yes, yes. How much money must I bring?"

"I'm not sure..."

"I will come, and I will bring money."

"Thank you."

Then the line went dead.

She sank onto the edge of the bed, thumping her temples with balled fists. This was exactly what she had never wanted. She was back in the township again, remembering those nighttime raids by the police. People jumping from their beds and running half naked in the darkness, hiding in sewage pipes to escape arrest. And there she was, trembling in a small bed, bursting to go to the toilet, growing more terrified as the barking dogs grew closer. Her father's whispers—"Use the bucket under the bed." Her, trying to pee as quietly as possible, petrified the police would hear the tinkling sound.

And still her father had insisted, "Not all whites are bad or racist. They are people like you and me. They cry like us. They laugh like us. It's the *system* that's bad, not the people." She had believed him. She had no alternative.

And she had so badly wanted Isaac to escape all this, to never know it. And he was so close. Today of all days, for him to be arrested. Someone was playing a cruel joke on her.

She stood up and pushed her hand between the mattress and box spring to reach her emergency stash of cash. She pulled it out and counted the notes. One thousand rand. Before Christmas she'd splurged and bought Isaac a fancy gold pen to sign legal documents one day. Obviously, she had gotten ahead of herself. The money would not be enough. There was only one thing left to do. She tucked the money into her bra, swallowed her pride, and went outside to the family.

At first, they didn't notice her. She waited in the shadows, reluctant and ashamed to disturb their happy gathering.

"So, on Mt. Athos," Master Nick was saying, "is that the only thing those monks do all day? Just sit around and pray? It seems like a waste of time."

"Don't underestimate the prayers of those monks," Father Theo said. "They pray all day and all night for us. Considering how bad things are in the world, can you imagine what it would be like if no one prayed at all?"

Well, those prayers hadn't done Isaac much good, she thought, shuffling from one foot to the other.

"Grace, what are you doing there? What's wrong?" Sofia was looking at her with a startled expression.

"It's Isaac, Madam." Her mouth was so dry that the words stuck in her throat, and she began to cough, unable to finish the sentence.

"Yes? Is he okay?"

"No. He's in jail. At John Vorster Square."

There was a stunned silence. Then everyone began talking at once.

"You see what happens in this country, Father Theo? They arrest innocent kids, and let the terrorists run wild," Dimitri said.

"Nick, you must go and find the boy," Sofia said.

"I'm not sure they'll give him to me," Master Nick said, already standing and scraping his chair back. "What did they arrest him for, Grace?"

"Damage to property. Or at least that's what he said."

"I thought he was celebrating?"

"That's what I thought, too."

"Dad, what difference does it make?" Natalie's voice was shrill. "Just go get him. You know what John Vorster Square is like."

Master Nick frowned.

"Please, Nick," Sofia said.

Master Nick looked from her to Sofia and then back to her again.

"Okay, Grace, I'll go and get him. Let me grab some cash and my checkbook just in case. Tell Johannes to bring the car to the front. Theo, are you up for this? Do you want to take a closer look at the *other* South Africa? Dimitri, come with us. Let's see if you learned anything in law school."

"Master, I have one thousand rand. I don't know if it's enough. But I can pay you back if it's more."

She tried to give him the money, but he pushed her hands away.

"No, put it away please, Grace." And then. "You don't want to come with us, do you?"

She did. She very much wanted to go to her boy. But the way he asked, she could tell he didn't want a woman with them at John Vorster Square.

"No, Master. It's alright. I'll finish cleaning up here. Do you think they'll let him out tonight?"

"Depends on how good a lawyer Dimitri is. Don't worry, Grace. Money talks. And we have a priest for good measure. I'll try to bring him home to you tonight."

"Okay, Master. Thank you. I'll pay you back every month, little by little."

"That's the least of our worries." He dismissed her offer with a wave of his hand.

Father Theo looked at her and smiled. "Everything will be fine."

"I hope so." She also hoped he would say a prayer that worked. Up till now, she had neither believed nor disbelieved in an invisible God. But at this moment she wanted to believe.

The men left and Peter stayed so that he and Natalie could drive Annelize home. Grace returned to the kitchen where Sofia had already rolled up her sleeves and tied an apron over her silk blouse. They worked in silence for a long time.

"I tried so hard for that boy," Grace said when they were almost finished.

"I know how you feel," Sofia said. "Sometimes I feel they ignore everything we tell them. Children don't seem to understand the sacrifices parents make. Until it's too late."

They continued to clean until the kitchen was spotless, and there was nothing left to do.

"Do you want to sit and watch television with me while we wait?" Sofia offered.

"No, Madam. Thank you. They might be very late. It's okay. You go to bed and I'll wait. You've also had a long day."

Sofia gave her a hug and left her alone. For a moment, Grace stood in the kitchen and felt a sting of regret for not accepting Sofia's offer. There was nothing she could do now except go back to her room and wait by herself. Why had Isaac done such a stupid thing? If they brought him back in one piece, she would give him a good slap, or *klap* as the Afrikaners would say. But he was bigger than her now. He wouldn't even flinch if she boxed his ears.

———

Her small room seemed to grow smaller as she paced up and down, and her fears grew bigger as time passed slowly. That copper clock was driving her crazy with its ticking. The sound seemed so loud. She stared at the familiar clock face shaped like the African continent. Ten-thirty p.m. Her eyes followed the movement of the second hand as it moved towards the southern tip. History was moving forward with the abolishment of apartheid, but she and Isaac were moving backward. A springbok bulged from the center of the clock as if it were running across the great plains of Africa. The deer's face looked startled, perpetually frozen in fear and surprise.

She couldn't stop the thoughts pounding inside her head. What if the university heard about this arrest? Would they kick him out? All these things had to be reported. What if they couldn't get him out of jail? "Try not to get arrested on a Friday night," she recalled Dimitri once saying. "Why?" she asked. "Because a person could sit in jail the whole weekend since there were no magistrates or judges available on a weekend to hear cases," he explained.

She should have stopped Isaac when he rushed out of the house. She had known it was a bad idea for him to go.

Frustrated, she got up and turned on the electric kettle for the fourth time, then switched it off. Not even a cup of tea would make her feel better.

She parted the curtains at her window. The outdoor lights lit up the empty verandah. There were a few leaves on the stone pavers. She picked up a broom from the corner and went outside. She swept the walkway between her room and the main house. And then she swept it a second time. A brown lizard scurried along the brickwork. It froze for a second under the light. It seemed he was examining her with the same scrutiny she gave him. It slithered onto the white windowsill, changed from brown to white, and disappeared into a hole.

"Grace, why are you sweeping at night? Are you alright?" Sofia was waving at her from her bedroom window on the other side.

"Yes, Madam." She stopped sweeping and went inside. Sofia would think that she'd taken leave of her senses. Maybe she was going mad.

It was after midnight when she heard the crunch of wheels on gravel. She sprang from her chair and peered through the curtains. One. Two Three. Four figures. Yes. They had him. She breathed a sigh of relief.

She could see Master Nick and Father Theo turn toward the main house while Dimitri escorted Isaac up the pathway to her room. She wanted to rush outside but held back for a few seconds. Isaac must have sensed her eyes because he stopped for a moment. He tried to smile but couldn't manage it. As a child, he'd always tried to cover his fear with a cheerful mask, hiding his wounds from the world. Tears began to stream down her face, and she rushed out.

"Thank you, Dimitri, thank you. Did they give you a hard time?" She ran her eyes up and down Isaac. He seemed to be in one piece. She wanted to kiss him and slap him at the same time. She did neither.

"Not really," Dimitri said. "We were lucky. My father happened to know the police captain. That was helpful. And when they saw we had a priest with us, they softened even more. No one paid any attention to me."

"Ah, Dimitri." She laughed, even though her heart was breaking.

"Isaac, go inside and wash up," she said.

"You might wish you were back in jail by the time she's finished with you," Dimitri said, waving goodbye and heading back to the main house.

When she closed the door behind her, they were alone. She wanted to point out that it was his white privileged friend who had brought him home and that his other maniac friends were the ones who had landed him in jail, but she kept quiet.

He sat at the table sighing loudly while she placed in front of him the food Sofia had given her earlier. She sat opposite and watched as he wolfed down the leftover meat and potatoes. His eyes were bloodshot.

There was a knock at the door, and she tensed. The police maybe?

"Grace, it's me," Sofia called out. She opened the door and Sofia stood there in her dressing gown.

"I thought Isaac might need a pair of pajamas," Sofia said. She held out a pair of Dimitri's striped pajamas.

"Thank you, Madam. He's fine." Grace knew this was Sofia's way of checking to see if Isaac was alright.

She took the pajamas and stepped back so Sofia could see for herself.

Isaac said nothing and kept his head bowed.

"Did they hurt you? Are you alright?" Sofia said.

"I'm okay," he said. "Thank you."

He kept his eyes lowered.

"If you need anything, call me," Sofia said. "Good night and sleep well." And then she left.

"You should have stood up when the Madam was speaking to you."

He continued eating. He was making her nervous. She didn't know how to handle his silence.

"I'm happy that you're home," she said at last. "But I don't know why you got into such trouble. Today of all days. Did you not hear De Klerk's speech this morning?"

Still no reaction. She stood up to stop herself from banging her hands on the table and answered her own question.

"No, I don't suppose you did. You were too busy running in the streets with hooligans."

She stood behind him, squinting at the top of his head, hoping he hadn't picked up something disgusting in those lice-infested jails.

"Do you not realize that the injustice in this country is almost over? Mandela will be released any day now. He made the sacrifice for you and all the other young people of this country. All you have to do is pass your exams, get your degree, and find a job."

He continued to ignore her.

"You should have been more careful. Is this how you're going to repay Mandela? By landing yourself in jail? He went to jail so that you could be free. Don't you understand the future is yours now? He gave it back to you."

At this, he let out a sarcastic laugh, pushing the small table, almost toppling it as she rushed to catch the plate.

"Apartheid might be over in the statute books, but it's far from over in reality. What about all the hurts of the past? Must we just forget about that? Forgive and forget? They've destroyed us for life. And I tell you one thing—the universities will continue to pass the white students and fail the Black students."

Suddenly, she understood. "*That's* what this is all about, isn't it? I asked you twice whether you passed that exam and I'm going to ask you a *third* time. Did you pass that exam?"

"I already told you. Yes, I passed the stupid exam."

She didn't believe him and felt a physical pain inside her chest. She clutched her hand over her heart and tried to ignore the agonizing soreness. It crossed her mind that if she had a heart attack and died at least she would be spared all of this.

"I'm trying to beat a system working against me."

"You're lying to me! And you're running around like a *tsotsi*, a thug, and blaming others."

"I'm not lying. And we need something radical to happen before people treat us right. Nothing is going to change in this country without a revolution."

She glared at this stranger. Was he crazy? The revolution was over. Could he be on drugs? These were not his words.

Someone had brainwashed him. She remembered those pamphlets she had found in his drawer one day, full of radical ideas she'd crumpled up and thrown away.

"Isaac, if you don't believe that something radical has already happened in this country, then we've wasted a lot of money trying to educate you. And which people are you talking about? You cannot change the whole country in one go. But *this* family has been so good to you. Master Nick got up from his dinner to get you out of jail. With *his* money. Not my money. The Madam got out of bed and came in her pajamas to bring *you* pajamas. They've paid for your school and university. And you say they're not treating you right?"

"*Master* and *Madam*! Please!" He almost spat out the words. "Where in the world today does one person call another person Master or Madam? In your mind, and in their minds, you'll always be the maid thanks to what the whites of this country have done to us. Even if you've read more books than most of them, you're still a maid. Look at you. You live in this tiny room at the back while they live up front in that big house."

This was not her child speaking. For sure, he was on drugs. She took a deep breath to calm herself. "You're wrong. Let me tell you about this Greek family—and you listen! I turned up on Sofia's doorstep with you tied to my back in a blanket after we were evicted from our home through no fault of my own. A friend sent me to this family for a job. And when Sofia opened her front door and you were crying, she took you and held you. I'd never seen a white woman hold a Black baby before. And she gave us a room without even knowing who I was. As for the Master and Madam thing, it's difficult for *me*, not them, to change the lifelong habit brought to us by the English colonizers. It means nothing when I say it. They're just stupid words. I love these people like they're family, the way I love you, my own son. Besides them and you, I have no one else."

He stood and paced around the small room, which didn't seem big enough to contain his rage.

"You think that because they're paying you a good salary compared to the other maids, that it's fine? That salary isn't enough for someone who's on call seven days a week. And you think Nick Levantis is doing us a favor paying for my bail money? It's nothing for him. How many cars does he have in his garage—six, eight, ten?"

She shook her head sadly. "I choose to be here. These people have been good to us, even if you can't see it. And the country will change, and things will get better. If you don't learn to let go of the past, you'll never be able to move forward."

"Mandela has been in jail for twenty-seven years! I can't just forget about that in one second."

"You're tired. Go to sleep. We'll talk tomorrow," she said.

She needed to lie down. She took out her other set of clean sheets and made a bed for herself on the small sofa.

"Sleep in my bed for tonight," she said, and tried not to think about the filthy jail floors where he'd been.

He made a few half-hearted protests, but she was no longer in the mood to listen to his babbling. This escapade of his had sucked the life out of her. He collapsed onto the bed without even changing into the clean pajamas. The old mattress groaned under the weight of his body. Within seconds his mouth gaped open and he began to snore. The sound of exhaustion, her father used to say, when she'd complained about his snoring. Within a couple of hours she had gone from wishing her father were alive to see the day the country was freed from apartheid, to being glad that he wasn't alive to see his only grandson released from jail.

Isaac's large feet jutted over the edge of the bed and as she stared at him, old African tales about the *tokoloshe* monster biting off toes crossed her mind. She pushed the superstitious nonsense out of her head and stroked his cheek, trying to soothe away the nightmares beneath his quivering eyelids. She had done her best with this boy, but clearly her best had not been good enough.

Eventually, she lay down. For a long time, she stared at the ceiling, listening to his agitated sleep. Just as her eyelids began to droop, a siren shattered the stillness. Rex and Lola began barking. She bolted from the sofa and Isaac jumped off the bed, hands above his head, shouting, "Don't shoot. Don't shoot."

"It's the alarm in the main house. Lie down. Don't move." Trembling, she pushed him back and pulled on her pink dressing gown. She peered through the window. Silence. Someone inside the main house must have switched off the siren. False alarm? Or not? Was it safe now?

She tiptoed barefoot to the door of their small flat and opened it, wincing as it creaked. The two dogs rushed to her, ears twitching and alert. She patted Rex and picked up Lola.

Father Theo's voice filtered through the darkness, calm and reassuring. "It's okay, Grace. It's me. I'm sorry. I made a mistake and set off the alarm. I woke up everyone. I'm sorry."

Followed by Master Nick's voice. "Grace, it's us. We forgot to tell Father Theo that the alarm system is on at night. He thought he was still at the monasteries of Mt. Athos and could just take a walk whenever he felt like it."

"Too much excitement for me, Grace," Father Theo said. "No wonder they couldn't find anyone to replace the old priest."

Relieved, she waved at them and shooed the dogs away. She went back inside. Isaac was still sitting on the edge of the bed, eyes wide open, like the deer on the African clock above his head. It was four in the morning.

"Go back to sleep, Isaac. Everything will be alright. One day."

"You're fooling yourself with lies. It's never going to be okay." He fell back on the bed and curled his large body into a fetal position.

She pulled a light blanket over him. By the time she lay down again, he had shrugged it off. Her fingers itched to straighten the covers, but her aching feet refused to budge. Was Isaac right? Was she fooling herself? She lay staring at the darkness pressing in on her, feeling the vastness of the African continent and remembering how Father Theo had looked as he prayed.

SEVEN

Two Steps Forward and One Back

Sofia

On February 11, 1990, South Africa and the rest of the world waited to see the man who had not been seen in twenty-seven years. At any moment, Nelson Mandela was expected to walk out of jail. It also happened to be the Sunday before Natalie's wedding and Sofia sat behind her desk in the study, trying to keep an eye on the family in the next room as well as the historical event unfolding before her eyes on television. Every few minutes her eyes flitted to the screen. Cameras zoomed in on the restless crowd gathering at the Victor Verster Prison outside Cape Town. Helicopters hovered above the yellow police vans lining both sides of the pathway Mandela was expected to take. One wrong move and the whole country could go up in flames. The clock on the mantelpiece showed that it was already an hour past the scheduled time for his release.

While she waited, Sofia scrutinized the seating chart on her desk and fiddled with the heating pad nestled around her neck. Her muscles were stiff and howling with pain. She'd spent hours hunched over, playing around with the best possible seating combinations for the guests.

"Natalie, why aren't you working on the seating arrangements? Why am I doing this?" she called out as Natalie tried to sneak down the passage. Everyone, including the Annelize girl, had gathered in the large TV room to watch the major event.

"Because the guests are mainly yours and Dad's," Natalie replied in a reasonable voice.

"Can't argue with that," Sofia muttered, turning back to her table arrangements.

"Why don't you come sit in here with us?" Natalie yelled across the passage.

Because Annelize is there, she wanted to say but pretended not to hear the question. The girl was becoming a permanent fixture in the house. One wrong move and she could lose her son along with the girl.

For a third time she drew a line through Theo's name, unsure where to place him. Reluctantly, she moved him from table number one back to the main table. She wished she could blot him out of her life forever, but, like Annelize, it didn't look like he was going anywhere. Apparently, the Greek community loved him. Everyone was begging Nick to make him stay longer.

A soft knock interrupted her dilemma. Grace stood in the doorway. "Can I watch Mandela's release with you?"

"Of course." She got up and moved to the sofa, glad for Grace's company. She took the seating charts with her.

"Do you think Dimitri will be upset if I place Mrs. Penny's niece next to him and Annelize at the wedding?"

Are you serious? Grace's raised eyebrows seemed to be saying. "Of course he will be upset, Madam. Don't do it," Grace said.

"Okay." Reluctantly, she moved the niece back to another table with single young adults.

"Where's Isaac?" she said, still circling her finger over the chart. "I haven't seen him all day."

"In my room. He wants to watch it there."

"The two of you should be watching this together. Does he want to come in here?"

"No, we're not speaking to each other. And he can't return to the campus until the police are satisfied with his paperwork."

Her heart went out to her. It wasn't fair that Grace had to suffer like this. "Nick and Dimitri are still trying to get the charges dropped. I wish they'd hurry up."

"Yesterday, I forgot to turn off the iron. I almost burned one of Master Nick's shirts."

"He has plenty of shirts. Don't worry about it. That's what happens when children drive us crazy."

"He can sit in my room for the rest of his life," Grace declared, wringing her hands together.

"Don't be like that," Sofia said. She remembered Isaac's face one time as a young child. He must have been about eight or nine. She'd been helping Dimitri with homework. Isaac's serious little face had suddenly popped up next to them at the kitchen table. *Can you please also help me with my homework?* Filled with guilt, she had glanced at Grace scrubbing pots and pans and pulled up a chair for the child. That was when she had decided she would pay for his school fees.

"Will Isaac stay for the wedding?"

"No," Grace said. "He's missed so much work already. The moment Master Nick sorts out those papers, he's on that bus straight back to the university. Maybe as soon as tomorrow." She crossed her arms over her chest in such a way that Sofia knew there would be no further discussion on this topic.

She glanced back at the television screen. "Mandela's late," she said.

"Ah, Madam. After twenty-seven years, what's a few more hours."

And suddenly there he was, a tall man who walked slowly from the gates of the prison. He held the hand of his wife, Winnie.

"That woman—" Sofia muttered. She was not a fan of the controversial Winnie Mandela.

"She's a handful—" Grace said.

They both leaned forward to see Mandela. Sofia removed her reading glasses. She saw an old man with a full head of hair that had gone gray. He stood stiff and stern in a dark gray suit and tie.

"I didn't expect him to be so tall. Nor so old," Sofia said.

"He walks like a king," Grace said, her voice thick with emotion.

Then he lifted his hand in a clenched fist salute, transforming the old man into a fierce warrior. His youth had been drained away by the years in prison, but his courage and defiance remained unbroken. Sofia trembled while the crowd roared with approval. She threw a sidelong glance at Grace, who was dabbing her cheeks and eyes with tissues.

"He's free. Mandela is free. And soon Isaac will also be free," Grace said. "Assuming he can stay out of jail."

"You mustn't be so hard on Isaac," Sofia said.

"Just like you were never hard on Dimitri and Natalie," Grace said, and gave her a sad smile.

She desperately wanted to believe that everything would be fine for both boys, but she felt her heart skip a beat as Dimitri's voice floated across the passage. "It's definitely time to leave the country. The past cannot be forgotten."

"There he goes again," she sighed, holding her head in her hands.

"Don't worry, Madam. Dimitri is only talking. You know how these boys are. When the time comes, he won't leave."

"My mother used to say that when the children are small, the troubles are small. And when the children are big, the troubles are bigger."

They sat together a little longer, following the former prisoner's motorcade to an uncertain destination. After a while, she grew restless but saw that Grace's eyes remained glued to the screen.

"It'll be a while before Mandela speaks," she said. "I'm going to check on the bachelor party preparations. We have Dimitri to thank for the last-minute relocation to the house."

"Yes, Madam," Grace said, her eyes still fixed on the motorcade.

In the kitchen, she stood by the window where Grace normally stood. Outside, Annelize and Natalie helped Dimitri and Peter arrange cushions on the extra chairs for the bachelor party. In the center of each table that surrounded the dance area, the girls had placed a bottle of Chivas scotch. Peter's bachelor party was the only task that had been assigned to Dimitri, and it had almost turned into a disaster. If only he would listen sometimes.

"I told you that Peter would never agree to a wild bash at Kinky Nightclub," she yelled through the window, unable to restrain herself.

"I bet you told him my plans and that's how I got caught," Dimitri said.

"I told Dimitri I'd elope with Natalie if he didn't cancel the nightclub venue," Peter said, and everybody laughed.

Half irritated, half indulgent, she watched her rebel circle the dance floor, testing the suppleness of the floorboards he'd managed to rent at the last minute. It always amazed her how Dimitri managed to land on his feet every time. He must have sensed her eyes because he looked up and flashed his see-I-told-you smile.

She rolled her eyes, wondering how much it had cost to cancel the other venue. He gave the dance floor a few more thumps with his heels.

"We can't be bouncing up and down on cement when the Greek dancing starts. It's hard on the feet," he said.

"I hope you haven't lined up some exotic belly dancer or stripper. I won't have such people in my house."

"Who, me?" He threw up his hands in mock surprise.

"Is there anything else I can do to help before I leave?" Annelize called out to her.

"No, but thank you for asking," Sofia said. "The caterers are bringing the food shortly." She tried to stem the coldness that crept into her voice every time she had to interact with her. The girl had done nothing to deserve this—except fall in love with her son.

She really was gorgeous, she had to concede, as she ran her eyes over the girl's soft gray-blue dress that clung in all the right places. The color enhanced the blueness of her eyes, making her more striking, and there was an openness in the beautiful face that seemed to convey a kind personality. She hated herself for being so mean-spirited.

"Well, I'll be leaving then, before it gets too dark. Dimitri hates it when I drive alone at night," Annelize said. Dimitri came up behind Annelize, nuzzling her neck.

With a sinking feeling, Sofia waved goodbye and watched Dimitri walk her to the car. He was more than smitten, and she had no idea what to do about it.

"I didn't realize until just a while ago that the bachelor party had been relocated to the house," Nick said, coming in from the verandah with a bewildered expression on his face.

"That's because you're never here," she said. "How would you know what's going on at home?" As soon as the words came out of her mouth, she regretted them. She knew she was being unfair. He had a lot on his mind. The labor unions were becoming more demanding, emboldened by the imminent change in government. Everything he had worked for was on the line if a militant government took over.

"It's because I'm out playing golf all day," he said. And she knew he was more worried than he was letting on.

"I'm sorry," she said. "I know you're stressed. It's all taken care of. Your son thought he was going to have the bachelor party at Kinky, but Peter refused. That's all."

He burst into laughter, shaking his head, and even she had to laugh at the absurdity of Dimitri's logic.

"I don't worry about anything as long as you're around," he said. He stood with her a few more minutes surveying the activity with a smile on his face. For one foolish second she thought he might stay and keep her company, but soon he was frowning at the contracts in his hands. He had completely forgotten about her. She watched as he walked back to his study at the other end of the house.

Exasperated, she tried not to resent his obsession with work. "Come watch Mandela's speech with me later," she called out, a little desperate. He continued walking without a backward glance. He hadn't even heard her.

The heck with all of them, she decided. She marched outside to check on the details Dimitri would have missed and almost stumbled over Isaac, barely managing to catch herself.

"Isaac, what are you doing there? I didn't see you." He was crouched on the ground, tucking wires and extension cords safely out of the way.

He stood up rubbing his knees. His smile was not as friendly as usual.

"I'm tidying up these wires. My mother said someone might trip over them. Are you happy with the way I set up the tables and chairs?"

"Yes, very nice. Thank you so much."

"Did you watch Mandela's release?" She felt bad that he was working on a day like this.

"Yes." He shuffled his feet and looked away.

He was not happy and she didn't blame him. She tried again. "It's an amazing day in history."

"Yes, but nothing is going to change."

"How can you say that? You sound like Dimitri."

"I'm unstacking tables and chairs and he's getting ready for a party. Nothing changes. Everything is still the same."

For a second she was taken aback by the bitterness in his voice. "But you'll party together later."

"I'm not invited."

"Oh!" Of course he wasn't. No one had been expecting him. He was only supposed to come home the following weekend for the wedding. "But you don't need a formal invitation. You're family. It's expected that you'll be there with the others."

"No, it's fine. I have to leave early in the morning anyway. Master Nick said I can head back to university. He'll sort out the papers."

"Surely you can join them for a short time. Even for just an hour or so."

"I don't know. I'll see."

"Isaac, everything will be okay. Don't be discouraged by one mistake. It's all over. The charges will be dropped. You must put it behind you and move forward now."

"Thank you," he said, and walked away.

Something was off in the way he had looked at her, but there was nothing she could do about it now. She wondered if she should apologize to Grace for Dimitri's oversight with Isaac. No, it would only make matters worse. She walked the rest of the verandah, smoothing down tablecloths, tweaking the balloon decorations.

A slight movement caught her eye through the open sliding doors that led to the study. Grace had disappeared, but she could see Natalie curled up on the sofa, the way she used to lay there as a little girl. Late afternoon rays slanted through the open door, catching the highlights in Natalie's hair. She lingered on the stone steps, enjoying the moment. Soon, her baby would be gone.

Natalie looked up, a tired smile on her face.

"Mom, can you believe I'm getting married next week?" There was a slight tremble in the undertone of her voice.

"Is that a touch of wedding nerves?" She sat on the sofa and pulled her closer. "Come here," she said, stroking her hair. "The house is going to be so empty without you."

A slight hesitation, and then, "Mom, what would you say if I told you that Peter loves me more than I love him?"

"I would say that you're a very lucky person. In every successful marriage, there's one person who loves the other a little more."

"Really? Somehow that doesn't seem fair."

"It's all about give and take. Some people give more, others take more. And the roles can reverse. Depending on the day of the week, or month, or the seasons of our lives. Or the circumstances that come your way."

"That sounds so boring and practical. I think Dimitri and Annelize might be the real deal. The perfect couple."

"Hah! The perfect couple. There's no such thing."

"Mom, when did you give up on love?" The indignation in her voice was sharp.

"I never gave up on love. I just don't believe in fairy-tale nonsense. Dimitri and Annelize are in the honeymoon stage, when it's all about each other. Then life gets in the way. No one knows if it's the real thing until you've been tried and tested."

"Sounds very unromantic."

"I've told you before, romance is a temporary thing. But you are a very fortunate young woman. Peter is a good and kind human being who will love you and look after you forever."

"Like you and Dad."

"Yes, we can always rely on each other. What more can you ask for?"

"The magic. The chemistry. I don't know," she said, getting up. "Don't listen to me. I'm having a severe case of wedding nerves, like you said." And with that she got up and walked away, mumbling something about the house being a men's only zone for the bachelor party and her having to catch up on some sleep.

"Have a good sleep and you'll feel better." Even Natalie was allowed to have a meltdown the week before her wedding. She turned to the television screen, wondering if Mandela was ever going to speak, and still hoped that Nick would join her.

Mandela finally stepped onto the podium. He began to read the long-awaited first speech as a free man: "Today, the majority of South Africans, black and white, recognize that apartheid has no future."

So far so good. He went on to praise De Klerk for his integrity, and then, in the next breath, his stern voice urged the international community to continue sanctions against the white government, stating that there was no alternative but to continue the armed struggle and the resistance movement.

What? No, be quiet. He was going to drive her son away for sure. With every word, she inched closer to the edge of her seat. This was not what she wanted to hear. She reached for a pen and notepad on her desk. Arrange extra security for the wedding guests, she scribbled. Rioting was the last thing she needed just before the wedding. Instead of calming the nation's fears, he was fueling them.

Nick poked his head into the study.

"Are you watching?" he said.

"Yes, a little inflammatory, don't you think?"

"Don't worry too much. He has to say these things. The people expect it. They'll sort it out. I have to get to bed because I need to be up early in the morning. By the way, when you come upstairs, I left something for you on the dressing table. Don't stay up too late spying on the boys."

"Alright, goodnight," she said, barely listening to him.

Greek bouzouki music filled the night air with lyrics of love and longing. She dimmed the lights in the study and drew the curtains, leaving just enough space to peek through the open patio doors. All the childhood friends had gathered together. The *kefi*, that rush of fun and high spirits, was powering up. She wrinkled her nose at the mixture of male sweat and alcohol.

Dimitri was badgering Peter. "*Ela Vre*, come on guy. Next week you'll be married. Who knows what restrictions my sister will impose. Dance now. Before it's too late."

Peter's cheeks reddened as he approached the center, stiff awkward movements echoing his discomfort. "You look like you're about to begin open heart surgery," someone called out.

More wild, raucous laughter. And yet, as he began to soak up the lyrics, she could see his body relaxing and he began to sing in Greek, "Pes Mou Pou Poulan Kardies"—"Tell Me Where Hearts Are Sold." She smiled and wondered if Natalie could hear this from her bedroom window. If Natalie wanted romantic, this was it. Peter was slightly off-key and had a few glasses of scotch in him, but the feeling was there. A circle of friends knelt around him, egging him on. Watching, she wrapped her arms around herself, snuggling into the shadows, enjoying the show.

The song ended and Dimitri walked to the center, needing no encouragement. No one could dance a solo *zeibekiko* like Dimitri, and the reserved Peter made a sweeping bow, slapped Dimitri on the shoulder, and happily handed over the spotlight.

Dimitri stood in the middle of the dance floor. A lock of hair fell over his brow and she watched as he looked down, then up, flashing that smile. Anyone would think it was his bachelor party instead of Peter's.

He raised his arms slowly, and she could tell he was savoring the music. "*O Aetos*"—"The Eagle"—his favorite song. He lifted his right leg and threw his head back. His feet and body surged into the music and he became the eagle. His muscular body sliced the air as he picked up the rhythm in circular movements. Two steps forward and one back. The tempo slowed and he dropped his body to a kneeling position, slowly lowering his chest to meet the ground. Someone slid a whiskey glass across the floor. He edged his face closer to the glass till he gripped it with his lips. Just as the music began to soar, he pulled himself up, defying the odds, swallowing the alcohol in a single gulp. Falling and rising. Everyone's struggle through life. A roar of approval. Again, he circled the dance floor, widening his circle, then breaking free, triumphant with the music, soaring like an eagle.

She had never seen him dance with so much passion. For a moment she wondered if he was imagining freedom in another place. Far away. America. Please, God, no. She wished she could make him understand that he would never be able to recreate this same circle of tight-knit friends again.

"*Opa*," somebody shouted. She peered into the darkness. Who was that? And then she recognized Isaac's voice. He stood behind the circle of friends, apart from the others. On his face, the fake smile of an outsider. Her heart went out to him. On the day Mandela had walked to freedom, her son had forgotten to invite Isaac to the party. Like the *zeimbekiko* dance, she thought. Two steps forward and one back. What a pity. She slid the patio doors towards each other, taking one last look. Dimitri was dancing again, arms outstretched, a dark silhouette against the night sky. She could barely remember that feeling anymore, being young enough to dance the night away without a care in the world.

Slowly she made her way up the stairs to her bedroom. Nick was fast asleep, and she tried not to wake him as she slipped out of her clothes. Pale moonlight slanted through the window, touching a red velvet box on top of the dressing table. Oh yes. She'd almost forgotten. Nick had said something about a box for her. This had to be it. She flipped back the lid without much curiosity, and then gasped. A diamond necklace shimmered in the moonlight. Pear-shaped, round, and marquise-cut diamonds formed numerous tiny blossoms, each floral motif intricately set and luminous. The piece was beyond beautiful. And beyond extravagant, even for Nick. Probably worth a fortune. He had stuck a hastily scribbled note to the inside of the lid: *I thought this would match your dress for the wedding.*

She lifted the necklace from the box and placed it around her neck, managing to hook the clasp on her own. She gazed at her reflection in the mirror. The diamonds shimmered under the moon's glow. She walked over to the bed and brushed her lips against his forehead.

"Do you like it?" he mumbled sleepily.

"It's stunning, thank you."

He smiled and fell asleep again.

She tiptoed back to the window. Greek music filtered upwards, and she breathed in the fragrance of jasmine and frangipani blossoms from the garden below. The evening stars were bright in a way that made her heart ache. Still wearing the necklace, she climbed into bed and curled herself around Nick's back, surprised by the warmth of his body against hers. But Natalie's question kept tugging at the edges of her mind: *When did you give up on love?*

EIGHT

The Wedding Day

Sofia

Joyful lyrics from the traditional Greek wedding song blasted through the house speakers. Sofia opened her eyes and found Nick standing at the foot of their bed, smiling at her.

"The music is so loud," she said, trying not to grimace. "You're going to wake everyone up."

"That's my intention." The belt of his navy dressing gown was loosely cinched and looked crumpled at his waist while his face looked pale in the morning light.

"It's our daughter's wedding day," she said, starting to feel a surge of happiness.

"I can't believe Natalie won't be sleeping here tonight," he said, surprising her with a tinge of sadness that seeped through his voice. His lips drooped at the corners.

"*Se parakalo*, please." She had heard about such situations, where fathers battled with the idea of their little girls leaving home. "When they come back from their honeymoon, she'll be down the road. At least once a week, they'll be over here for dinner."

He smiled, but she could see that beneath his cheerful veneer, the heart of an ageing man was aching. She didn't blame him. Soon it would be just the two of them.

"*Ela*, come. Pull yourself together," he said, as if *she* was the one who had just been moping. "It's going to be a beautiful wedding." He kissed her forehead. And she had to smile. The male ego.

"Well, I've done everything I can to make sure the day is perfect," she said. "Do you think our son will realize how important family is? Maybe he'll change his mind about leaving the country?"

"Let's enjoy Natalie's wedding day, and then we'll worry about Dimitri later. One at a time." He kissed her one more time. "Come on, mother of the bride. You need to get dressed."

She swung her legs over the edge of the bed. "I'm up," she said. "Let's get moving. This is the day I've been working toward for a year."

"A year? Your whole life, I think." With a cheeky grin, he ducked the cushion she threw at him, and left the room.

Within a few hours the house hummed with noise and people. Voices and laughter echoed off the marble floors. Florists traipsed in and out. They delivered bouquets, wrist corsages, and miniature roses for the men's buttonholes. Photographers and videographers hauled clunky camera equipment, and she gritted her teeth as she watched them dodge furniture, scrape her white walls, and bump cocktail tables laden with refreshments and drinks. Ecstatic bridesmaids and flower girls rushed up and down the stairs, dragging makeup and clothing bags behind them while hairdressers asked her how many people they had to style and where they should set up. Perfect chaos, she thought.

Before long, it was time for the photographs. She nipped into the dressing room to check her dress in the long mirror one more time. As mother of the bride, she knew she'd be scrutinized from top to toe. The light yellow silk, scooping low on her shoulders, had turned out well and the necklace from Nick was perfect. Her mother would have approved, and for a moment she was overcome with longing. If only her mother were here to see this day. It would have made up for the sorrow she had caused so long ago.

Enough, she decided and headed straight to Natalie's room. Natalie sat at the dressing table, dressed and ready, with the *koumbares* and maids of honor fussing over her hair and veil while photographers snapped away as discreetly as possible in the background. Natalie appeared calm and relaxed. She had never seen a more beautiful bride than this daughter of hers. Without turning, Natalie caught her eyes and smiled at her from the mirror's reflection. Sofia blew her a kiss.

"Take a quick picture with your daughter," the chief photographer suggested.

"Yes, please." She leaned in close to Natalie, grateful for the suggestion. These were precious moments.

When the photographer was done with her, she saw Grace waiting patiently by the door.

"Grace, you look beautiful." Grace wore the stunning blue taffeta gown they had chosen together.

Grace beamed and waved over a junior photographer. "Madam, please, let's take a photo of the two of us. I already took one with Natalie. Once they start with the big family group, they might forget about me."

"How could I forget you, Grace?" She slipped an arm around Grace's waist and they posed and smiled as the photographer clicked away.

"I know you're sad about Isaac not being here today," she said. "But after Natalie's wedding, you can take some time off and go check on him."

"Yes, thank you, Madam. I will," Grace said.

And then a grating voice came booming down the passage, "Well, don't the two of you look like the new South Africa." Anna Economou pushed her carefully styled head in between her and Grace. Sofia took a deep breath, ignored the comment, and stared at Anna's bright red gown. Well, at least she's not wearing white, Sofia thought.

"Sofia, I can't believe you're allowing the bride and groom to see each other before the wedding," Anna said. "Shouldn't the photographs be done *after* the church ceremony. Everyone knows it's bad luck for the groom to see the bride before the church service."

God help me, Sofia thought. Soon, the two of them would be related. "It isn't practical *after* the church," she said, as calmly as possible. "It's not just a couple of photographs. It's more like a two-hour production. The guests become tired and restless waiting for the couple to arrive at the reception hall."

"Well, you know best," Anna said, even though her tone conveyed the exact opposite. And off she went, flouncing down the staircase in *that* dress. Nobody could miss her.

"I hope she doesn't become worse," Sofia muttered. "My poor daughter."

"Madam," Grace said, and placed a warning finger over her lips before walking away and shaking her head.

As long as Natalie and Peter were happy together, that was all that mattered, Sofia decided and headed down the stairway.

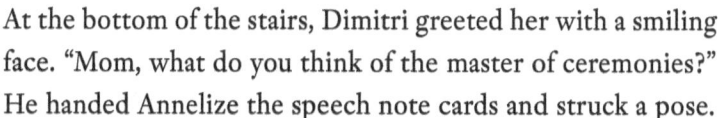

At the bottom of the stairs, Dimitri greeted her with a smiling face. "Mom, what do you think of the master of ceremonies?" He handed Annelize the speech note cards and struck a pose.

"Very handsome," she said, and felt her heart bursting with love and pride. In the buildup to the wedding, she had neglected this boy. Never mind, she would make up for it afterwards. She tweaked and straightened the miniature rose pinned on his tuxedo lapel, and observed Annelize as discreetly as possible over his shoulder. Her long blonde hair was knotted loosely at the nape in a French chignon, and she wore an understated long black dress with quiet confidence. Elegant, Sofia grudgingly conceded. For any other function, she might have given her a ten, but for a Greek wedding, no. It wasn't customary to wear black at a Greek wedding. Still, with her blonde hair, blue eyes, and black dress, the girl was a stunner and stood out. There really wasn't much hope that any other Greek girl might catch Dimitri's attention. Then a thought struck her. Surely, Annelize's parents were also less than thrilled about the idea of their beautiful daughter moving halfway across the world to be with Dimitri?

Before she could consider this further, one of the flower girls raced down the stairs. "She's coming. She's coming. The bride's coming!"

In that moment, she forgot about her son and his girlfriend and followed the ripple of attention. All eyes were focused on the staircase landing. Nick joined her and as they waited, he threw a quick glance at the necklace she wore.

"Whoever bought *that* for you has excellent taste and must love you very much," he said.

"It's beautiful. Thank you, but way too extravagant."

"You're worth it," he said, and kissed her lightly on the cheek.

Suddenly Natalie appeared, every inch a fairy-tale princess with a sweeping circular train billowing behind her. Peter couldn't take his eyes off his bride. I know you'll look after my girl, she thought, as she watched his eyes glisten with tears.

Nick squeezed her hand tightly and she squeezed his hand back and swallowed her tears. This was the moment they had both been waiting for. To see their daughter as a bride.

Everyone followed the bridal couple and moved outside in a swirl of gowns and giggles, tuxedos and laughter, until the photographer took over and restored some order. Within minutes he was orchestrating groups. She was glad she had stuck to her guns about choosing him. Of course, Anna Economou had tried to impose her photographer, but she had pushed back hard. My photographer is the best in the country, she had told Anna firmly. No one had even heard of the one Anna was suggesting.

She watched as he expertly lined them on the stone steps leading up to the house. He snapped instructions to his young assistants and sweet-talked his subjects, coaxing smiles and loosening stiff poses.

She lingered on the side, enjoying the show and watching Natalie. Obliging as always, Natalie carried out the photographer's directions, smiling, twirling, kissing Peter, and stroking the hair of excited little bridesmaids. That severe case of wedding nerves had been forgotten. And when Natalie's future mother-in-law came and stood next to her, she made herself smile sweetly. "See, Anna, I told you photographs takes a long time."

"Yes, but he hasn't taken any photographs of Peter and I together," Anna said.

"Don't worry. It's on the Wish List we gave him. You're just not right at the top of the list."

"That's fine," Anna said. "I'm only the mother of the groom. Nothing important."

She ignored the sarcasm, and the two hours passed quickly. Soon it was time to leave for the church. Nick leaned over the verandah railings. "Off you go, mother of the bride. As the group combinations finish, I'm packing them into the waiting cars, otherwise we'll be late. You're with the bridesmaids."

She hurried along to the front of the house, past the kitchen, where Grace was already closing up, locking doors and windows.

"Go, Madam. I'll be the last one. Johannes will bring me. Don't worry. I'll take care of everything."

Only the Mercedes and the white Rolls-Royce remained in the circular driveway. Two white ribbons extended down the length of the Rolls bonnet and met at the front tip, by the wings of the miniature lady poised to fly. The ribbons sagged ever so slightly in the middle. Not quite as tight as she would have liked. Her fingers itched to undo and fix the ribbons.

"*Aman esi*, you're unbelievable," Nick grumbled under his breath as he came up behind her. "I know exactly what you're thinking. Leave it alone." She dropped her hands and gave him a sheepish grin before sinking into the back seat of the Mercedes amongst the chattering flower girls. Who cared about the ribbons, anyway?

"Ready, Mrs. Levantis?" the driver asked.

"As ready as I'll ever be." A row of sparrows lined the sliding gates. The gates rumbled open, and the birds flew upwards in a flutter of feathers. She hoped she hadn't forgotten anything and crossed herself as they set off for the church.

———

The driver pulled right up to the front steps of the church entrance and Sofia waited for the little girls to bundle out first. They held up their long skirts and flower baskets while a trail of rose petals and rice spilled after them. At this rate, they'd be lucky to have any petals left for the guests to throw. It is what it is, she thought, taking a deep breath before stepping out to follow the girls.

A unanimous "*aahh*" rose from the crowd as she stepped out of the car. A playful breeze lifted the bottom layers of her gown and she put on her most dazzling smile. I can do this, she told herself.

A surge of murmurs rose from the gathered guests, and she felt a hundred pairs of eyes examine her dress, hair, makeup, and of course, the necklace. "How much do you think it cost," she heard someone say.

She weaved her way through the compliments, scrutiny, good wishes, and what she imagined to be envious eyes. Her late mother would have censed the bride and the whole family with burning incense to counter the effects of envy. She wished she had remembered to do this ritual.

As she lifted the sides of her dress and climbed the steps leading to the main entrance, she paused and looked up. Theo stood at the top, waiting for the bride. Framed by the arched mahogany doorway, he made an imposing figure in his dark red cloak embroidered with golden crosses. A mosaic icon of Christ, embedded in the stonework above the doorway, gleamed in the sunlight.

For one split second, she wondered if a man of the cloth, who took his faith so seriously, could have lied about those letters she never received. And even as she thought this, she gave herself a mental slap for allowing it to cross her mind on such an occasion. Nothing was going to spoil her happiness on this day.

She reached the top of the stairs and greeted him warmly, kissing both of his cheeks.

"Well," he said. "Every Greek mother's dream, right?"

"Yes, to see their children married and living happily ever after."

"And it looks like every Greek in the City of Gold is here, showing off their gold," he said.

She laughed, remembering just how funny he could be. She scanned the courtyard, which had become a showcase of designer gowns, tuxedos, and expensive jewelry. The South African Greeks could hold their own among any glamorous group in the world. Even Hollywood would meet its match here. The guests had turned up in grand style for the wedding of the year. It wasn't often that they had a good excuse to haul out their gold and diamonds, normally locked in safes and bank vaults. Their faces shone along with the dangling earrings and sparkling cuff links as they enjoyed the opportunity to flash their wealth, and their chatter grew louder as they exchanged greetings and gossip.

Across the road in the church parking lot, expensive cars gleamed competitively next to each other while security guards she'd hired patrolled up and down. A few homeless people lingered outside the church gates, pressing their faces against the iron bars.

"This country of yours is definitely a different sort of place," Theo said, his eyes also drawn to those living on the streets.

A raucous burst of laughter interrupted the quiet moment. Dimitri was keeled over with laughter while Peter looked stiff and anxious. The glazed expression on Peter's face told her that Dimitri was doing a terrible job of keeping the groom calm, so she marched over.

Peter's eyes darted left and right as he clutched Natalie's bouquet of white roses and lilies, oblivious to Dimitri's back-slaps and the banter of the other best men.

"Relax," she said to Peter, and touched his cheek.

"I can't," he said. "Not now. Maybe later."

She wished Natalie would hurry up. What on earth was this girl doing? She had been ready hours ago.

A gentle tap on her shoulder. She turned to see Michalis. He greeted her in silence, like he always did, and the twinkle in his eye outshone the permanent scowl on his face. His familiar outfit, black pants and black shirt, had been slightly modified to black pants and a white shirt, carefully pressed and starched in honor of the wedding.

He placed a basil sprig into her hand. A memory of her father with a piece of basil tucked behind his ear jumped to mind. She had once told Michalis that this royal plant used by priests to bless people and homes had been her father's favorite. He must have remembered, and she was deeply touched by his gesture. This was Michalis's way of wishing them well.

"Thank you, Michalis," she said. She stared after him as he sprinted back inside the church, shoulders hunched against the world. It seemed to her that Michalis was always dashing to a secret task as if his life depended on it.

She tucked the basil into her purse and turned her attention back to the guests. The crowd had grown larger and louder. Only Theo stood quiet and still, his eyes focused on the road leading up to the church.

And then Anna came rushing up the stairs, pointing to her wristwatch. "She's rather late, Sofia, don't you think?"

Before she could reply, Theo jumped in. "I've been a priest for over thirty years. Brides are always late. It's nothing unusual."

Suddenly the sound of screeching brakes announced the arrival of Nick's black Mercedes. Why was Nick driving like a maniac? He was supposed to come with the bride in the Rolls. She felt a tightness gripping the area of her heart. Something was very wrong.

Nick bolted up the steps, two at a time, without a bow tie, without a jacket. She began crossing herself. People had noticed him and grew quiet. Peter's *koumbaro*, his best man, was the only one still chattering, and he stopped when Peter hushed him. What was it? A carjacking? A robbery?

Panting, Nick reached the top, white-faced, and with beads of perspiration dripping down his forehead. He gripped her elbow.

"What's wrong? Where's Natalie?" She could barely get the words out of her mouth.

"We must cancel the wedding."

"Why? Is she sick?"

"Natalie changed her mind." His voice was so brittle, it was barely a whisper.

Peter and his parents stared at each other and then at her. She grabbed the nearby pillar, trying not to fall over. She heard Dimitri let out a low, soft whistle and watched Theo grip his gold cross.

Peter remained rooted to the spot, looking at her. "What's going on?" he asked, clutching the bouquet. His parents moved closer, forming a protective flank on either side of him.

She swallowed hard. She felt her head spinning and looked up at the blue sky, unwilling to believe that God would allow this to happen. How could she not have seen this coming?

"Peter..." Sofia began. His whole body shook. She loved Peter like her own son, but she was powerless to stop his pain.

"It can't be," Peter said. "Please tell me this isn't happening."

She placed her arms around his stiff shoulders, rigid with shock.

"Your daughter is a fool," Anna hissed in Sofia's ear.

For once she agreed with Anna. Or maybe *she* was the fool for not seeing this coming? She felt her knees buckle, and she grasped again at the pillar. She had wanted this marriage more than anyone. More than Natalie, she realized.

"Please take these. I don't know what to do with them." Peter thrust the bouquet into her hands.

She stared at the white roses interlaced with imitation pearls. Somewhere she had read something about pearls being bad luck on a wedding day. What was it? Pearls and tears. Something like that. She felt herself becoming lightheaded and dizzy.

Dimitri came to her side and gripped one arm. "It's okay, Mom. I'm here."

"You're all I have now."

He turned to Theo. "Father, do you want to tell them or shall I?" he said, inclining his head towards the crowd.

"You tell them, Dimitri," Theo said. "I'll take Peter inside the church."

"I'll take your mother home," Nick said.

She watched Peter stumble down the aisle, next to Theo instead of Natalie. She wanted to run after him, but her legs refused to move.

"Ladies and gentlemen...," Dimitri began addressing the guests with some sort of explanation and apology.

Dear God. She didn't want to hear this. Nick steered her down the steps, hurting her elbow with the tightness of his grip, as he tunneled a path through the crowd. People moved aside and she felt their eyes trailing after her as she passed. She bowed her head and kept it down, making sure she didn't trip on the pavement cracks.

She stumbled into the car, and when she glanced back she could see heads shaking. A cacophony of rumors had to be spiraling into the air. For a brief moment she thought that maybe this was happening to another family, that she was watching everything from above. But then she looked at Nick's ashen face next to her. No, it was happening to them.

"What did Natalie say to you?" she asked, as he slammed his foot on the accelerator, and the speedometer swung sharply to the right. He leaned forward, his knuckles white as he gripped the steering wheel.

He kept quiet.

"What did I miss?" she said.

No answer came from Nick.

She wracked her brain. "Do you think she's in love with someone else? Someone she doesn't want us to know about? Maybe she's sick? How can she do this to Peter? And to us?"

Questions tumbled from her mouth. Nick's lips remained a tight thin line.

"You should have seen this coming," he said at last.

"Me? What about you?"

"You're the mother. You should've picked up on something."

"Oh yes, that's right. I forgot. Because I'm at home more than you." She sank back into the leather seat. Sometimes he could make her feel so alone, even when she was sitting right next to him. She turned away and looked out the window. The sun had dropped behind the buildings and long shadows cut across the road. On the street corner, dustbins overflowed with rubbish. She watched the city slip away as they entered the highway, and she wondered how a morning that had begun with so much promise and joy could turn upside down in a matter of hours.

At the guard house, Johannes stared at them with a confused expression on his face. A few hours ago he had been clapping his hands and shouting, "Happy, happy."

They pulled up to the front of the house. Perhaps there had been a mistake. Maybe Natalie had been overcome by a sudden illness, a fever, or something that had made her delirious, and Nick had misunderstood. A faint stirring of hope rose inside her as she thought about these possibilities. But as she gazed at the front door, the house looked eerily quiet, as if it were also in shock. The white ribbons on the Rolls had come undone and flapped aimlessly in the breeze.

Then Grace opened the front door, still dressed in her beautiful blue taffeta gown. She was wide-eyed and frantic as she ran down the steps.

"Madam, Master," she said. "Natalie's gone. She took one of the cars and left. I'm so sorry. I couldn't stop her."

God, I want you to know that you have let me down. Sofia kicked off her heels, yanked up her gown, and knocked over a flower stand, sending stargazer lilies and roses flying across the room as she sprinted up the stairs.

Surely, she would find Natalie upstairs. *Please God. Don't do this to me.* She flung open the door. Everything was immaculate, except for the satin gown that lay in an empty heap on the carpet. She bent down and picked it up, hugging the dress to her chest, trying to embrace the girl who was supposed to be inside it.

The air didn't feel right. She couldn't breathe. The ceiling seemed to be spinning above her head. Terrible thoughts raced through her mind. Natalie had been kidnapped. There was no other logical explanation. Any minute now, they'd call, demanding ransom.

Grace's footsteps came pounding down the passage.

"Madam, Father Theo's on the line." Grace stood in the doorway, handing her the receiver.

"Theo?" she grabbed the phone.

"Sofia, everything's fine," Theo said.

"How can everything be fine?" she screamed. "Natalie is gone. She's not at the house. Theo, I think they've kidnapped my child."

"No, calm down. She's with me. Natalie is at my house."

"What?"

"She couldn't go to a friend's house because all her friends are at the wedding. She had nowhere to go. So she came to me."

"Is she okay?"

"Yes. She's a little upset, but I spoke with her, and she's sleeping in my guest bedroom now."

"And the wedding is definitely off?"

"Yes, I'm afraid so."

"But what's the matter with her? Did she say why? She's hurt Peter so badly. Such a good boy. And she humiliated him in front of the entire Greek community. Why did she do this?"

"I didn't ask too much," Theo answered. "I thought it would be better for her to rest."

"I'm coming there right now."

"No, please, let her rest. She's not in a state to see anyone. She's very upset about what she's done. She said she needs to get away by herself. She's leaving on Monday. For New York. She said something about staying with her cousin Eleni."

"What? My God, she's totally lost her mind. I have one child wanting to leave the country. Now this one has beaten him to the punch? I cannot believe this."

"I'll try to get her to speak to you when she wakes up. But let her rest now," Theo said.

"Let her go." Nick's voice boomed through another telephone receiver. "She must not come back here. I don't want to see her. I can't believe my daughter would do something like this."

There was a click from Nick's side, and she gave the phone to Grace, who was hovering nearby.

She stumbled her way to Natalie's bed and sank into it. To deal with all this *and* Nick's rage was too much. She closed her eyes.

"Madam, if Natalie is with Father Theo, then she's okay. Let me help you out of your dress. Then you must lie down, and I'll make some tea," Grace said.

Thank God for Grace. Grace's strong arms unzipped the tight-fitting gown. She slipped into Natalie's pale blue pajamas, inhaling the familiar scent of her perfume, before she climbed under the covers. She pulled the sheets over her like a shroud. The day's exhaustion had seeped into every bone and muscle, and her whole body was now aching.

Why hadn't she seen this coming? She was a terrible mother, that's why. Nick was right. This was all her fault. The girl had tried to tell her, but she'd refused to listen. She felt herself drifting in and out of sleep, but her mind kept churning up images. Brides running. Grooms crying. Crowds of people. Hands cupped over whispering mouths.

She had no idea how much time had elapsed when she heard a soft knock on the door and opened her eyes. She squinted. Theo stood in the doorway, wearing the somber black *rasa* he normally wore. She sat bolt upright.

"Theo, what's wrong? Has something else happened?" She flipped back the bed covers and swung her legs over the side.

"No. Everything's fine," he assured her. "Natalie's asleep. Peter's okay. He's at his parents' house. I went past there first, and then came here to check on you and Nick."

She stared at him for a few seconds, and even in her dazed state, she sensed there was more.

"But there's something else?'

"Yes, I wanted to tell you in person."

"Tell me what? She's met someone else?"

"No, nothing like that. She came to me earlier in the week, full of doubts about the wedding. I told her to listen to her heart. I don't know if I caused this . . ." His voice trailed off.

"You what?" She couldn't believe what she was hearing. She gripped the edge of the mattress and stood, horrified.

"Why didn't you tell me?" she said.

"She asked me not to tell anyone."

"But you encouraged her to break up with him? How could you do that?" She could feel herself trembling.

"I didn't encourage her. I told her to listen to her heart."

"You caused this," she screamed at him. "I told Nick he never should have invited you here." She began pacing up and down the length of Natalie's room, stepping around the discarded wedding gown. "You're a priest for heaven's sake. You're supposed to keep people together, not break them up."

"That's unfair, Sofia, and you know it," he said. "Did you really want your daughter to make a mistake that she'd be stuck with for the rest of her life?"

"Who says Peter is a mistake?" Something inside her snapped. Was he suggesting she'd made a mistake with Nick? "I'm her mother and I know what's best for her. Not you. Who the hell do you think you are? It's rather strange, don't you think, that when you're around, the wedding plans of the women in this family change overnight!"

From the corner of her eye, a slight movement behind Theo caught her attention. Nick stood just inside the doorway, slightly unsteady on his feet and clutching a glass of whiskey. How long had he been there?

"Why don't you tell us why you changed *your* wedding plans. I'd love to hear," Nick said in a quiet voice that she'd never heard before.

Christe mou, God help me. Guilt overwhelmed her. He must've heard the whole conversation, or certainly the last part. And Theo was looking at her as if he, too, wanted to know.

The hell with both of them. "I've done nothing wrong. And I don't owe anyone an explanation. Theo and I were very young. That's all."

"But not too young to make marriage plans," Nick said.

There was a coldness in his eyes, and she realized her whole life was coming undone. She was losing the children. She was losing her husband.

"*You're* the one who invited Theo. Not me," she reminded him.

"I invited him as a priest and a friend. Not to come wreak havoc in my family."

"I am a priest. And I am a friend," Theo said. "And for those reasons, I'm walking out right now. You're overreacting, Nick, and you'll realize it when you've calmed down."

"*I'm* over reacting? My daughter has just abandoned a perfectly good boy on the steps of the church based on *your* advice, and apparently my wife had a cozy setup with you before she came to South Africa to find a fool like me. You're lucky you're a priest, otherwise I'd punch you in the face."

Theo stared hard at him, then turned, and left without a word.

"That's right, cause chaos and walk away!" she shouted after Theo.

Nick's furious eyes bore into her.

"Were you going to marry him?" Nick said.

"Are you being serious? Are you really asking me what an immature eighteen-year-old girl was thinking thirty years ago? Our daughter has just abandoned Peter in front of five hundred guests, and you're asking me about rubbish? *Ma ise sta kala sou*? Have you totally lost your mind?"

"I've had one too many surprises today. I know he always loved you, and I know that you felt something for him, too, but I thought that if I gave you everything, you would forget the past and learn to love me. Up till now, I was so sure of myself—and of you. I thought I had nothing to worry about."

"You don't have anything to worry about. I love you. Maybe not right now at this moment, but I love you when you're in your right mind."

His face remained skeptical.

"It's our daughter we have to worry about," she said.

He slammed the door so hard that the light fixture shook, and she stood for a long time shivering and watching it swing back and forth.

⇒

After a while, she picked up a framed photo of herself and the children in Cyprus. Alone, of course. Always without him. She couldn't help feeling bitter. She had been faithful to him all these years, and now he was furious about something that had happened when she hadn't even been married to him.

The children's suntanned faces grinned up at her. Without Dimitri and Natalie, her life was meaningless. These children were her life. If she didn't hold it together, her family would come apart, and the life she had worked so hard to build in South Africa would disintegrate. She lay down on the bed and held the photo against her chest.

Another knock. Grace marched in and set down a tray of tea as well as her knitting.

"Madam, what's going on? I just saw Master Nick and Father Theo. Master Nick's cheeks were so red, and Father Theo walked past me without even saying goodbye." Grace had changed back into her maid's uniform and stood there, hands on hips, eyes full of worry and concern.

"Oh, Grace. My life is falling apart. All this time I was worrying about Dimitri. But now Natalie has made the biggest mistake of her life. And my husband is worried about a time when I was even younger than Natalie and made the biggest mistake of my life."

Grace poured a cup of tea and handed it to her.

"It's not that bad, Madam. I don't think Natalie made a mistake. Any time *before* a wedding is not too late to change your mind. And Master Nick, you know him. He gets angry quickly and then gets over it just as quickly. He'll get over his jealousy when he calms down."

Grace took a sip of tea. "Anyway, you've been married for so long. It's too late for either him or you to change your minds now."

"Whenever that priest is around, things go wrong," Sofia said.

"I don't think Father Theo brings the problems. He just happens to be there."

She sighed heavily as she watched Grace draw the curtains in that no-nonsense way of hers.

"Grace, sit with me a while."

"I'm not going anywhere," she said, pulling the chair from Natalie's dressing table next to the bed and reaching for the remote. "Do you mind if I watch the television with the volume off?"

"No, go ahead."

"Grace?"

"Yes, Madam?"

"Thank you."

"For what, Madam? We are always there for each other."

"Grace, why do you think Natalie changed her mind?"

"I'm not sure. Maybe she realized she didn't love Peter enough."

"But there was nothing wrong with Peter."

"I know, but sometimes even the best match in the world isn't the right one for the heart."

"It's all my fault, Grace. I should have seen this coming. I don't know how I missed this. I'm a terrible mother."

"No, Madam, even I didn't see this coming. You're not a terrible mother. Children surprise us every day."

They sipped their tea in silence as Sofia replayed the day's events, examining everything over and over in case she had missed something. Suddenly, she remembered Michalis.

"Grace, could you please pass me my clutch? It's lying over there somewhere."

Grace leaned over and handed her the small sequined purse. She fiddled with the clasp and extracted the basil stem Michalis had given her. Was it only a few short hours ago? It seemed like a lifetime had passed. The fragrance permeated the air.

"It smells beautiful," Grace said.

"It was my father's favorite." She closed her eyes and breathed in the fragrance that always brought her father close. She thought about her mother's suffering as a young widow, and her sacrifice in sending an only child to South Africa.

She opened her eyes. "Grace," she said, "everything I did to my mother is coming back to haunt me a hundred times worse."

"Go to sleep, Madam. We can't control our fate."

Isn't that the truth, Sofia thought. She had tried everything to spare her children the struggles she had known. And yet she had failed. And if she had failed her children, she had failed at everything that mattered. She closed her eyes, listening to the rhythm of Grace's knitting needles and aware of the light shimmering from the television screen. In her worst moments, Grace was always there.

NINE

The Sewing Basket

Sofia

Sofia felt herself frowning as she opened her eyelids. Images of Peter's anguished face floated before her eyes. She breathed a sigh of relief. It had been nothing but a nightmare. For a few blissful seconds she lay there and believed this to be true. Then she edged up onto her elbows. A shimmering mass of empty tulle and satin lay discarded on the floor. Natalie's wedding gown. With a jolt, she sat upright. No. She was living the nightmare.

Next to her, Grace dozed in the chair, head tilted to one side, with soft snores escaping from her open mouth. Somewhere in the house, a phone rang. *Go away*. Probably some woman hungry for gossip and faking concern.

"I'll get it," Grace said, now awake and alert.

"Tell them I'm not here."

Grace hurried out of the bedroom. Within minutes she heard Grace's scolding tone float down the passage on full volume.

"Natalie! Your mother is so heartsore. How could you do such a terrible thing?"

Natalie! She sprang out of bed and bolted down the hallway.

"It's alright, Grace. Let me speak to her. Give me the phone." She coaxed the receiver from Grace's grip. Please, God, maybe Natalie had come to her senses.

"Natalie, what happened? You should've seen Peter's face. Standing there all alone, abandoned on the steps, waiting for you." She sank onto the carpet, pressing her back against the cold wall.

Grace disappeared then reappeared, easing a blanket between her shoulders and the wall.

"Mom, I just couldn't do it. He deserves to be loved more than I can love him."

"But why, Natalie? Why can't you love him? He worships the ground you walk on."

"That's the problem. I don't feel the same way."

"And you only realized this *on* the day of the wedding? Are you in love with someone else?" She pressed the phone against her ear, trying to hear what was not being said.

"I tried to tell you, but you wouldn't listen. You said it was nothing but nerves. But it's more than that. And no, there's no one else," Natalie sighed, sounding exhausted.

"Then what is it? I don't believe you could change your mind just like that for no reason," Sofia insisted.

"I didn't want to disappoint you and Dad. Or him. I've spent my whole life pleasing people. It's hard to break that habit. Then I found the letters."

"What letters?"

"The love letters."

"Peter has someone else? He wrote love letters to another woman? That no good son of a—"

"No, Mom. Not Peter. I was looking for something blue to keep the wedding traditions and I found this beautiful blue shawl. The letters were tied together inside the shawl."

"A blue shawl?" She could feel herself breaking into a cold sweat. "Where?" As far as she knew, *that* shawl was in Cyprus.

"In *Yiayia's* sewing basket. Remember how you shipped some of her things here after she died. You kept everything in one of the guest bedrooms. I found her sewing basket. She kept beautiful fabrics stashed in that basket."

"Yes, I never got around to sorting out all her things. But what letters are you talking about?"

"Yours, Mom. The letters are addressed to you. I put everything back the way I found it. I didn't mean to pry, but after I read those letters I knew I couldn't settle for less. That's the kind of love I want."

"I have no idea what you're talking about," she said, as an uneasy feeling settled over her.

"Mom, you know what I'm talking about. You must have read those letters. I know it happened a long time ago, and I understand that it's personal and private, but you don't have to pretend with me."

"I haven't read any letters and I'm not pretending."

"They're from Father Theo to you. Before he became a priest. You should read them. They're beautiful. I put everything back. I'm sorry, Mom."

The letters she had never received. But how could they be in her mother's sewing basket? She had pulled that basket out of the rolltop desk a long time ago. The smell of naphthalene moth balls had caused a sneezing fit, so she'd pushed it back for another time.

"Mom, can you please come to Father Theo's house? I need a suitcase and a few clothes. I'm going to New York and staying with Eleni. I can't handle all the Greeks right now. The whole of Johannesburg will be gossiping about me."

"Oh, *now* you're worrying about the Greeks." She closed her eyes. Why was God doing this to her? She had been so afraid that Dimitri would leave, and now she had Natalie asking for her suitcase.

"I need to get away and clear my head. Please, Mom. I need your help."

This was crazy. She no longer had the strength to argue with these children. Let them do as they pleased. "Alright, I'll see you in a few hours," she said. The receiver went dead and she looked up. Grace hovered over her with a worried expression. "She wants to go to America. She needs a suitcase."

"Yes, I heard. Another one for America. Maybe you and I should also go. It seems to be a popular place. Anyway, I'll check the suitcase she already packed for her honeymoon. I'll take out the bathing suits and all the sexy things and replace them with jackets, gloves, and sweaters. It's winter there, right? The opposite of here?" Grace said.

She nodded and stayed on the floor, unable to budge. "Grace, I don't know what I've done wrong in my life. I don't understand why God is punishing me like this."

"Come, Madam." Grace held out her hands and pulled her up. "You haven't done anything wrong. It's just life."

Lola scurried down the passage. Her eyes looked large and sorrowful as if she knew that all was not well. A tiny bundle of fur with a big heart.

With the blanket around her shoulders and Lola at her heels, Sofia walked slowly to the guest bedroom. She pushed back the curtains and let in the light. The mahogany rolltop desk stood in the corner. She shrugged off the blanket and rolled up the desk lid. There it was. She extracted the fabric-covered basket, a deep red, with flowers embroidered all over. It was larger than a normal sewing box and she had forgotten how heavy it was. She could feel her heart pounding as she lifted the latched hoop of the lid.

An unmistakable scent of naphthalene, bitter and sad, nipped her nose, and she shrank back into a coughing fit. Holding the basket at arm's length, she peered inside. Whatever a person might need for sewing lay neatly stacked in the top storage tray: stainless steel scissors, multicolored reels of thread, needles, short and long, silver thimbles, and measuring tapes. Her mother had always been organized.

She lifted the top tray. Beneath it, beautiful fabrics—red silk, white satin, black velvet—leftovers used to create new and beautiful pieces. At the bottom of the pile, something blue caught her eye. And there it was, the blue shawl she had forgotten at Theo's house a lifetime ago. It was wrapped around a small bundle, and she could still see the faint tear down the middle. With trembling fingers she untied the knot. A stack of yellowing envelopes lay inside. She stared at the writing on the top envelope. Natalie was right. These were Theo's letters. She recognized his cursive S for Sofia.

A horrible truth hit: Her mother had deliberately cut Theo out of her life. She had chopped him off like a piece of excess fabric that she didn't need and created a different design, far away across the ocean.

She sank into the swivel chair and spun across the Persian rug in a kaleidoscope of memories, clutching the bundle against her heart. Lola scampered away, dodging the wheels, and watched her from a safe distance with worried eyes.

Now she understood what she had seen on Theo's face at the airport. He had looked at her as if she were the one who had lied. All these years, both of them had been wrong. Neither she nor Theo had betrayed the other. Her mother had betrayed them both.

Every day for a month, she had waited to hear from him, desperate for one of these letters. But nothing had ever arrived. She scrutinized the top envelope addressed to Sofia Stylianou, her maiden name. She flipped through each one. There were seven envelopes for Sofia Stylianou, the girl she once was—young, innocent, naïve, and desperately in love. A girl who, once upon a time, had viewed the world as a place filled with joy and endless possibilities.

Now she stared at the hands clutching the letters. These hands were no longer smooth or wrinkle-free. They belonged to a woman who did not trust love or happiness and who viewed the world with caution. She began to sob, her tears falling onto the faded postmarks.

When she was all cried out, she sat still for a while and held the letters, not daring to look. Lola inched closer, softly whimpering and watching her with small brown eyes full of sympathy. *She wants me to open the letters*, she thought, gently patting Lola's head. She began to flip through the brittle remains of the past, from August through September 1959.

She took a deep breath and opened the first envelope, pulling out a single sheet of paper. It was dated August 27th, the feast day of St. Fanourios, the patron saint and finder of all things lost. She choked back a sad laugh. She had lost so much more than a shawl on that date, the last time she had seen Theo. He must have written the letter the same night.

27 August 1959

Agapi mou,

How will I ever make this up to you? My father found your blue shawl and realized we had been together. I could not lie. The old man was furious and insisted I leave for Mt. Athos to "cool down" as he put it. I will do as he says but my love for you will never die. My happiness depends on you. Wait for me, just as we discussed. Once my father has calmed down, I will attend the theological school in Athens as planned. As soon as I graduate, we will marry.

I'm sorry for the pain I've caused you by this abrupt departure. I promise I will make it up to you one day. I thought I loved you when I left you that night. I was wrong. That was nothing. Now, I love you a thousand times more.

You are always with me, seared into my heart and soul. Nothing can separate us.

I love you forever,
Theo

"*Nothing can separate us.*" She repeated those words. Except her mother. She turned to stare at the woman who smiled innocently from the framed photograph on the bedside table.

"*Yiati?*" she whispered. Why? "You had no idea what you were doing."

Lola whimpered as they stared at the photograph.

She kept reading and rereading the letter, listening to the voice behind the words, till she knew them by heart.

Agapi mou. Wait for me. I thought I loved you when I left you that night. I was wrong. That was nothing. Now, I love you a thousand times more.

She went through all the letters. There was another one from August, short but sweet.

30 August 1959

Agapi mou,

I've arrived safely in Athens and will be leaving for the Holy Mountain shortly. Everywhere, people are smiling at me in this bustling city. I realized they are returning my smile. My love for you overflows and I cannot hide my feelings from others. My joy is contagious. Whenever I think about you (which is all the time) I cannot contain the happiness which spills onto my face.

Look after yourself. Don't be sad. The gossip will stop. My only regret is that you have to endure it alone. Time will pass quickly. And people will forget.

I love you,
Theo
PS I will give you an address in my next letter

She read through all of them until she got to the last letter, a longer one.

14 September 1959

Agapi mou,

I've heard nothing from you, and I'm beginning to worry that my letters are not reaching you. Or maybe your letters are not reaching me on this remote peninsula at the edge of Greece. Communication with the outside world is deliberately cut off here.

I must confess that even though this sacred space has been set aside for the worship of God, I think of you all the time. I sense your presence everywhere. In the air that I breathe, in the silence of the monaster-

ies, in the chanting of the hymns. Yesterday, the abbot pulled me aside. I will never forget his piercing blue eyes. Like small marbles, they bore straight into me. He said, "There is a woman who occupies too much space inside your head." I don't think they will accept me here.

Still, I wish there was some way I could share with you the beauty of the place. My words are inadequate. Midnight, the time for prayers, is the most beautiful hour. They wake us up by drumming a small hammer on a piece of wood. We come out of our cells and walk in silence along the icy corridors to the warmth of the candle-lit churches.

By the time the liturgy ends, the sky is lightening from black to gray. Yesterday, I watched the sun rise over the Aegean, changing the dark blue waters into soft hues of pinks, purples, and reds, and the breathtaking beauty of God's creation reminded me of you.

I will keep writing until I hear from you.
I kiss you with my words.
I love you,
Theo

She sensed in his words, the struggle of his heart: God or her. It did not have to be like that, except that her mother had ordained it that way. She folded the brittle paper carefully and a few fragments splintered off the fragile edges. She felt a tightness in her heart. Thirty years of misplaced anger vanished in a second and a sharp rush of sadness poured into the void, followed by a tiny drop of joy. He had never abandoned her. She slipped the shawl around her shoulders one more time, feeling its delicate softness. In the mirror, she caught sight of her reflection from the back, and saw the huge tear down the middle. She ripped it off and gave it one final tug, tearing it in half and pushing the two pieces back into the sewing basket. As she did this, her fingers felt another sheet of paper, folded, lying flush against the side. She extracted the single sheet and smoothed it out. No date, no nothing. Just her mother's spidery handwriting:

> *Sofia mou,*
>
> *Forgive me. I did what I thought was right at the time to save you from the gossip and the scandal. I always meant to give you these letters. Somehow, I never found the right time. Or the courage. If I did wrong, I am so very sorry. When I see you with your beautiful children and your husband who loves you more than life itself, I have hope in my heart that I did the right thing. No one knows how things might have worked out if we had made different choices. Therefore, we should try to live with no regrets. My wish for you is that you will always be happy and surrounded by love.*
>
> *Always with love,*
> *Your Mother*

"I can't fight with the dead," she said to Lola, who whimpered softly.

She picked up Theo's letters, glancing once more at her mother's photograph. "The problem is," she explained to Lola, "this truth which I hold in my hands has also upended Natalie's life. And I think Natalie gave up a good man."

Lola's eyes filled with sympathy.

She lingered a few more minutes and then picked up the letters. She would return them to Theo. It felt like the right thing to do. She closed the door behind her and walked down the passage with Lola trotting beside her.

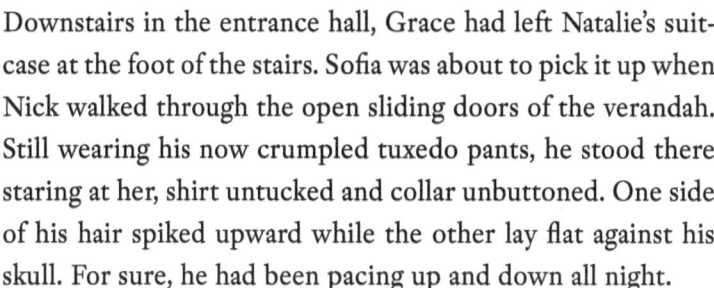

Downstairs in the entrance hall, Grace had left Natalie's suitcase at the foot of the stairs. Sofia was about to pick it up when Nick walked through the open sliding doors of the verandah. Still wearing his now crumpled tuxedo pants, he stood there staring at her, shirt untucked and collar unbuttoned. One side of his hair spiked upward while the other lay flat against his skull. For sure, he had been pacing up and down all night.

Across the gleaming width of the entrance hall, morning light intersected his shadow with hers. All around, the marble tiles reflected hundreds of drooping flowers from the wedding that never was.

"Where are you going with that suitcase?" he finally said, his face strained but controlled.

She dropped the handle of the suitcase and set it down.

"In my perfect world, I'd be going to the airport to drop it off for Natalie and Peter. Instead, I'm going to Theo's house to take it to your daughter so she can run off to New York, alone, and find herself." She could hear the sound of her voice echo off the marble tiles. It sounded shrill, as if it belonged to somebody else.

"You should eat something," he said, and crossed the space between them. He was holding a small white container from International Bakery. He flipped back the lid and offered her a half-empty tray of *kourabiedes*, the cookies meant for the wedding guests. He must have found the extra boxes in the pantry.

"Who ate all these?" she said. Powdered sugar dusted the tip of his nose and the bottom of his unshaved chin. She stretched out her hand to dust his nose and stopped halfway.

She redirected her hand to the tray. She picked up one of the *kourabiedes* and popped it into her mouth. Thank God, he had finally calmed down.

"You're still wearing your necklace," he said, straightening it around her neck. "I always wanted you to have beautiful things. Maybe that wasn't enough."

She had forgotten she was still wearing it, and she touched his hand as he adjusted it. "You and the children are all I need."

He watched her finish the cookie and then he said, "Here, if you're going to Theo's house, you might as well give him this."

He extracted a letter from his pocket and handed it to her. "What is it?"

"You know what it is. A letter from Theo. I found it in Natalie's room. I assume there are more, and that you'll give them all back to him."

The shoulder bag containing the rest of Theo's letters suddenly felt heavy on her arm, and she gripped it tightly. Oh. My. God. No wonder he had gone crazy yesterday. He had read one of those letters.

"She must have dug them out somewhere in your mother's room," he said. "This must be what unsettled her. The fantasy for that one great love. Although it's not really a fantasy. I found it. I don't know about *you*, but I did."

Could this get any worse? she wondered.

"Why don't you read it?" he said.

Dear God. This could not be happening.

"I'm sure there's nothing important in it. Just the ramblings of a young man."

"Read it," he said. "It's not too wild. Actually, it's quite logical."

So she swallowed hard and opened the letter with fumbling fingers.

October 5th. Just after she had left for South Africa. A distinct change of tone. Theo no longer addressed her as *Agapi mou*. Relieved, she gulped back tears as she read it out aloud:

5 October 1959

Dear Sofia,

This will be my last letter to you. My father told me that you left for South Africa to marry Nick. Now I understand why you didn't reply to my previous letters. I always feared that I might lose you one day. I knew that your dreams matched Nick's big dreams better than my humble ones.

It was unreasonable to expect you to wait so long for me. Four years is a long time. You did the right thing. Nick will be an excellent husband and you will never lack for anything. You and I both know that he has always loved you.

I would have liked to look into your eyes one more time before you made this decision, but it was not meant to be.

Please believe that I hold no grudges, and with time, I will accept God's will. I will be fine, just as I know that you will also be fine. I wish you both everything of the best, and for God's richest blessings to be showered upon you.

You remain in my heart and in my prayers, and I hope that you will also keep me in your prayers.

Always with love,
Theo

Tears streamed down her face for the man she had lost and for the one in front of her. She folded the letter and put it in her bag with the others, glad that Natalie had not left any of the others lying around.

"Theo seems to have made peace with this a long time ago," he said, watching her face carefully.

"Have *you*?" she said.

"Yes, and I'm sorry. Natalie caught me off guard yesterday. I took it out on you."

"I've been married to you for thirty years. I know you by now," she said, and picked up the suitcase. In all their married years, he had never apologized to her for anything. Not once. This was a first. He must really feel bad, she thought.

"Have *you* made peace with it?" he said.

She put down the suitcase. "Is that why you invited him here? To see if I'd made peace with it?"

"No. He was a practical solution to a problem. I needed a priest for my daughter's wedding. The wedding that never happened. But that's beside the point now."

"Okay. But I chose to marry you," she said. "Not Theo. Whatever happened between him and me was a long time ago between two young people who didn't know any better. I have loved you as much as I am capable of loving another person."

"As much as you are capable of loving," he said, repeating her words. "Fair enough." But still, a flash of uncertainty flickered across his face. Something had shifted in their relationship, like the foundation of an older house that had settled over time and displayed a few cracks.

He opened his mouth to say something, then changed his mind and caressed her cheek instead. The gentleness of his rough palm against her skin made her want to cry. She knew their foundation was still strong enough to weather a few storms.

"You had better find out what's going on with your daughter," he said. "Let me carry this to the car." He picked up the suitcase and walked with her.

"She's your daughter too," she reminded him.

From the balcony, Dimitri's voice called out. "Mom, do you need any help?"

"No, I'm fine. Thank you, my boy."

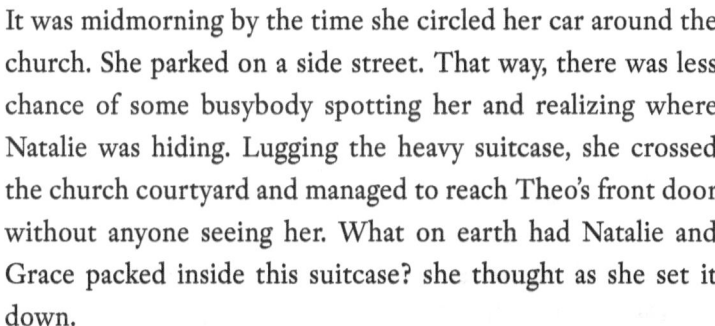

It was midmorning by the time she circled her car around the church. She parked on a side street. That way, there was less chance of some busybody spotting her and realizing where Natalie was hiding. Lugging the heavy suitcase, she crossed the church courtyard and managed to reach Theo's front door without anyone seeing her. What on earth had Natalie and Grace packed inside this suitcase? she thought as she set it down.

She rang the doorbell and looked behind her. Judging by the few cars in the parking lot, not many people were attending Sunday liturgy. They were probably all busy discussing the Levantis family drama. She imagined people sitting around their breakfast tables, sipping coffee, shaking their heads as they talked about the bride who had left the groom at the altar, and everyone glad that it hadn't happened to their family. What a scandal.

Where is this girl? The sound of a car slowing down made her jump. She pressed her finger on the doorbell and kept it there till she heard footsteps.

"I'm so sorry, Mom," Natalie said as soon as she opened the door.

Her beautiful hazel-colored eyes looked dull, and her normally bright voice was flat and lifeless. Her hair was still partially swept up, interlaced with diamanté, like the bride she should have been, but wisps had escaped and black eyeliner ran down her cheeks. She stared at her daughter and images tumbled through her mind: A toddler in white leather shoes taking her first unsteady steps, a preschooler's face lighting up at the sound of a doorbell announcing a playdate arrival, an adolescent girl modeling an off-the-shoulder dress. All her anger, frustration, and embarrassment melted away. "Come here," she said, hugging her tightly.

"Tell me what happened." They went inside and sat down on a worn chenille sofa in the small front parlor. Through the lace curtains, she could see the dome of the church bathed in morning sunlight.

"I just couldn't go through with it," Natalie said. "I saw those letters from Father Theo and realized that's what I wanted. The kind of love where happiness glows on your face."

"Oh, Natalie," she said, and felt more guilt sit on top of her other guilts. "You're going to base your life on one impulsive romance I had as a young woman. And a bunch of old letters?" Somehow Natalie's future had collided with her past into a horrible present.

"I wanted something more. Not just some arranged marriage."

"First of all, your marriage wasn't arranged. You and Peter met at the Cypriot dance. Secondly, I can't believe you were influenced by the silly letters of two young people who knew nothing about the world, or each other. It was an infatuation, a first love, that's all. Everyone has a first love they remember. It's a rite of passage into adulthood."

"I think it was more than just a first love," Natalie said. Her voice was adamant and her expression surprisingly stubborn.

"Natalie, sometimes there are things that happen in a person's life that are best left in the past." She sat back and crossed her arms, unwilling to go there, not even for Natalie.

"But don't you have any regrets? I don't want to have any regrets when I'm fifty and old one day."

"First of all, fifty isn't old, even though I feel old today. And in life, there will always be disappointments. But you can't live in the past. You pick up the pieces when something gets broken and you soldier on."

"But why did *Yiayia* hide those letters?"

"I don't know," she said. "But mothers think they know better and sometimes they cause chaos. She had her reasons, I suppose. And luckily my life still turned out well."

She rummaged in her bag for her wallet and extracted a small photograph. She handed it to Natalie.

"I don't have regrets. Look at this."

Natalie cupped the family photograph in both hands.

"I remember that time," Natalie said. "Our whole family was together in Cyprus. Even Dad. Look how young and beautiful you were, and how happy we all look."

"Yes. Once you create a family, you have a place where you'll always belong, and there's nothing more important in the world."

And then.

"I'm still going to New York, though."

Dear God, why are You doing this to me? She got up and walked to the window. She could see the church bathed in noon daylight, shimmering white and serene. She turned back to Natalie, unable to restrain herself.

"Why in hell do you want to go and live alone in a foreign country?"

"I'm not going to be alone, Mom. I'll stay with Eleni. And I'm not going for an extended period like Dimitri. I just need to get away for a couple of weeks and I'll be back. No big deal."

"Why don't you go to our apartment in Cape Town? It's a two-hour flight."

"Mom, if I went to Cape Town, you'd be there in a day or two."

"Oh." She sat back, stung to the core. Natalie was running away from her, too. Not only Peter.

"It's not you. I just need space and time to think," Natalie said. And then. "Mom, do you think I'll ever find it, that one great love?"

"I don't know. It's rare. And even if you're lucky enough to find that one great love that strikes like a bolt of lightning, or *keravnovolos erotas* as the Greeks say, at some point you're going to look at this person and see an ordinary man who gets sick or angry or depressed, who has fears and insecurities and doesn't look that great when he wakes up in the morning. It's not all about the idea of being in love."

"I know, but at least I want the romance *now*, in the beginning," she said, twisting her engagement ring to the tip of her finger.

"Natalie, if you reject all the good men, holding out for that one great love, there is a strong possibility that you could end up alone."

"I'm willing to take that chance."

"I hope you won't regret it."

"I won't. The only thing I regret is hurting Peter. How's Dad?"

"He's fine. He found one of the letters, though. You accidentally left one in your room."

Natalie's face became a paler shade of white.

"It's alright. It was the last one. Less romantic than the others. The best one for Dad to find."

"I'm sorry, Mom."

"Don't worry about your dad. He and I have been through a lot together."

"And Father Theo?"

"Father Theo is a priest and belongs to God. The young man who fell in love with me and wrote those letters no longer exists."

"So you're not sad about what could have been?"

She swallowed hard. "How can I be sad when I share an extraordinary life with your father, and I have you and Dimitri?"

"Maybe God used *Yiayia* to keep Father Theo for himself. He's a great priest, Mom. I really like him. Maybe God needs him full-time in the church, without a wife and children for distraction."

"Maybe."

Natalie suddenly jumped up and looked at her watch. "Mom, I have to go. I need to return this ring to Peter. Father Theo told me he'd be home as soon as the liturgy was over. Please tell him I'll be back later." She kissed her quickly and with that she was out the door. A second later, the door opened again and Natalie dragged the heavy suitcase inside. "We forgot this baggage outside. I'll just leave it here for now," she said.

She nodded and continued to stare at the door for a few minutes after Natalie left. Slowly, she walked back to the sofa and sank into it, half afraid that she might never be able to get up again.

She wasn't sure how long she sat before she heard the sound of a key in the lock. The door opened and Theo stood there for a few seconds. She couldn't read his expression because the sun's glare through the window obscured his face. All she saw was the black cassock.

He spoke first. "Sofia, are you okay?"

"I'm not sure. Both my children are leaving me," she said.

"You must let Natalie find her way," he said gently. "Give her a little bit of breathing space." He sat next to her, and she could smell the faint scent of incense clinging to his clothes.

"It seems like I have no choice," she said.

"You look so sad," he said.

She bit her lips to stop the tears and reached into her handbag.

"I have something for you," she said.

She handed him the letters.

"What's this?"

"Your letters."

"My letters?" he said, as confusion spread over his face.

"The ones you mailed thirty years ago. I never got them until today. I think it's best if you keep them."

She watched the color drain from his face. He crossed himself and slid his fingers over the relics from the past.

"Where did you find these?"

"Natalie found them in my mother's sewing basket. My mother had kept them hidden all these years."

"Natalie read these? And you read them now only? For the first time?" he said in a flat voice.

She nodded, holding back her tears.

"And Nick read the last one you wrote. Only that one."

His eyes widened with shock.

"May I?" he said.

The same hands that had once dashed off youthful love letters trembled now as he opened the first letter. In silence, he began to read his own words, and she wondered if this man who had devoted himself to God remembered any of the emotions he had once felt.

After a few minutes, the longest minutes ever, he leaned his head against the headrest and said nothing. A vein twitched in his neck and his fingers pressed hard into the armrest, leaving little dent marks in the chenille. She tried to say something, but the words came out wrong so she kept quiet. For a long time, neither of them spoke. Somewhere in the distance, the sound of an ambulance siren broke the stillness of the Sunday.

After a while, he asked in a quiet voice, "Would it have made a difference if you had received the letters when I sent them?"

"At the time, yes," she said. "I kept waiting and hoping. You should have realized that something had gone wrong."

He squeezed his eyes shut.

"I'm sorry, Sofia. I never stopped worrying about you or what happened that night. I thought the gossip had become too much and that you had chosen to go on with your life without me. But you are right. I should have come for you."

"I have a different life now with my husband and children. And I wouldn't change it."

He stood and walked to the window. His fingers clutched the cross around his neck. He stared at the church outside for what seemed like a long time, and she joined him at the window. She followed his gaze to the top of the dome. The sun's rays reflected off the gold cross crowning it, and she thought about how its shape pointed in every direction, north, south, east, and west, nothing beyond its reach.

"I also wouldn't change my life," he said after what seemed like a long time. "God's ways are not for us to understand, Sofia. It never crossed my mind that your mother might do something like this."

"According to Natalie, God used my mother to keep you for Himself."

A skeptical line creased his smooth brow.

"Natalie says she wants to hold out for a love like the one you described in your letters."

"That's not a bad thing," he said with a sad smile. "So my letters tipped her over?"

"Yes, but it's rare what we had, and I told her that. She might not find it. And I don't know if I can ever forgive my mother," she said. She walked slowly back to the sofa and sank into it.

He dragged a dining room chair across the room. The metal legs scraped the floor, jarring her stretched nerves even more. He positioned the chair in front of her, turned it around so that its back came between them, and straddled it, his face so close to hers that she felt his warm breath brush her cheeks. In that one mad moment, she wondered what it would be like to kiss him again. She saw his ache for her reflected in the depths of his eyes.

"Listen to me," he said, breaking the spell and moving back. His voice was quiet and beseeching. "The fact that she kept these letters for so long means she had remorse. Let God be the judge of her actions, not you."

"All those years of not knowing the truth, believing you had simply abandoned me," she said, shaking her head.

"I would never abandon you. Not then. Not now. Not ever. I will always be there for you. Remember that. Please."

"But we can never be the way we were."

"No, we can't. And there's nothing we can do about it now. But do you know why it was so perfect?"

"No, tell me."

"Perhaps because we never got the chance to test us in real life. You might have hated living with me. I'm truly sorry, Sofia. It was my fault, too. I should have chased you down. But I want you to try and be happy. Accept God's will. Promise me?" The shadows in the depths of his eyes betrayed the confidence in his voice, and she tried to smile through the tears that were threatening to spill.

"We would have been fine," she said. "Now there's always this feeling that something is missing. Like a constant absence."

"That's normal," he said. "God planted that feeling in all of us, even in me, so that we'll keep searching for Him. There's no perfect paradise anywhere here on earth. We're all foreigners here. Wherever we go, it makes no difference. We're always going to be restless. Even in our own countries sometimes, we feel as if we don't belong. Our purpose here on earth is to walk each other home, and by that I mean our one true home."

"Alright, if you say so, *Father* Theo," she said, deliberately emphasizing the word Father. "But I still can't forgive my mother."

"No, don't say that. You don't know whether God has forgiven her. If God has forgiven her, then who are you not to forgive her?"

"It will take some time," she said. She got up slowly. It was time to leave.

"And, by the way. Natalie has done the right thing," he said.

"I'm not so sure about that, but I need to get home," she said. "Is the church still open? I want to light a candle before I leave."

"Yes, only Michalis is there. Everyone else has left." He walked her to the door, and she dabbed a few more unexpected tears with the back of her hand.

"No regrets," he insisted. He cupped her chin in his hand and kissed her softly on both cheeks. The gentleness of the gesture and the tears in his eyes made her cry even more. "You've created a beautiful family and planted deep roots here. I'm very proud of you."

"No regrets," she said. She could sense him watching as she walked away.

"How is that husband of yours, by the way?" he called out as she crossed the shaded churchyard.

"He's fine," she said. "I've spoken to him and he's calmed down. Just like you said." She wanted to tell him that *she* wasn't fine, that she needed him, that she couldn't do this, but she kept on walking.

―

At the church entrance, she pushed against the door and it remained closed. Then she leaned in hard and it opened, as if recognizing the curve of her body. Like a fugitive, she slipped inside the refuge and was immediately soothed by its womb-like darkness. Dazed by her life that seemed to have spiraled out of control, she sat down with a soft thud on the wooden bench, and let her eyes adjust to the dimness and her heart to the stillness. All around, the flowers from the wedding still looked fresh. She breathed in their fragrance. What a waste. Masses of white roses spilled over the pews, the arches, and the steps of the solea. Yesterday seemed like a faraway place.

"Okay, God," she whispered. "I give up. I offer all these flowers to You, and everything else—my worries, my problems, my disappointment, and yes, even that temptation You placed in front of me a few minutes ago, because I don't know what to do about anything anymore." A shaft of light poured through one of the upper windows and fell directly onto the altar. The light reflected off a votive candle, red and gleaming, inside the small tabernacle on the holy table. Eternally lit. As she stared into the red heart, she felt as if time had collapsed on itself, dissolving the two thousand years between her and Christ. She was there and He was there. Time was no longer running forwards or backwards. And neither was she. She was simply in the center of it, where she wanted to stay forever.

And then the moment disappeared. She noticed a prayer booklet jutting awkwardly from the pew pocket in front of her. She reached out to straighten it but instead picked it up, flipping through the pages. Her eyes skimmed over the Troparia prayers recited before Holy Communion and landed on the words: "You have smitten me with yearning, O Christ, and by Your divine love You have changed me." God had certainly smitten her with yearning, she thought, placing the booklet back in the pew pocket. What was it that Theo had said? Something about God deliberately planting this yearning inside, compelling His people to search for Him.

A hand touched her shoulder and she looked up, startled. Michalis stretched out his hand, offering her a special piece cut from the *prosforon* bread—the offering to God. Part of the Holy Gifts for the people of God. He had wrapped it in a paper napkin for her.

"I didn't bake this week," she explained, hesitant to take the piece Michalis normally reserved for the week's baker. "Remember? I was busy with the wedding."

He pressed the blessed bread into her hands and shook his head, pointing his finger at her.

"Oh, it *is* from one of my breads?"

Yes, he nodded. He must have selected one of her loaves from the stash he froze for emergencies. If one of the parishioners forgot their turn to bake the bread, Michalis always had a backup for the priest.

He curved his right hand as if to clutch a pen and pretended to write in the palm of his left hand.

"You gave the names of my family to be lifted up in prayer this morning?"

Yes, he nodded. He pointed to Peter's photo in the wedding brochures lying on the pews.

"And you included Peter?"

Again, he nodded.

"Thank you." She smiled and gave him a thumbs-up. Of course, he'd included Peter. He was family. Almost.

She unwrapped the *prosforon* piece and placed it reverently in her mouth. When she looked up at Michalis, she was surprised to see her reflection in his eyes. He touched his hand to his heart, his familiar gesture, and gave one of his rare smiles, crinkling his face into a hundred wrinkles. Then he turned and walked back to the solea where he'd left his cleaning materials near the *iconostasis*, the wall of holy icons that separated the congregation from the altar. He bowed his head and crossed himself at the icon of Christ before picking up a cloth from his basket. Ever so gently, he began to wipe Christ's face. No wonder he never seemed lonely, she thought. He was always in the church surrounded by the angels and saints. He lived in Christ, and Christ in him. What was it like to live only for God? she wondered. Could she ever become like Michalis? Silent tears began to pour down her cheeks again.

And then, another hand on her shoulder, "Mom?"

She looked up to see Dimitri and Annelize leaning over her. Dimitri looked worried, and the girl's big blue eyes radiated concern and kindness.

"Are you okay? Dad said you might be here so we came to check."

"Come sit," she said, patting the pew bench. He slid in beside her and took her hand. Annelize sat next to him and he held her hand, too.

They sat like that for a while, not talking, and her eyes were drawn to their intertwined fingers resting on Dimitri's knee. Young lovers. She shifted across the bench and moved closer to the couple.

TEN

The Fafi Runner

Grace

Grace clutched the receiver in one hand and the university's letter in the other. She was afraid to ask what she wanted to ask. Surely, the people had made a mistake.

"May I help you?" the woman on the other end repeated. Her voice sounded impatient.

"Yes, my name is Grace Molepe." She swallowed hard and gathered her courage. "I received a letter from you. The letter says that my son Isaac is no longer registered with the university. You also returned a check for his fees."

"And how can I help you?"

"This can't be right. My son has one more year to complete his studies and graduate. There must be a mistake." She hoped they had not found out about his arrest that night.

"Let me double-check," the woman said.

After what seemed like a very long time, the woman returned to the phone. "There is no mistake. Isaac told the dean that he was quitting."

"Oh." A sick feeling churned in her stomach.

"Is there anything else I can help you with?"

"Yes. Can you please tell me—did he pass the supplementary exam he wrote in December on criminal procedure?" She knew he hadn't, but she wanted to be sure.

"I'm looking at his student record right now on my computer screen. I'm afraid he did not pass that exam."

A sinking feeling spread through her as the lady confirmed that which she'd known all along. "Please, if I make him change his mind, can he come back?"

"I don't see why not," the woman said. "Of course the dean will have to agree to this. But you realize that it would then take him longer than a year to finish his degree."

"Yes, I understand, thank you." She hung up the phone and sat on the edge of her bed. She was not ready to give up. The idiot was probably running around Alexandra township with those no good friends of his. If it was the last thing she did, she would find him and drag him back to class by the scruff of his neck.

―

"Grace, where are you going in the rain without an umbrella?" Johannes said, as he waved her down. She knew he wanted to talk about the wedding drama, but right now she was on another mission.

"Argh, Johannes," she said. "It's not only the Levantis children who are doing crazy things. It's my son, too."

"What do you mean?" He opened an umbrella and held it over both their heads.

"Johannes, I had so many dreams for this child." She dug out a Polaroid of a young Isaac from a side pocket and handed it to him. He stared at the gap-toothed smile and grinned.

"Before he was born, I was nothing. The government didn't even acknowledge my existence as a human being. But when I held this baby in my arms, I became a person with a reason to live. I was a mother."

"What's happened?"

"He dropped out of university!"

"What? No way. But he only has one more year to go?"

"Exactly."

Johannes stared at her in wide-eyed disbelief.

"I have to find him," she said.

"Yes, of course you must go." He thrust the umbrella into her hands and opened the gates. "Good luck," he called out after her.

⁓

In the pouring rain, she made her way to the taxi ranks. She waited beneath a dripping canopy. Big fat raindrops smacked the ground, soaking her shoes as she stared through the gray mist. Rows and rows of white minibuses lined the ranks. Funny how they called them Black taxis when all the buses were white. Of course, it had to do with the fact that they were the lifeblood of South Africa's Black workforce. Still, it was odd.

It had been years since she had taken one of these taxis. She led such a sheltered life inside Sofia's house. Johannes was her driver whenever she needed him, and truth be told, she hated taxis. The reckless drivers raced down highways and swerved across multiple lanes as if there were no other cars on the road.

Each time she had disembarked at the leafy, white suburbs with wide streets, she had stepped out feeling dignified, a lady. Each time she had boarded one back to the dusty, crammed township, her world shrank, and she had felt small and insignificant. Now here she was, going back to the life she had left behind. Certainly not the life she had wanted for herself or Isaac.

With a heavy heart, she boarded a minibus heading to Alexandra.

"Come, come, Mama, speed it up," the driver urged, tucking a hand-rolled cigarette behind his ear. A bumper sticker on his cracked windscreen proclaimed *In God We Trust*.

The minibus was already overloaded, but she squeezed her way to the back where a young man gave her his window seat. He looked so much like Isaac. The woman next to Grace moved her knees sideways and beamed up at her as if to take credit for the boy's politeness. Surrounded by boisterous laughter still lingering from Mandela euphoria, and the day's political banter bouncing back and forth between the passengers, Grace leaned her head against the hard windowpane.

She remembered how Sofia would play Monopoly with Isaac and Dimitri. They would roll the dice to calculate their moves around the game board, and Isaac used to laugh when he collected houses and hotels to buy and trade. But when he ended up with the card that said Go to Jail, he would cry, and she and Sofia would laugh. It's only a game, they reminded him. Now here they were. Sofia was sitting at her house crying about her children, and she was sitting in the Black taxis she hated, crying about her son. If only life were a game, she thought.

She sighed and looked outside as they waited for a red light to change. A shirtless man rummaged through rubbish bins on the street corner. He extracted a loaf of bread and bit hungrily into it. She turned her head away. Once, she had hoped that Isaac would become like her and develop a love for learning.

But no such luck. She now had to go and collect him from the gutters and she had no idea where to begin.

The lady next to her was watching the same man digging in the trash. "Looking for food where the dogs eat is a terrible thing. Now that *Madiba* has freed our people," she said, "we won't live like that anymore."

Unless you're an idiot like my son, she thought, and smiled politely at her fellow passenger as the maniac driver shot forward. She clutched the seat edges, trying hard not to slide off.

In less than twenty minutes, they had arrived in Alexandra, so near and yet so far from Sofia's home. She stepped down from the minibus into a swarming mass of people who all had somewhere to go. She had been absent for so long that she was now a stranger in the streets of her childhood. The gray drizzle continued to fall, and she remembered how the rain in the townships always seemed to arrive as the workers set off in the mornings or when they returned in the evenings.

Somebody jostled her, and she instinctively clutched her bag, even though she'd stuffed her money into her bra. Nobody carried cash in their handbags here. She had not forgotten how to survive on the street. *Tsotsis* and gangsters prowled everywhere in the townships. And in the *shebeens*. Those beerhalls provided a haven for Black men who were forbidden to drink in white neighborhood bars. She could still hear her father's warnings about the thugs and the prostitutes who frequented these places. *They go there to drink themselves into oblivion and forget their miserable lives.* Could Isaac be in one of these places?

Warily, she peered inside the first beerhall, adjusting her eyes to the darkness. The rambling banter of drunks and bums and tired workers floated outside while stray dogs and children played in the dirt near her feet. Two women, probably *shebeen queens* who owned and ran unlicensed bars, leaned against a wall, staring at her in a menacing way.

"What's the matter?" they shouted. She could smell the alcohol on their breath from where she stood. "You think you're too good for us? What do you want? What are you looking for?"

She pretended not to hear and scurried away. She passed the houses, which all looked the same, made more similar by the shadows: scraps of iron on the roof, cheap wooden planks for the doors, cardboard and sheets of plastic in the broken windows. A silent reminder of everything she didn't want for Isaac.

On the next corner, she almost collided with a sprightly old woman who, in spite of the heat, wore thick black stockings and white running shoes.

"Come," the old woman said. "Place a bet with the *fafi* runner. Ten rand and you could win big tonight."

The last thing I need, she thought. Fafi, the popular betting game, had never attracted her. She dodged sideways but the determined runner began to mirror her movements with backward steps, and they started a discordant dance down the dusty road.

"Come on. Trust me. The game's organizer is just down the road. I'll run the money over to him in a minute. The last bet usually wins. It's your best chance tonight." She flashed a coaxing smile.

"I have to go somewhere. Leave me alone. Get lost. *Hamba*."

"Give me ten rand. What's your lucky number? I'll play it for you and I'll find you if you win."

Why did this strange person have to pick on her? Desperate to get away, she shoved some notes into the outstretched hand. "Here, take this and go away."

"What's your lucky number?"

"I don't have one. I'm not lucky. Leave me alone. Please."

"What did you dream about last night?"

"Robbers." She said the first word that popped into her head, hoping to get rid of her.

"Ah, that's a good number. Seven. Seven is for robbers. That's what I'll play for you. You know what? I like you. I have a good feeling. You're going to win big tonight." And finally the determined little woman waved cheerfully and disappeared.

She staggered away in the opposite direction, close to tears, as if she were a drunk rolling down the road. She was not off to a good start.

But then, diagonally across the road, the name of another shebeen caught her attention: Sibongwe's Shebeen. That's it. She remembered now. The home of Isaac's friend was behind Sibongwe's Shebeen. She had heard Isaac speak about that place. Many times, Isaac had skipped school and gone to a friend's house close to this place. She would start there. Maybe someone could tell her something.

She stood outside, wanting to run away. Should she go inside? If he was there, what then? She peered inside. A group of men were laughing and drinking under a cloud of cigarette smoke. Their beer breath filtered through the air. One of them stood up.

"Come in, *Mama*, come in," he called to her. "Everything is legal now in the new South Africa. Don't be shy."

Embarrassed, she ignored their catcalls and ducked around the corner to get away from them. And there it was. She recognized the house because of its yard. She had gone there many times in the past to collect Isaac. It had been a dump then, and it was worse now. A junkyard.

She entered from the rear, hoping no one would see her. Chickens and roosters scattered, squawking and kicking up a dust storm. Their useless wings flapped up and down as she sidestepped her way through the dirt, past broken bicycles, flat tires, and an abandoned toilet. It stank like hell, she thought, and covered her nose with one hand as she tried to breathe through her mouth.

Among the collection of junk, she spotted a bucket. She grabbed it and placed it upside down near a grimy window. Wobbling slightly, she climbed on top of the bucket and balanced on tiptoe to peer inside the house. The reek of marijuana hung thick in the air, creating a hazy curtain. Hoping against hope that he wasn't inside, she squinted through the broken window.

Shapes and faces came into focus. Laughing, drunk, and stoned out of their minds, a group of men passed a tin container from one to the other as they squatted on the filthiest and most disgusting floor she had ever seen. Their clumsy hands spilled what she guessed to be foamy beer while a dog circled and licked up the spills. And then she saw him. Isaac sat outside the inner circle, on a sofa that looked oddly grand in the shabby surroundings. He doesn't look as bad as the others, she consoled herself. Somehow, his eyes seemed less glazed. He looked more alert.

She began to tremble and clung to the window ledge. Shit, she thought. Shit. Shit. Shit. They were all shits, all of his lowlife friends who had led him down this path were pieces of shit. But Isaac was the biggest shit of all. She stared at the six-foot man sitting awkwardly on the sofa while his *tsotsi* friends stumbled around. For a few seconds, she saw the child who had looked at the world through frightened eyes, always in a constant state of anxiety that he would fail to please her, that he would fail his exams, that he would fail at everything. And that's exactly what he had now gone and done. A bitter taste stung the back of her throat.

Teetering slightly, she climbed off the bucket, using the umbrella for support. And when her feet touched the ground, she bent over and threw up. She wished she had a cloth, but she wiped her mouth as best she could with the back of her hands and walked to the front door.

"Who's there?" A startled voice called out before she had even knocked.

"It's me, Isaac's mother," she said, pushing open the creaking door and swinging the umbrella in her hand. "If anyone touches me, I'll hit them with this umbrella." There was a stunned silence as she walked inside.

"Mom." Isaac stood.

"You need to come home. You are going back to university," she said.

"I can't. I failed. They won't take me back. And it will take me two years to finish now."

"You can. And you will. I've spoken to them. They will take you back. We can pay for another year. Whatever it takes, we'll do it. Let's go."

He hesitated. All eyes were on him.

"I need your help," she said, realizing that he had to save face in front of his idiot friends. "I'm not sure I can find my way out. Let's go. Now."

"Fine," he said, and grabbed a dirty-looking sweater from the sofa.

She turned to the others. "You should be ashamed of yourselves. Your poor parents are working day and night. And here you are drinking. This is the thank you they get."

As they left she could hear snickers of laughter growing into raucous jeering. Let them laugh. She didn't care. As long as she could save Isaac and get him out of this hellhole.

She led the way, and he followed in silence. When they reached the end of the street, she stopped. It was dark. She had forgotten there were no streetlamps in the townships. But she looked up and a bright full moon beamed over them.

"This is not where I want you to live," she said.

"It's hard for me to pass those exams," he said.

"I know. But you can't give up. You must suffer a little more and push yourself a little harder. Anything is better than this. And it'll be worth it in the long run. One day you will thank me."

Suddenly, a woman's voice called after them, "Wait. Come back here."

She turned, trying to see in the darkness.

"There you are, Lucky Lady! I found you. You won. Your number came up—seven, the robbers. I told you. Remember? Didn't I tell you?"

The fafi runner. Like a shadow boxer from another world, she stood there waving her arms and clutching fistfuls of crumpled notes.

"It's fine, keep the money. I don't want it."

"It's two thousand rand. Are you mad? About four months' wages." The fafi runner stared at her in obvious disbelief.

"Give it to my son. He needs to catch a taxi back to university in the Eastern Cape."

Isaac looked more astonished than the fafi runner, but he took the money and kept quiet.

"You're lucky," the fafi runner called out in a more subdued tone as they walked away. And then, "Young man, don't screw this up now."

Neither she nor Isaac looked back until they reached the taxi ranks. She was glad the woman had not followed them, but she was also glad for the stroke of luck with the money. The platform was less crowded than before, and she pointed to a bench beneath the awning.

"Let's sit," she said.

For a while they didn't talk.

"Nice sneakers," she said, as she stared at his long feet stretched out in front of him. "Mrs. Sofia gave them to you the Christmas before last, remember?"

"Yes," he said.

"So what do you want to do? Come back with me to the Levantis's house, or go straight back to the university and tell them you've decided to finish your studies?"

"I'll go back," he said. "I have enough money for the taxi and to pay the first semester fees."

"Good boy," she said.

They sat in silence a little longer.

"You know," she said, after a while, "you arrived in the world the same day Nelson Mandela was removed from the world. On your birthday, June 12 of 1964, he was sentenced to life imprisonment."

"Really?" Isaac said.

"Yes, for me, it was a remarkable coincidence. I had followed Mandela's trial every day, afraid he would get the death penalty. When he received life imprisonment instead of the death sentence, I thought it was a good omen. For him. For you. For the whole country. I looked at your tiny arms and legs, and thought, by the time this baby grows up, Mandela will be released from prison, and there will be freedom for the people, and you will lead the life denied to me."

She saw tears in his eyes, and she was glad. Maybe she was finally getting through to him.

The minibus pulled up. It was the same one that had brought her earlier. She recognized the sticker *In God We Trust*.

"Do you want me to wait with you until your taxi arrives?" she asked.

"No, I'll be fine," he said. "You go ahead. You must be tired."

"Don't let me down again," she said, swallowing her tears as she stood up to board. "I don't have much money, as you know, but I've done my very best for you."

"You are a good mother," he said. "I won't let you down."

"Promise you won't let me down?"

"I promise." She squeezed his hand and climbed into the minibus.

The taxi was less cramped now, so she sat near the front. It began to drizzle again and she stared out the window, watching the rain wash over her reflection. Her body swayed back and forth as the driver swerved across slippery roads. She should have waited with Isaac but she was so tired.

When she got back to Sofia's house, she trudged up the long driveway. Johannes came running, a worried look on his face.

"Grace, you didn't find him?"

"I found him," she said triumphantly.

"Hai, Grace. I'm so happy. You are a superwoman. Tell me everything."

He joined her under the umbrella, and she told him about Isaac as he escorted her back to her room. As they passed the main house, she glanced up at Sofia's bedroom window. The light was still on. Up there, another mother was crying. Soon, Natalie would be leaving. She knew she ought to go upstairs and check on Sofia. But right now, every muscle in her body ached. She had traipsed all over that township. She would see Sofia in the morning. Nothing would change overnight. And deep down, she was afraid that her heart might not be able to hold Sofia's pain as well as her own.

ELEVEN
A Small Gathering
Sofia

Although two weeks had passed since Natalie had left for America, Sofia was still struggling. Grace would come to her bedroom, trying to make her eat something. Madam, you cannot carry on like this, she would say. And of course, Grace was right. But she could not fall asleep until the early hours of the morning. And when she woke up, she spent a lot of time alone in her bedroom, just sitting and thinking. The same thoughts over and over again: The morning Natalie had left, Nick had been inconsolable, and in the end he had refused to go to the airport; Dimitri had driven her and Natalie; and the worst was when Natalie had walked down the passenger walkway to the plane and stopped midway to look back. She had wanted to run after her child, and it had taken every ounce of willpower to restrain herself. As well as Dimitri's hands. Mom, it's going to be okay, he repeated, holding her back.

But it wasn't okay. *Had she caused this?* And just as she asked herself this question for the hundredth time, Dimitri popped his head around the bedroom door. "Mom, she's not gone forever."

She looked up from where she sat in the armchair by the window and couldn't help but smile. He had an innocent boyishness about him. The sight of him made something flicker inside her, and she realized what it was. A sliver of joy. Thank God for Dimitri. "You're all that I have right now," she said.

"Mom, don't be so dramatic. Nobody died. Natalie broke up with Peter, that's all. She'll come home again, just give her time. And you have to get out of the house. You cannot stay cooped up forever. You'll go crazy."

He was right, of course. Except for Grace, Nick, and Dimitri, she had stopped seeing people. She had cancelled her regular beauty and hair appointments, stepped down from the church and educational committees, and withdrawn behind the safety of walls. She had never felt so alone in her life, and yet she couldn't stand the thought of being with people.

Dimitri pulled up a chair next to her. Suddenly, she was frightened. What did he want to tell her? America? And she felt that tiny spark of joy leaving her. She was too afraid to ask, so they sat in silence for a while. She didn't want to hear what she didn't want to hear.

He would never do that to her, she thought. At least, not right now. But there was a question in his eyes. He was bursting to ask her something.

"What is it?" she finally said.

"Mom, I need you to do me a huge favor. *Please*."

She sat up straighter. She would do anything for him.

"Annelize and her parents are having a small gathering at their house on Sunday, and they would really like for you and Dad to join *us*," he said.

Us. She flinched. What did he mean by that? Did he regard himself as one of them? Already? *Them* and *Us.* She tossed the words around in her head, testing them, and squirmed in her seat. Dimitri was *her* son. Not *theirs.* But she saw again Annelize's fingers entwined with his, locked together that day in church. And she remembered what her mother had done to her and Theo.

"So it's a luncheon?" she said, and sat forward.

"Yes. It's a kind of get-to-know-you type of thing. And it would be good for you to get out."

"I suppose so," she agreed, no longer sure what she was resisting.

"It's going to be a *braai,* very casual," he continued, and she watched his face brighten. *God, how she loved that face.*

"Her father really knows his meats, and no one can cook meat better than he does."

She tried to be happy for him. A braai was the South African way of grilling meat over an open fire with friends. Not too different from the Greek way of cooking a lamb over an open fire.

"Fine, if that's what you want, your father and I will come."

For a moment Dimitri looked stunned, even more surprised than she felt by her unexpected surrender, but then his face broke into a smile, and a surge of love overwhelmed her. He bent over and smothered her with kisses until she pushed him away, "Don't you have any work to do?"

"It doesn't suit you, by the way, the pitiful face," he said in a gentle, mocking tone. He sauntered off, looking pleased with himself. He must really love this girl, she thought, swallowing a lump in her throat.

There was a slight nip in the air, but the sky was a startling blue when she and Nick set off to visit the potential future in-laws in Pretoria. She could tell he was thrilled about her first steps back into society after the wedding fiasco, and she wondered if she truly deserved his love. He seemed to be over that ridiculous jealous rage. Maybe they could get back to some sort of new normal.

Within an hour, they were near Pretoria and the posh suburb of Waterkloof. Nick slowed down as they drove through the prestigious neighborhood of the capital city.

"Remember when we wanted to buy a house here?" she said. She remembered how it was known for its ambassadorial residences and hilltop homes occupied by the Afrikaner elite and high-ranking government officials.

"You mean when I wanted to buy a house here. You had kicked up a fuss. It wasn't good enough for you," Nick said.

"Nonsense," she said. "I just wasn't comfortable in a city where Afrikaans was the dominant language. I could never wrap my tongue around that language."

"I'm surprised you agreed to come to Pretoria today for this party," Nick said amiably.

"Do I have a choice?" she said. "I tried to control my daughter's life and look what happened. I'm not going to make the same mistake twice. If he's serious about Annelize, I suppose we must get to know her parents."

"If you can't beat them, join them," Nick said.

"I don't know about that," she said. "But the girl is not a bad girl."

"Are you trying to convince yourself or me?" he said.

She stared straight ahead, annoyed with him for knowing her so well.

"I'm teasing you," he said. "You're right. She's not a bad girl. And the neighborhood's not too shabby either."

They pulled into a tree-lined driveway. The remote-controlled gates rolled open and she noticed the cameras on top of the wall, just like the ones they had at their house.

They parked near other luxury cars, close to a private tennis court, and she extracted a bouquet of protea and strelitzia from the back seat. All around them, huge oak trees and natural rockeries complemented the African flavor of the Cape Dutch home that graced the property. In spite of herself, she grudgingly admired the thatched roof and the white-plastered, central gable of the home.

"It's an impressive house. A stunning example of the early French and Dutch architecture," she said.

"Not a bad place for a wedding venue," Nick said.

"Let's not get ahead of ourselves."

The delicious aroma of *boerewors* drifted across the lawn as they reached the dark-stained double doors.

"Smells good," she said. She would never admit it to anyone, but she actually liked the South African grilled sausages better than the Cypriot grilled sausages, or *loukanika* as Nick called them.

Nick also sniffed the air appreciatively as they reached the verandah steps. "Try to behave yourself and not cause a scene," he said. She rolled her eyes and before she could answer, the front door swung open and two people whom she guessed to be Annelize's parents stood there with outstretched arms and broad smiles. Dimitri and Annelize hovered in the background, anxious and wide-eyed.

She stared at them. The father was one of those tall, good-looking Afrikaners. Definitely he had played rugby for his school and university, she thought. The mother could easily have been a former Miss South Africa in her heyday. But not without a little bit of pleasure, she noticed an ever so slight thickening around the woman's waist.

"*Welkom*! Welcome to our home," the burly Afrikaner extended a giant hand, and his wife said, "*Aangename kennis*, a pleasure to meet you. I'm Elmarie and this is my husband, Andre."

She winced. A feeling of dislocation came over her with the Afrikaans, a language she'd never mastered. But she plastered a smile on her face and thrust the bouquet into Elmarie's hands.

"*Hoe pragtig, baie dankie*. Beautiful, thank you so much," the woman gushed. "I must get a vase for these." Elmarie hurried off while she stood there feeling lost.

Dimitri winked at her and seemed to be bursting with happiness. She smiled. For you, *I'll kill the bull*, she thought, surprised at herself that an idiom used mainly by the Afrikaner people had popped into her head. She remembered the Afrikaans builder who had said this to her a long time ago. She'd driven the man crazy with challenging construction requests. He had patiently fulfilled all her wishes and taught her that phrase when she'd apologized for her excessive demands.

Nick's eyes darted playfully around the room, taking it all in. He's already enjoying himself, she thought. She, too, would try to relax for the sake of the children.

Within a few minutes, Elmarie returned. "I just love everything Greek," she gushed. "I adore Greek people and Greek dancing. Andre and I went to Greece a few years ago. Mykonos, Santorini, Crete. I love the Greek islands and the Greek people. So passionate. And your son is gorgeous, like a Greek god."

She didn't know whether to laugh or cry at this outpouring of flattery, and looked at Dimitri. *See what I have to suffer for you?*

Nick poked her in the ribs with his elbow and gave her a playful wink. Leave me alone, she wanted to say, but then Annelize linked her arm through hers and whisked her away.

"Come, Mrs. Levantis, let me show you around," and she was pleased by the girl's instinct to rescue her from the mother.

As they walked through the tastefully furnished house, Annelize pointed out various photos and awards accumulated over the years. Academics, equestrian shows, tennis tournaments, modeling competitions. So many awards. This girl had been primed to succeed. For the life of her, however, she could not understand how the parents would be okay with their beautiful daughter leaving the country to live far away with Dimitri. Of course, not all parents thought like she did, she reminded herself.

As they passed the dining room table, she skimmed her eyes over the desserts, certain that Elmarie would not be able to match a Greek spread. She recognized the famous South African Malva pudding. She loved that sponge cake seeped in apricot jam. Oh, and Elmarie also had the traditional *melktert*. This was not quite as delicious as the *galaktoboureko*, the Greek milk pie with its creamy semolina filling, but still, the Afrikaans version had a silky milk-based center that was also tasty. Aha. The selection could not be complete without an exotic fruit salad. This was a must-have for South African luncheons. And look at that: Elmarie had the fruit beautifully layered in a tall square dish of clear glass. What a good idea. Row upon row of delicious fruit. You could see everything: pawpaw, grapes, blackberries, strawberries, and blueberries.

The woman had even topped the final layer with passion fruit cut into flower shapes.

"How many people is your mother expecting?" she asked, unable to stop herself from feeling impressed.

"Just us," Annelize said.

"What? Wow, your mom caters like a Greek. There's enough food here to feed an army."

Annelize beamed, and she was beginning to like the girl.

By the time they all gathered around the table, she felt that she might be able to get on with these people. It won't be so bad, she told herself. Maybe they could even teach them to speak a little Greek.

Nick was halfway through his second serving of grilled steak when Dimitri tapped his fork on a glass. "Everybody, I have a small surprise that I want to share with you."

Oh, dear God. Surely he wasn't going to give her a ring without even having discussed the matter with her or Nick.

Everyone put down their forks and looked at him.

"I have two first class tickets to New York," he said, whipping the tickets out of his pocket. He waved the paper as if he were presenting a winning lottery ticket.

She drew in a sharp breath. What on earth had made her think he'd put this idea on hold, at least for a short while? Had she missed something when he'd asked her to attend the luncheon? Desperately, she tried to remember the details of what they had said that day.

Around her, there was a stunned silence. She was dimly aware of Nick glaring at Dimitri, Andre growing red in the face, Elmarie open-mouthed, and Annelize looking as if she were about to burst into tears. A whirring sound in Sofia's head seemed to make the ceiling move further and further away as she gripped the table's edge.

"I haven't discussed this with my parents yet." Annelize broke the silence.

"I know," Dimitri said. "But so much has been happening, and I had to give my final answer to the university or I'd lose my spot. I'm definitely going to study there, and I thought I'd just surprise everyone."

"Surprise is the right word," Andre said, and pushed back his chair as he stood up. "You can go wherever the hell you like. If you want to study overseas, good luck to you. My daughter is not leaving. You go by yourself. *My* daughter will *not* go with you."

She finally had an ally on the emigration matter, but instead of feeling happy, she felt sick to her stomach.

"But why do you want to study overseas?" Elmarie asked. "Can you not just do another degree here? At Unisa or Cape Town or somewhere here?"

"It's not just the studies," Dimitri said. "It's the crime. Not so long ago, I buried my best friend. He was murdered for nothing. There's no future here for young people."

"Of course, there's a future. If you take adequate precautions, nothing will happen to you," Andre yelled and slammed his fist on the table, making the plates and silverware shake.

Annelize got up, no longer able to stop crying. "Please excuse me," she said, and left the table. Elmarie ran after her.

"My son has never been known for his timing," she said, at a loss for words.

Nick also pushed his chair back and stood. "Dimitri, we weren't expecting this so soon after your sister left."

He then turned to Andre. "Thank you for lunch, but I think we must leave so that the family can talk privately about these personal matters."

"Yes," Andre agreed, without a moment's hesitation.

Dimitri continued to sit at the table, white-faced. "I'll see you later," he said, head bowed.

She wanted to hug him, but Nick was pulling her by the hand.

Clutching each other for support, Sofia walked unsteadily next to Nick until they reached the parking area. A gardener was busy watering the hard-to-reach rockery plants. He stopped and waved cheerfully at them. Neither she nor Nick waved back. They climbed into the car and drove off in silence.

After a while, Nick said, "Well, at least it wasn't you who made the scene."

"When I walked around their house looking at their family photos, I knew they wouldn't be able to cope if their daughter left the country. I just knew it."

When he said nothing, she carried on. "I won't be able to cope either if Dimitri leaves."

"You'll have to find a way to cope. He's a grown man and needs to make his own decisions without your melodramatics, or Andre's, or the girl to influence him," he said.

"Maybe the girl will keep him here," she said.

"Maybe," Nick said. "But he has to make up his own mind."

"Fine," she said, and folded her arms.

"Don't interfere."

"Okay."

"I'm serious," he said. "Don't say okay if you don't mean it."

"Okay," she said. But it wasn't okay. He knew it. And she knew it.

Neither of them spoke another word the whole way home, each in their own separate world of shared pain.

TWELVE

The Uninvited

Sofia

The next morning Sofia was awake before seven, convinced that Nick was wrong about her staying out of it. If she didn't get involved, who would? Dimitri was *her* son. She would call him later and tell him to come home for lunch. Then she would sit with him and talk about the whole thing. No tears, no raised voices, no drama. Just a calm, reasonable discussion.

Already, she felt better now that she had a plan. She got up, dressed, and headed to the kitchen where Grace was clearing away breakfast dishes.

"Master Nick and Dimitri were up early," Grace said. "They left for work."

"They're avoiding me," she said.

Grace poured some coffee and handed her the morning newspaper. "I noticed that Dimitri was quiet this morning."

"You won't believe what happened yesterday," she said. "Sit for a few minutes, and I'll tell you." Grace pulled out a chair, and Sofia told her about the disastrous luncheon, the airline tickets, and Andre's reaction.

When she finished, Grace shook her head sadly. She poured more coffee for Sofia, and made a cup of tea for herself.

"Madam, let me tell you about my visit to Alexandra township yesterday."

When Grace finished her story, they looked at each other and Sofia could tell what Grace was thinking. "Yes, our boys are having a competition to see who can wear down their mother first," she said. Grace let out a long soft sigh and got up to clear the table.

Sofia turned back to the newspapers. "Look, Grace, Mandela is also in the United States; he's visiting New York, Boston, Miami, Atlanta."

"Hah, everyone wants to go to America," Grace said, peering over her shoulder. One standing, one sitting, they both skimmed the article. Mandela was still pushing for sanctions against South Africa until a non-racial democracy was secured.

"He's lobbying the international arena, preparing for the final push before acceptance of a political settlement," she said. "It's going to happen any day now. If only I could convince Dimitri to be patient a little longer."

She put down the newspaper. "Grace, I'm going to call Dimitri and tell him to come home for lunch so we can talk. Maybe I can persuade him to postpone his study abroad idea for a year."

"Monday is always a bad day at the office," Grace warned.

She ignored Grace and picked up the phone. Dimitri answered immediately.

"I want you to come home at lunch or as soon as you get a gap in your day."

"Mom, I have meetings—"

"I don't care. Cancel them and come home. I need to speak with you."

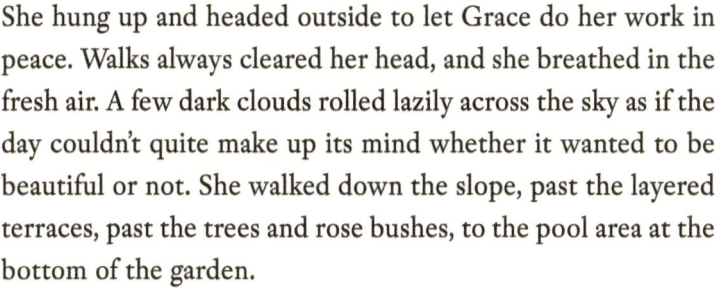

She hung up and headed outside to let Grace do her work in peace. Walks always cleared her head, and she breathed in the fresh air. A few dark clouds rolled lazily across the sky as if the day couldn't quite make up its mind whether it wanted to be beautiful or not. She walked down the slope, past the layered terraces, past the trees and rose bushes, to the pool area at the bottom of the garden.

She loved water. It had a calming effect on her. Angels liked to be near water. Her father had once told her this. Two square-shaped pools, one shallow, the other deep, shimmered in the morning light. A waterfall flowed over the edge of the one into the other, merging the two bodies of water. She had always dreamed that one day her grandchildren would swim in the shallow pool. But the way her children were going, she was never going to see grandchildren in her lifetime.

Sighing, she slipped off her sandals and sat by the steps of the shallow pool, slowly lowering her feet into the water. It took a few minutes for the cold sharpness to feel comfortable. She wondered what time Dimitri would come home. She knew he would come. He had a soft spot for his mother.

Suddenly, a shadow cut across the water. She froze. It wasn't Dimitri. She had just spoken with him. It wasn't Freddy. It was way too early for him. Without looking up, she saw dark outlines slicing the white cement that edged the pool. Six figures surrounded her image in the water. Her reflection stared back, bobbing helplessly up and down on the water. *She was in big trouble.* This was the moment all South Africans feared.

She was going to die. She would never see her children or her husband again.

The sun glinted off the diamonds of her wedding band, and she thought about sliding it off her finger. No, rather not, she decided. She kept still and stared straight ahead. Her breathing sounded very loud in her ears. Just a few feet away, the ten-foot wall surrounding the property towered above her. Early morning rays bounced off the jagged glass and electric wires embedded into the concrete walls, precautions that were supposed to protect her. From the other side, the wind carried over the laughter of the neighbor's gardeners. She could hear them mowing the lawn, as if it were an ordinary day in Johannesburg's suburbs. *Over here*, she wanted to shout. *Please help me. Over here.*

She watched the shadows of the intruders grow shorter. They were moving closer to her.

"Don't make a sound or we'll kill you." A muffled voice reached her ears.

A gloved hand clamped her mouth.

"Get up."

He yanked her up and stale sweat assaulted her nostrils as he pulled her against his muscular body. Clutching her around the neck, and with her back rammed against his chest, he turned her to face the others hiding behind balaclavas pulled over their heads. Except for one, they all carried guns, and she wondered if they could hear her heart threatening to explode through her rib cage.

"Take us to the safe in your bedroom. You are a rich lady," the one holding her said.

My God, how did they know she had a safe in the bedroom?

"Is anyone else in the house with you?"

"My maid. Grace."

"Okay. She's not a problem. I'm the boss now. Do you understand?"

He pushed the gun barrel between two of her ribs as he steered her up the patio stairs. No one spoke. Only the sound of their heavy breathing followed her. Two stone angels stared at them from the gushing water fountain. The sweet, spicy aroma of vasiliko rose sharply from the potted plants, and an image of her father flashed through her mind. *Dad, where are you?*

They entered the house through the kitchen. Grace was standing just inside the pantry doorway reaching for a glass jar. She watched Grace's back stiffen before she slowly turned her head. The glass jar dropped from Grace's hand. A loud crash. It rolled and shattered across the marble tiles, splattering diced tomatoes everywhere. Grace stood motionless, her hand frozen midair in an empty grasp while her eyes bulged with terror.

With the crashing of the glass, the attackers froze in their tracks. She felt their fear spilling out hot and wild, charging the air with terror. The words of the Jesus Prayer came to her mind, *Lord Jesus Christ, Son of God, have mercy on me a sinner*, and she silently repeated this phrase over and over.

One of them grabbed Grace. He yanked her arms behind her body. "We'll kill you if you try to be clever, old woman. Come with me." He steered her down the hallway, forcing her to walk with shoulders pinched back as he pinned her wrists in a tight grip.

"Please," Grace begged. "Please don't hurt my Madam."

Her tall figure looked short next to the giant ramming her forward.

"Shut up," a muffled voice ordered, and a loud thud resounded as one of them shoved Grace into the wall.

Quiet, Sofia silently screamed at Grace. *Don't do anything to aggravate them. Just obey.*

"You too," the leader said and gave her a hard shove. "Where's the master bedroom?"

"Upstairs," she said.

The red eyes of the motion sensors blinked as they reached the landing at the top of the staircase. If only the alarm system would self-start, but they never activated it during the day.

Everything seemed to be happening in slow motion as the armed thugs marched them down the hallway. They reached the master bedroom, where just a few hours ago she had woken up safe and secure. How did these intruders get inside the house? What happened to the dogs? Johannes? Not a peep. How did they get past them?

The tall one gave a low whistle. "My whole house could fit into this room."

"Show us the safe," the leader said. He released her hands from behind her back.

Her wrists were red where his fingers had dug into her. Trembling, she pointed to the built-in cupboard inside the closet.

"The safe is inside the cupboard," she said.

He ripped the door open, and smiled. The steel box sat encased in the white cupboard.

"The keys?" He waved a huge open palm under her nose.

Her mind went blank. *The keys? Where the hell were the keys?* She had no idea. Small droplets of sweat trickled down her neck. A loud slap sent her reeling across the room. Another pair of arms caught her and hurled her to the ground. Carpet fluff filled her nose and mouth.

"The drawer of the dressing table," she gasped, hoping and praying she was right. She hadn't opened the safe since

Natalie's wedding. For the life of her, she could not remember where she had put the keys.

One of them lunged towards the drawer while the others began wrenching out built-in drawers, smashing hinges, dumping contents everywhere. Bras, panties, stockings flew through the air. The glass, heart-shaped container with her wedding crowns lay cracked and broken near her face. Icons and silver-framed photographs landed near her cheekbone. Upside-down faces of her family and the *Panagia* looked at her. *Help me*, she begged. *Mother of God, please help me.*

Finally, she heard a batch of keys jingling wildly. Thank you, she whispered into the carpet. She could hear the leader grunting and cursing, forcing the keys into the unyielding lock. *Oh, dear God. They must not be the right keys.* Someone kicked her in the back, a blow so powerful it sent shock waves all the way down to her toes. Bile rose in her throat.

"Get up." The leader forced her into a kneeling position, gripped her by the hair, and pulled her neck as far back as it would go.

"I'm tired of playing games, do you understand? Open your mouth," he said.

Dear God. Why? What did he want?

"Open your fucking mouth," he repeated.

She tried to part her lips. Her mouth was so dry her tongue stuck to the roof of her mouth. He shoved the gun between her lips, and she cried out as the metal clanged against her teeth. She tasted blood on her tongue.

Grace was sobbing loudly.

"Shut the fuck up!" she heard another man shouting, followed by a loud blow and a groan from Grace as her sobs subsided into whimpers.

"Now tell us where the keys to the safe are." The gangster wriggled the gun inside her mouth, his face so close to hers that she could see a red maze of tiny veins crisscrossing the whites of his eyes. Vomit rose again in her throat. *Always give them what they want.* That's what everyone said. But she had no idea where the damn keys were.

"This is your last chance," he said.

She gestured a thumb to her mouth. *She couldn't talk.*

Slowly, he removed the gun.

"There." She pointed a trembling hand to the bedside table. "The keys must be there."

Please, God, let the keys be in that drawer.

"If these keys don't work, I'll show you how I'm going to kill you," the leader hissed into her face. He placed a pair of her silk stockings around her neck.

"South Africa does not belong to the whites anymore. I hope you realize that. And you must learn to share and play nicely with us," he said.

He looped the two stocking legs together and began tightening the noose as one of the men found a batch of keys. The pressure on her throat was beginning to numb her mind. She turned her face away from his hot, stale breath. To her side, another thug towered over her. She stared at that one's shoes. Dark blue Italian loafers. Two-bit bastards with imported shoes.

And then. Outside. The crunching sound of wheels on gravel. Everyone froze. The grip around her neck loosened.

Oh. My. God. No. Dimitri. She had told him to come home. She recognized the sound of his car, the way he carefully closed the door of the car he pampered. *Please, God, please. Anything but this. Don't let them kill my boy. Take me. Not him.*

"Who's that?" his voice demanded, jolting her head up and down in the silk noose. She could feel his terror seeping into her, blending with her fear, and she stared helplessly back at him. *Lord Jesus, Christ, Son of God, have mercy on us.* He flung her head to the ground as he stood up, pinning her down with his shoe digging into her neck.

Suddenly, the sound of a screeching siren exploded into the air, bouncing off the walls like a crazed banshee, and he jerked his foot back sharply.

"Fuck!" he shouted. "Run."

They all bolted toward the French doors that led to the balcony. Loud manic kicks. Dark-clad legs smashed at the locks. Within seconds, the metal latches snapped like twigs. The doors flew open and the lace curtain blew inwards, brushing her cheek as she lay trembling on the carpet. More cursing, shouting, and scuffling. *The balcony was too high for them to jump.* Someone kicked the railing hard. Then the sharp thud of a body landing on the awning below. Followed by a second and a third heavy thud. A hesitant voice. The clanging of metal. A scraping sound. The others were sliding down the drainpipe. Thank God. They were leaving. But had they all left? She turned her head. No. One remained. He was pointing a gun at the bedroom door. She could hear Dimitri's footsteps coming closer and closer.

Oh my God. Please. No.

She saw Dimitri's shocked face framed in the doorway. The gunman stood less than a meter from her. She pushed herself onto her elbows. A force like nothing she'd ever known catapulted her into the air. She lunged at the gunman's back. Then, a deafening sound. A bullet cracked through the air. Dimitri's body lifted, and then crashed to the ground. The shooter stepped over him, slammed the bedroom door, and thundered down the hallway. She crawled across the floor, digging her nails into the reddening carpet. A halo of blood spread around Dimitri's head.

"My boy." She stared at his beautiful face. She couldn't see where the bullet had gone. But there was blood everywhere.

"Please, God, no. Why are You doing this to me? What do You want from me? Don't take my child."

She beat her fists into the bloody carpet.

Grace's screams filled the room, exploding inside her head.

"I can't hear You, God."

"I can't hear You!"

"Can You hear *me*, God? Please!"

All she could hear were Grace's cries and the sound of someone screaming. It was a sound so terrible, so out of control, that she barely recognized her own voice.

THIRTEEN
Holy Water
Grace

Grace sat on the staircase, crumpled on the first step, cradling her head in both hands. She dragged a sleeve across her face, dabbing her nose, and saw she had smudged blood over her clothes. *If Dimitri died, she wanted to die too. Sofia's baby. Her baby.* She had rocked him to sleep so many times on her back. And covered for him so many times when she knew Sofia would be upset with him. Today, when he needed her most, she was powerless to help him. She had never seen so much blood in her life. *Blood everywhere.* Not even when she had lived in Alexandra township, surrounded by beatings, brawls, and police raids, had she ever seen anything like it.

All around her, people were coming and going. Police, television, and newspaper reporters. In no time, the news had spread through the Greek community and familiar faces were walking through the front door every few minutes. She recognized Mrs. Stathakis from down the road. She could see their fear, in the way they walked with shoulders hunched, in the way they huddled in small whispering groups. And in the way they looked at her.

"This is how it's going to be from now on," Mrs. Andreou was saying in Greek. "The Blacks are going to chase us out of the country. It's going to get worse." And Mrs. Pappas nodded and said that the maid had to be involved. It could only have been an inside job, they said.

I can understand every word you're saying, she wanted to scream at them. Each word stabbed her. She had worked for this family for thirty years. How could these people think she would endanger the lives of her family?

Upstairs, she could hear the sergeant's voice booming, instructing his officers to look for footprints, fingerprints, spit, anything. Downstairs, nobody bothered her. Not until a pair of shoes, light brown and well-polished, appeared in her side vision. She studied the dark brown laces protruding beneath the cuffs of khaki trousers approaching her and remembered the fear that overwhelmed her as a child when she spotted that color. Khaki. The color of the oppressor. The fear of being arrested for something she hadn't done always came with this color. She looked up as the captain's shoes stopped in front of her. His bulky arms strained against his shirt. Also khaki. He clutched a notepad and a tape recorder.

"Okay, Mrs. Grace Molepe. Come with me. I've finished with Johannes and Freddy. Let's sit at the kitchen table, and you can tell me everything you remember." His polite veneer was edged with aggression. "English or Afrikaans?" he said.

She stood on wobbly feet. The glint in his eyes and the set of his jaw warned her to brace herself. What about the other twelve languages of this country, she wanted to say, but kept quiet. She was in no position to be clever. "Whatever you prefer, Sir. *Ek kan ook Afrikaans praat.*"

As soon as she told him in Afrikaans that she could speak his language, he said, "English it is, then."

"Sir, before we begin, can I ask you: Do you have any news from the hospital about Mrs. Sofia and Dimitri?"

"Nothing yet. But it didn't look good to me."

She looked away. This was not what she wanted to hear. If anything happened to them, she did not want to live. And then she noticed that the sliding doors were wide open, which filled her with fear again.

"Sir, it's starting to get dark outside. Can I lock the sliding doors on this level? If the police are finished taking fingerprints here?"

"I don't think the robbers are coming back any time soon, but, yes, we are finished with our work on the bottom level. Go ahead," he said, stroking his neatly trimmed moustache and watching her carefully.

She walked over to the sliding doors and clicked the last latch into place, staring at the peaceful lawns from which the devil robbers had seemed to sprout earlier. And then a thought struck her: Where were the dogs? They hadn't made one sound during the robbery.

"Sir, the dogs. I haven't seen the dogs. There are two. An Alsatian and a small white one, a poodle, Lola."

He stared long and hard at her before answering.

"The Alsatian is dead. Someone gave the dogs poisoned meat. Do you have any ideas who might have done that?"

She gasped. "No, I have no idea. But what about the little one, Lola?"

"The small one will live," he said. "The vet has her. The poodle didn't eat anything, or very little."

"That makes sense. Master Nick always feeds Lola. Lola doesn't eat from anyone else's hands. Not even mine."

He was looking at her as if she had poisoned the dogs, and she sank into the chair and took a deep breath. She began to tell him what had happened. The captain took notes the whole time she spoke. The scratching sound of his pen on the legal pad sounded very loud.

"Nobody hurt you, I take it?"

"No, sir. They pushed me a little and hit me once or twice."

"How do you think they got inside the house?"

"I don't know, sir. It's very difficult to get inside this house. The wall around the property is high, and we have Johannes guarding the front gate."

"They tied up Johannes," he said. "According to my men, he didn't give them the code to open the gate. Johannes says they knew the code. Who besides the family has access to the code?"

"Only myself, sir."

"Have you ever given the code to anyone?"

"No, sir."

"How long have you worked for the family?"

"Thirty years."

"How do you feel about these people?"

"Feel? How do you mean feel? I don't understand."

"I mean do you like them?"

"Do I like them?"

She would lay down her life for them. They were as much her family as her son.

"Sir, these people have been very good to me. They are paying for my son's education." She paused. "They are my family. I wish it was me whom the robbers had shot."

He sat back in his chair, regarding her carefully.

"Can you tell me anything about the robbers? Do you remember what they looked like? Were they wearing anything that stuck in your mind?"

Something tugged at the edges of her memory, but she couldn't grasp the thought that was bubbling to the surface. She sighed and shook her head. "No, sir. They were all wearing masks and gloves and dark long-sleeved clothing. Like overalls."

"Do you have a husband?" he asked.

"No. He was killed in the mines a long time ago."

"A boyfriend?"

"No."

"Any friends that come here to visit?"

"No. I know some of the maids who work for the other Greek ladies of Johannesburg, but we don't sit around and drink tea together. Johannes is the only one I talk to sometimes."

"What do you do on your day off?"

"I work or I read."

He leaned forward in his chair, narrowing his eyes.

"Let me understand this properly. On your day off, you work some more or you read? Is that correct?"

She nodded. "It's all I know how to do."

"How many children do you have?"

"One son. His name is Isaac."

"Where is he now?"

"The University of Fort Hare in the Eastern Cape."

"What is he doing there?"

"He's studying to be a lawyer."

"Oh." He arched his eyebrows. "He will be an important person one day. In the new South Africa."

She moved back in her chair and swallowed hard. She wanted to tell this Dutchman to go jump in a lake. But Isaac had failed that deferred exam and dropped out. He had returned to school only because she had dragged him back by the scruff of his neck. Maybe the Afrikaner's scorn was justified. She bit her lips and said nothing.

He changed the subject. "It's very unusual for a house such as this one, with this type of security, to be robbed by people who are unknown to the employers."

"That's exactly what I'm thinking," she said, looking him straight in the eye. She could feel her resentment growing.

He pushed the document across the table.

"Here, sign on the bottom line."

She picked up the papers, hesitating.

"It's your affidavit," he said, his voice impatient.

"I know what it is, sir."

Something inside her flared, and she could feel the heat flush through her body. She wanted to tell him that she was not stupid or illiterate. Quietly, she said, "I must read it first. But I need my reading glasses. May I fetch them from my room?"

"You don't trust me?" he snapped.

She looked at him. Was he joking with her? An Afrikaner felt insulted because he thought she did not trust him? She sighed loudly, unable to restrain herself.

"It's not a matter of trust, sir. This is a legal document. I must be careful. Actually, I can just borrow my Madam's reading glasses. They are right here in the kitchen drawer behind you." She stepped behind him to get the glasses.

"How good is your English anyway?" he said, tapping his pen in an irritated manner. He watched her slide the glasses onto the bridge of her nose.

"My English is very good." She began to read aloud so that he could decide for himself. After a while, he stopped tapping. She glanced up quickly while continuing to read. He was staring at her with his head cocked to one side. She wondered whether it would annoy him if she pointed out his spelling errors and decided against it.

"I will sign it now," she said.

"Where did you learn to read like that? Did you finish school?"

"No. I have no education. I learned to read by myself, with my father's help. He was a chauffeur for a rich man. He used to bring me books and magazines and comic books from the man's house. That's how I lived under apartheid. Through the lives of other people I read about."

He pushed his chair back and stood, handing her a card. "Here. If you remember anything, phone me. My number is on this card."

She took the card and memorized his name: Captain Johan van Rensburg. Then she said it aloud, and with the proper Afrikaans pronunciation.

"Is it alright to clean the blood on the carpets upstairs, sir?"

"Yes, you can clean up everything," he said. His eyes drifted to her apron. She touched the red blood stains blotting the lace-edged pink apron.

"Dimitri. He was bleeding a lot."

"I know. I saw him. We have everything we need for now, thank you. Of course, you understand that you are not to leave this area until our investigation is over?"

"I have nowhere to go," she replied quietly. She wished she had somewhere to go. This family and Isaac were her life.

As soon as he left, she began rechecking doors, windows, and bolts. Everyone had gone and the house was now silent, as if it, too, were traumatized. Upstairs, on the second floor, chaos waited. She knew she had to clean up.

Instead, her feet carried her to the front gate. She was tired of struggling. Her whole life had been one big struggle. And nothing was changing. Not even Mandela could change it. Dimitri was right. They were all living in a fool's paradise.

And there was this other thing gnawing at her. Something that she knew she had seen. Too quick for her eye to catch, but her brain had snapped it up. All she had to do was find it somewhere inside her head.

The trees loomed dark in the distance, and although it was warm, she shivered from the cold sweat drenching her body. She stared into the darkening horizon. The huge wrought-iron gates were closed. Johannes sat in the guardhouse. She narrowed her eyes. He looked exhausted but alert, and clutched his gun as he waved her over. "Grace, come here. I haven't stopped shaking since they attacked me. Can you believe it?"

She waved back, shaking her head. She could tell he was desperate to talk, but she was all talked out. As she turned to walk back up to the house, she stopped. There it was. The thing that had been nagging at her. It had finally surfaced. She remembered it, and now she wished she hadn't. She hugged herself and walked slowly up to the house.

Back inside, she stood at the bottom of the staircase. A mountain would have been easier to climb. She began the ascent, dragging herself up the stairs, clutching the banister. At the top, she stopped to catch her breath.

She took a deep breath and went straight to Dimitri's bedroom. She stood in front of his closet, hesitating. She touched his work suits, stroking the luxurious textures of wool, cotton, and linen, each one nicer than the next. His shirts, blues, grays, and whites. Sharp, neat, pleated, all ironed by her. She had dreamed that someday Isaac would also wear suits like this. Sofia had promised that as soon as Isaac completed his degree, she would take him shopping in Sandton City.

She knelt and began to pull out shoeboxes from the shelves beneath the suits, one by one, till she placed her hands on the box she was hoping did not exist. It was different from the other boxes. She remembered it well. An imported box. Green, red, and white, the colors of Italy. She held her breath and opened the lid. *Navy.* There they were. *Those shoes.* Size 12 Italian loafers. *Pantofola d'oro.* A very expensive Italian brand, over a thousand rand. Not something that just anyone could afford. She reeled back, sinking down onto her haunches, shutting her eyes tightly. She remembered Isaac's feet at the taxi rank, stretched out in front of him. One foot crossed over the other. He had been wearing these exact same sneakers.

No. No. No. This could not be true. She opened her eyes. There they were, still in her hands. *The navy shoes.*

She could scarcely believe that life would rob her like this again. When her husband had been trapped underground with the other miners, she had come close to losing her mind. After three weeks they pulled the bodies of the dead men from beneath the collapsed ground. Pulling out these shoes was almost worse. Her world was caving in again.

She remembered that Sofia had bought two identical pairs, one for Dimitri and one for Isaac, the Christmas before last. The ones in her hands were Dimitri's. But during the robbery, she had seen the other pair. Isaac had worn them. In the chaos, her mind had barely registered what her eyes had seen. But now she knew. Isaac was the one whose shoulders had flinched when the leader had slapped her.

She stared at Dimitri's shoes, clutching the box, and felt herself sinking into a deep, dark hole: *If I tell Sofia, it will be the end of Isaac's life. If I keep quiet, I might as well have been the one who fired the gun at Dimitri.* She shoved the box back onto the shelf and swiped at a stupid spider's web in the far corner. The silky white threads dangled limp and broken on her fist.

Slowly she walked down the passage, her head exploding with memories from the past. The township alleys, dogs barking, police lights flashing, and the foul stench of the sewers where they hid to escape. She could hardly think straight for fear of going back to the gutters.

At the doorway of the master bedroom, she froze. It looked like a tornado had ripped through the place. Clothes and shoes, brushes and combs, broken drawers and glass scattered all over. And everywhere, the blood. Their world destroyed.

She lowered her exhausted body onto the floor and lay face down, over the bloody outline of Dimitri's body. She felt his blood soaking into her clothes. And then she let out a long howl that sounded, even to her ears, as if all the pain of this tortured land had collected in the bowels of the earth and was being released back up through *her* body.

She lay for a long time in the dark, until the house grew cold and her body was numb. She knew she had to get up. She needed to clean and wash and scrub everything before Sofia came home. She got up and walked with heavy steps to collect her cleaning materials downstairs.

As she walked down the hallway, the icons on the wall stared at her with large, sorrowful eyes. She shook her head at them. These saints and the invisible God Sofia believed in were a mystery to her. Perhaps in Greece and Cyprus, it was easier to reach God. But here, at the southernmost edge of Africa, God had forgotten the people.

She stopped at the end of the hallway, staring at the small icon stand against the wall. She had walked past it hundreds of times but never paid much attention, except when she cleaned the images to keep them dust free. On the ledge, a small oil lamp cast a soft red glow over the faces of the Virgin Mary and Child, almost bringing them to life. She moved closer now, staring curiously at the faces. The baby Jesus reached out a tiny hand to his mother's face. How many times had she and Sofia rocked their boys to sleep, oblivious to what lay ahead. There was something else in this picture. The child's face was actually an adult face. She sensed a pulse behind the image, as if *she* were the one being viewed, and something stirred inside her.

"Man and God," she whispered. "That's what you look like. Man and God." She did not know anything about prayer. It was difficult to believe in an invisible God who had let her down. How could she trust him? But she had seen Father Theo pray. And surely all these saints, who had once been alive, had not martyred themselves for nothing, for something that did not exist. So she got down on her knees the way she had seen Sofia do many times. At this point, she had nothing to lose. She began to pray, whispering the words aloud:

"Mary, you are also a mother. If you can hear me, you will know my pain just as I see the pain in your eyes. Please, if you can ask your Son to help us, I will be grateful. He might listen to you because you're His Mother and he knows you. Please ask Him to help Dimitri. He doesn't deserve to die. He's a good boy. His mother is a good woman. She has always helped my family. Isaac has done a terrible thing. I don't know what to do about this. I tried to be a good mother but I failed. And now I have a bigger problem. How can I betray my son? If God could please tell me what to do, I'll do it. I'm not very good with prayers because I've never prayed before. If God has something to tell me, if He could please make it clear so I can understand. Thank you."

As expected, she didn't hear anything from God or from His Mother, so she filled a bucket with soapy water and scrubbed away throughout the night. Her breathing became one with the circular motion of her hand, and the repetitive rhythm soothed her shattered nerves. She was good at cleaning; that's what she did best. Slowly the carpet became almost white. She sat back on her haunches and examined her work. The carpet would never be perfect, but it was much better. She scrubbed a little more. She was still on her hands and knees when she became aware of someone calling her name.

"Grace? Grace? Grace?"

Father Theo stood in the doorway. The morning light was just beginning to slant through the windows, washing his face with light that showed how exhausted he was. He looked confused, as if trying to remember something he had forgotten.

"I'm sorry. I didn't mean to frighten you. Are you alright? I've just come from the hospital. Sofia gave me the house keys. She wanted me to check on you. Do you need anything?" he said.

He stretched out his hands to help her as she heaved herself up.

"Dimitri, is he alright? Is he alive? Please tell me, Father," she begged.

"He's alive, but he's unconscious. The doctors are worried. The bullet has lodged near his spine. It will be a very difficult operation. The surgeons are not willing to touch it at this point."

"But he will live?"

No answer. He was marching to the windows, focusing hard on something she could not see, tracing the sign of the cross in the air with his right hand.

"And what about Mrs. Sofia? Is she alright?"

He waved one hand in the air making circular motions. It was the Greek way of saying something was a disaster. When words failed a Greek, Grace knew the situation was very bad.

"I want to do an *agiasmo*, Grace. I need to sprinkle holy water in this room."

He was flinging the windows wide open as if to expel any demons and terror still lingering in the air. "Can you please bring me a bowl of water, and some vasiliko from the yard?" he asked.

"Of course, Father." She knew this church tradition, and she knew that vasiliko was the basil plant Greek priests used to bless homes with holy water.

By the time she returned, Father Theo had placed an icon on the table and arranged a stole over his shoulders. He began to chant in Greek, and the sound was soothing. He walked around the room and she followed carrying the bowl, careful not to spill any water. He dipped the leafy basil stems in and out of the bowl, flinging his arm wide, showering the four corners of each room with water. By the time he finished, water was trickling down her forehead and droplets clung to her lashes. She blinked furiously, and he smiled as he took the bowl from her.

"It's good for you, Grace. Holy water sanctifies and heals everything. We must not throw the remaining water down the drain. It's been blessed. It's holy now. We need to pour it over a plant. Or drink it."

"Don't worry, Father, I know about this. I will take care of it."

She would drink it all later. She needed as much help as she could get. "Father, can I tell you something?" she blurted out, surprising herself.

"Of course. What is it?" He was rolling up the stole he had removed from his shoulders.

"If I tell you something in confidence, even if it's a bad thing, as a priest, you cannot tell anybody else? Is that correct?"

He stood still and stopped rolling up the stole. He let it unroll and placed it over his head again. The two ends hung down equally in front, just beneath the knees, and her eyes fixed on the golden tassels that fringed the bottom edges.

"Now that I'm wearing this, yes, that's correct." He lifted the ends of the stole, and a slanted rectangle of sunlight from the open window shimmered on the golden tassels. "See these golden tassels hanging on the edge, they represent each and every person who comes to me. I'm responsible for all these people. As a priest, I cannot discuss with anyone whatever you tell me in confidence."

"Even if I'm not an Orthodox Christian?"

"Correct. This conversation is a sacrament."

"I have a big problem, Father."

"I'm listening."

"My son was one of the six criminals who came here today."

She heard his sharp intake of breath and a shadow flickered across his face.

"*Christe mou*," he said and crossed himself. "Are you sure?"

"Yes," she bowed her head. "I recognized his shoes. Mrs. Sofia bought those shoes. They're from Italy. Very expensive. You can't find them in the shops here. Mrs. Sofia bought them while traveling in Italy."

"Was Isaac the one who shot Dimitri?" he asked in a voice so quiet she had to strain to hear him.

"No. He was standing at the back watching the others. He said nothing the whole time. He didn't touch anyone. But he must be the one who gave them the access code to the front gates. I had the numbers written on a piece of paper in my room, in case I ever forgot. I had the paper hidden in a drawer. He must have found that piece of paper."

"I'm so sorry," he answered. "But why would he do such a thing? It doesn't make sense. These people have been so good to him."

"I don't know. I believe he got mixed up with a bad crowd at university. They filled his head with lies and nonsense. They changed him. I'm sure that's also why he got arrested that night when you arrived from Greece, remember? He is struggling with his studies. Maybe I'm the one to blame for pushing him so hard. It's all my fault."

"It's not your fault, Grace." He made the sign of the cross on her forehead and touched his lips gently to the top of her head.

"If Dimitri dies, Mrs. Sofia will not be able to live. Her life will be finished. What should I do, Father? Please tell me what to do?"

"Grace, I can't tell you what to do. All I can tell you is that loving people means that you give up things for them. Sometimes, it means that you even have to give up the person. For their own good."

This was not what she wanted to hear. No mother brought up a son to throw him into jail.

"Nothing has to be decided right now. Try to get some rest," he said.

"I can't rest, Father. I'll go shower and change, but first let me pack some clean clothes and toiletries for Mrs. Sofia. Are you going back to the hospital? She was covered in blood when she left in the ambulance. She'll need clean clothes."

"Of course, Grace. I'll take them to her," he said.

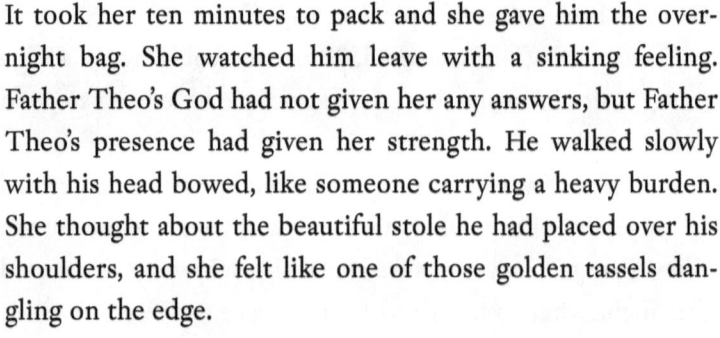

It took her ten minutes to pack and she gave him the overnight bag. She watched him leave with a sinking feeling. Father Theo's God had not given her any answers, but Father Theo's presence had given her strength. He walked slowly with his head bowed, like someone carrying a heavy burden. She thought about the beautiful stole he had placed over his shoulders, and she felt like one of those golden tassels dangling on the edge.

FOURTEEN
A Weeping Icon
Sofia

Sofia still could not believe what had happened. But when she leaned her forehead against the glass panel that separated the Intensive Care Unit from the hallway, Dimitri lay on the hospital bed, deathly still. She watched the monitors attached to him. Red dots flashed and beeped. Graph lines peaked and dipped. He was slipping back and forth between this world and the next. She was the one who had told him to come home.

Her breath created a hazy mist on the glass as she stared at her boy. She lifted the tip of her index finger to the glass and drew a heart shape in the thin film of condensed air.

"Sofia, what are you doing standing in the passage? Why did you leave the examination room?"

She spun around to find Nick. His eyes were sunken and hollow. "I'm fine. They gave me something for the shock. I don't need anything else. Nick, had I not called him, he would not have come home at that time."

"Your son probably saved your life."

"I would rather they had taken me and not touched my son."

"What a choice," Nick said, leaning his head against the glass pane. "My wife or my son. Everyone should leave this godforsaken country."

For a while they watched the doctors and nurses in green overalls attend to their son. Nick could not stand still for long, and his sighing and fidgeting were getting on her nerves.

"Don't you have somewhere to go? When are you fetching Natalie from the airport?" she asked.

"Not for a while yet." He walked away and began to pace up and down the long passage. She was sorry that she had snapped at him.

As soon as one of the nurses left the intensive care room, she took the gap and slipped inside. A doctor looked up and glared at her. *Too bad, I'm his mother.* She ignored the objection written all over his face and stared at Dimitri, entangled in a web of IVs, tubes, and wires. *My God. His throat.* Her eyes fixed on his neck. They had cut a hole in his beautiful, long neck. A ventilator breathed for him. The boy who entered a room and filled it with life now had a machine breathing for him. She stroked his cheek and smoothed his hair.

"Dimitri, open your eyes. Please."

Nothing.

She knelt down and leaned her head against the cold metal of the guardrail. Pray, she told herself. Pray. But no words came. She banged her head against the railing, desperate for a smidgeon of faith. She begged God for a tiny crumb of hope.

The doctor nudged her gently.

"Mrs. Levantis, let him rest now. He needs to rest as much as possible to allow his body to recover."

"I want to be near my son."

"Mrs. Levantis," the doctor said, not unkindly, "please, do as you are told so I can do my job."

A nurse led her out of the room. In the hallway, Nick continued to pace up and down, like a person possessed.

Another nurse. "Mrs. Levantis, can you and your husband please follow me. The doctor wants to speak with you about your son's X-rays."

They followed the nurse down a long hallway. An orderly was pushing an empty wheelchair down the passage and a cold shiver ran down her spine. They passed a nurse's station where two nurses sat chatting. One chomped a sandwich, the other sipped coffee from a Styrofoam cup. Behind them, a TV flickered. According to the newscaster, violence in the townships was spilling into the cities, and the president was considering a state of emergency. The matter-of-fact voice angered Sofia, and she wanted to throw a coffee cup at the presenter's carefully made-up face. Not that it was the presenter's fault. The damned politicians had caused the country's problems, and now the people were paying the price.

At the end of the hallway, they stopped in front of a door and the nurse said, "Go ahead, knock and go inside. Dr. Pretorius is waiting for you."

Inside, the doctor looked stiff and serious in his white coat. Her heart sank. *This was not good.* The doctor skipped the niceties and pointed to the chairs by his desk. When she sat down next to Nick, she couldn't stop trembling.

The doctor pointed to a set of X-rays lit up on the screen. "We've tried to control the bleeding, but the bullet has lodged itself here." He tapped at a space between two vertebrae on the screen. "It's right next to the spinal cord."

She drew a sharp breath. Oh God. This was worse than she had thought. After that she caught only random words.

Hematoma. Pressure. Paralysis. Removal could cause more harm than good. She could not catch everything he was saying. He was speaking too quickly. Her head felt foggy and thick.

"Who is going to do the surgery?" she interrupted. Her son could die and this man was wasting time, delivering clinical facts like a robot.

"That's what I'm saying," he began again. "It's not an easy surgery. We have to weigh the pros and cons very carefully."

"I want to speak with the surgeon." She almost said I want to speak to a real doctor, not a robot, but thought better of it. When he didn't reply, she repeated herself and added the word *now*.

"If anybody is going to do this surgery, it should be Professor Kingsley," he said. "He's away, on a teaching conference in America. He'll be back in a few days."

"In America? In a few days? But my son—" She didn't want to say the words *could die*.

"I've already spoken to both Dr. Randall and Dr. Viljoen. At this point neither one of them thinks it's a good idea to attempt the surgery now anyway. We have to wait."

"And if the bullet remains?" Nick said.

"Also not good. At this stage we cannot tell how much paralysis there is. We have induced a coma to help him rest."

"So what options are you offering?" Nick asked.

Again, the man kept quiet, and she felt something inside her shutting down.

"I see," Nick said after a long silence.

"Let's get the patient through tonight, and then we can regroup again in the morning," he replied quietly.

Sofia looked at Nick, willing him to do something. Nick could fix anything. Except this. He sat there helpless and stunned. The man she regarded as invincible looked worn down and defeated, like a boxer flung against the ropes. His cheeks were wet with tears. She had never seen him cry before, and this scared her almost as much as the sight of Dimitri in the ICU.

"Can my son be moved?" Nick finally said.

"No. Under no circumstances," the doctor replied.

She looked at his steely blue eyes and felt the strength drain out of her body. She didn't like this doctor, but how could she argue with him, and where would they move Dimitri anyway? This was the best private hospital in Johannesburg. Her son's life was in the hands of this man and they were at his mercy.

So she changed her tone. "Please, you must try to help my boy. He's a very active person. Full of energy. Full of life. He plays soccer and rugby and basketball. He's the best Greek dancer I know. You should see him dance. He could never be in a wheelchair."

"Mrs. Levantis, let's take things one step at a time," he said, moving towards the door. She could not understand his coldness. Why was he being like this, ushering them out?

Desperate, she grabbed a framed photo from his desk. A woman and two young men, carbon copies of each other, beamed up at her. These had to be his sons.

"If one of your boys was lying in the ICU, what would you do?" she asked, holding the picture close to his face.

"I would get hold of Professor Kingsley as fast as I could, which I've already done for you. I left an urgent message. I've worked with him, and he's one of the best surgeons in the world," he said. "I'm waiting for him to get back to me. He's the type of doctor who will cut a trip short to help us here."

"Fine," she said, still not encouraged. "I guess there's nothing else we can do until then. Thank you." She was unaccustomed to people not bending backwards to accommodate her wishes.

She handed him the framed photo of his two boys, and they walked back to the ICU in a daze. Men and women went about their business. No one turned to look their way. Her son was dying and nobody cared, including the doctor.

———

A young woman sat in the waiting area outside the ICU. She was hunched over, holding her head with both hands. Her long blonde hair fell over a profile that reminded her of a classical Greek or Roman sculpture molded in sorrow. The girl lifted her head as they walked past. Oh my gosh. She would recognize those blue eyes anywhere.

"Annelize."

"I'm so sorry, Mrs. Levantis," Annelize said in a hoarse voice.

"I'm the one who's sorry," she said. "I'm the one who made him come home at that time."

"No, it's not your fault. It's my fault. He phoned me and said that you had called him. I encouraged him to speak with you. I didn't want to leave South Africa. I wanted Dimitri to stay." Her voiced tapered off.

For the first time, she no longer heard the voice of a girl trying to trap her son into marriage. She heard the voice of a grieving woman who loved her son.

"If anyone is to blame, it's Sofia. Not you," Nick said.

She turned to stare at him and could feel pieces of herself breaking apart, shattering inside, at the sound of these words. Earlier, he had said that she was not to blame. Now, he had changed his mind. He was right, of course, but the truth hurt more than the physical blows of the thugs. She struggled to remain standing. The ceiling began to close in. Her knees were buckling.

"No one is to blame." Another voice. It was Theo. She hadn't noticed him coming down the passage.

"Here, Sofia, this is for you." He handed her an overnight bag. "It's from Grace."

She peeped inside and felt her eyes becoming moist again. She could still hear Grace begging those monsters not to hurt her.

"Grace must go," Nick suddenly declared.

"What?" *Maybe she'd heard wrong.*

"She has to go. Either she or her son were involved in this crime."

"No, Nick. There is no way Grace had anything to do with such a terrible thing."

"Well, then it was Isaac. Either way, she has to go."

"Grace has been with us for thirty years."

She looked at Theo. *Help me.* He shook his head, eyes squeezed shut, as if trying to drown out both their voices.

"I don't give a damn how long she's worked for us. She must go."

Theo looked from her to Nick and back again.

"Stop this," Theo said. "This is not the time."

Nick suddenly leaned forward, his eyes narrowing.

"Your neck. What are those red marks around your neck? There are two circles, all red and raw."

The horror flashed back at her, the bloodshot eyes of the gunman, his arms pulling a silk noose tight around her neck.

He touched his fingers to her neck, and for a moment she felt that constricting pressure again, squeezing her throat. Darts of pain began digging into her like needles.

"Nothing. It's nothing."

She pushed his hand away.

"Is that from the attack?"

"Yes, yes. But it's nothing. It'll disappear soon."

Tears welled up in his eyes. "I could have lost you both, and all you're worried about is the maid."

He reached out for her, trying to hug her, but she pulled back, astonished how unmoved she was by his tears.

"Don't do this to me, Nick. I cannot go through this ordeal without Grace."

"She's a maid. That's all. Get somebody else."

"She's more than a maid. She's probably spent more hours with me than you have."

"I don't care. Either she or her son are responsible for what happened."

"Please, be reasonable."

"My son's life is hanging by a thread and you're telling me to be reasonable?"

A nurse interrupted them. She needed papers to be signed.

"I'm not signing any papers," Nick shouted. "If something happens to my son, no lawyer in the country will be able to defend any of you!"

He shoved the clipboard with such force that it went flying from the woman's hands and clattered down the hallway. He stormed off in the opposite direction.

"Like a child," Theo said, shaking his head.

The nurse shrugged and Sofia cringed. Her hands were shaking, and her mind was not far behind. It crossed her mind that her husband had taken leave, and a maniac had stepped inside his body.

"Please, we need someone to sign these documents," the nurse persisted.

"Waiver. Of. Liability," Sofia read aloud. There was a roaring sound in her ears as she flipped through the pages, twenty-five in total. She bit her lips and ignored her heart beating like a frantic fist. Page after page, she scribbled her name, Sofia Levantis. She repeated her name each time, trying to keep herself together, until the ink grew faint.

"I'll get another pen," the nurse offered.

Sofia rummaged in her handbag. She knew she had a pen somewhere. The purse slipped from her trembling fingers. Lipsticks, identity cards, money, mints, and combs clattered across the disinfected tiles, rolling under plastic covered chairs. Everything spilled out, and she wondered why she carried all this junk. Then she began to cry.

"Theo, everything is coming apart. I'm going to lose my son. God has completely abandoned me."

"Shh... I'll pick up everything," Theo said. And through a haze of tears, she watched this cathedral of a man, crawling around on his hands and knees, picking up bits and pieces and placing everything back inside her black leather bag.

"If there is a God, why is he allowing this to happen?" she said. "Can you explain that to me, Theo? You who pray day and night, and you who have given your life to God, can you please tell me?"

"Sometimes," he said, sighing as he heaved himself up, "pain is God's gift to remind us how much we need him."

"It's a horrible gift. I don't want it."

"Only God can help you through this."

"Theo, I can't pray. I tried, but I can't. Something has happened to me. The words won't come. I need you to please pray for Dimitri. God has abandoned me. If He's going to listen to anyone, it's going to be you."

"God will never abandon you, Sofia. Come. You're exhausted and still in a state of shock. There's a little chapel in this hospital. We'll pray together." He took her by the hand, and she went because she didn't know what else to do.

Nick sat alone on a bench at the end of the hallway, head in his hands.

"Call him," Theo said.

"Do I have to?"

"Yes, he's in pain, just like you."

She touched Nick's shoulder, and he looked up, meek as a child. His eyes were glazed with fear.

"Come," she said.

He tried to stand but collapsed back onto the bench. He pushed them away when they tried to help. He stood up and followed them without a word.

The hushed chapel with its bare walls didn't feel much like a church. It still felt like a hospital.

She sat down in the front pew next to Nick. "I can't pray, Theo. You pray. I'll just sit here."

"That's fine," Theo said. He knelt down at the foot of a huge wooden cross and slowly began to repeat the words of the Jesus prayer: "Lord Jesus Christ, Son of God, have mercy on me a sinner." In unison with the prayer, he started to prostrate his tall frame over and over again, touching chest to ground, bending his body to the will of God. And she hoped that God's will was that her son might live.

Softly, she began to repeat his words, but they came from her head, not from her heart. Everything on the inside of her felt dead. She could not think or feel. How could Theo be so certain? she wondered, almost envying his faith. But his calmness seemed to envelop her, and she soon felt a gentle pressure around her. It seemed to hold her in place, and she relaxed into it, losing track of time until she was aware of him rising from the ground to sit next to them. They sat in silence for a while.

"Theo, what if none of this is true?" Nick said. He'd been quiet the whole time, slumped in the pew, not saying a word. And now he sat on the edge of his seat. "What if there's nothing on the other side, just a big black hole and it's all a story, a lie, to make us feel better?"

"No," Theo said. "I can't believe you just said that, Nick. We grew up together in the same village. In the same church. With the same faith. Please, don't say that again."

"But how can He let this thing happen?" Nick's voice was hoarse.

Theo stood up and placed his hands on Nick's shoulders, shaking him. "I don't know. But I'm your friend and I would never lie to you. I would not have given up my life for a God that doesn't exist. I've experienced Him and I know Him. It would make no sense for me to withdraw from the world for nothing. Even if you don't believe, I'll believe for you, okay? Trust me. Just hold onto me."

"I don't even have the strength to hold onto you," Nick said, pushing Theo's hands off his shoulders.

"That's okay. I will hold you," Theo said, gripping Nick by the wrists. "If I hold you like this, then you can't let go."

Nick shook his head.

"That's why it's called faith rather than history or science," Theo persisted. "Without faith, there is nothing."

The air was suddenly perfumed with the unmistakable fragrance of basil. Sofia looked around. There was no one in the chapel except the three of them.

"Theo, do you smell something?" She crinkled her nose, sniffing.

"Is that a stem of basil next to you?" Theo said.

He pointed across her lap, and Nick handed her the basil sprig on the other side of him.

"Do you think someone left it here? I didn't notice it when we came in," she said. Her fingers trembled as she twirled the stem in her hand. It filled her with memories of her father—and hope.

"I don't know. But I do know that God has never abandoned you. He is always with you," he said with a smile.

"It's a sign, Theo. I just know it. I feel it. God is going to help Dimitri. Thank you, Theo. Thank you." She clutched the basil and inhaled deeply before stowing it carefully inside the zippered compartment of her bag.

Slowly, they walked back to the ICU and sat down on another bench in the long, narrow passageway. There was nothing more left to do except wait. She braced herself for a long night, and when the double doors at the farthest end swung open, she barely glanced in that direction. Until she realized that somebody in a white coat was heading towards them. She could not make out which doctor it was. Dear God, she thought. Not more bad news.

And then she could hardly believe her eyes. Peter Economou stood in front of them. It was the first time they had seen him since the wedding, and she hurt for him all over again. If the doctors were to cut open her heart and look inside, they would find Peter embedded right there, next to her children.

"Mr. Levantis, Mrs. Levantis, I heard what happened. I'm so very sorry. One of the residents on duty phoned me. I came as soon as I heard," Peter said.

She threw her arms around him. He was a breath of fresh air in this cold, clinical place where no one gave a damn.

"Nothing bad is going to happen," he said. "I told Dr. Pretorius you were family. He allowed me to look at the X-rays and CAT scan. Kingsley got back to him already. They are busy speaking right now. Kingsley is one of the best neurosurgeons in the world. He specializes in this type of spinal cord injury. Once Kingsley gets here, he'll have a better idea of what to do."

Tears were streaming down Nick's face. She glanced at Theo, who was crossing himself over and over again. She sank back into the chair, unable to stand.

"Thank you, Peter. Thank you," she said.

He bent over and hugged her. She kissed him on both cheeks.

"Those marks on your neck need to be looked at," he said.

"Never mind my neck. It's nothing. Dimitri is all I care about. Thank you for giving us hope."

"I'll keep you posted," he said. "I must run. Try to get some rest."

Thanks to Peter's intervention, she was allowed to stay in Dimitri's room for the night. Nick left to fetch Natalie and she sank into the vinyl La-Z-Boy chair in the corner, pulling a hospital blanket around herself.

She had a little hope now. She reached for her bag and felt inside for the stem of basil. She inhaled its fragrance and lay back, closing her eyes. Immediately, the eyes of the attacker stared at her, dark bottomless pits, eyes without a soul. No sleep for me, she decided and sat up. For a long time, she watched the nurses who watched her boy.

The nurse on duty checked on him every hour. Each time the nurse stood, her shoes squeaked on the polished linoleum floors. The monitors flickered and blinked, and the ventilator breathing for Dimitri whooshed softly.

A commotion of thoughts continued to hammer inside her head. There was no way Grace could have been involved. And Isaac? She had done everything to help him since he had first arrived on her doorstep as a baby. Nick was wrong.

Suddenly a machine beeped and a red light flashed. She jumped up and held her breath. The nurse said, "Don't worry, Mrs. Levantis. It's nothing. I have to change the IV drip."

But even as her heart calmed down, her stockinged feet splayed out, and she lunged at the bed railing, accidentally pulling one of the wires that looped between the medical equipment. An alarm screeched, and she froze in horror. *They're going to throw me out of here.* The nurse leaped into action pressing buttons, untangling wires, and finally plugging all the cords back into their proper outlets.

"Sorry," she mouthed to her.

"It's okay," the nurse said and pointed to the chair. "Sit down."

The trauma of the past twenty-fours was beginning to sink in. She felt as if this was happening to somebody else and she was floating somewhere near the ceiling, looking down. A small icon lay on top of the nightstand. Theo must have left it there. She picked it up and stared at the Panagia with the Christ Child. Shocked, she saw tears streaming from the Panagia's eyes. Gently, she brushed the tears away. Then she realized the tears were hers.

FIFTEEN

The Hand of God

Sofia

Professor Kingsley sat at the head of the table, apart from the others. Sofia watched him closely. He was small in stature and easy to miss had you passed him on the street. Although he wore a relaxed air of confidence, like a comfortable jacket, his dark brown eyes glowed with an unmistakable intensity. She could tell that his quiet manner was misleading and imagined many a nurse or young resident squirming under this man's stern gaze or reprimand. But when it came to the patient's relatives, he listened to their questions as if he had all the time in the world before answering in a voice so soft, it forced her to lean forward and listen harder.

Nick was also listening with close attention but couldn't stop coughing. His nerves, Sofia thought. On the odd occasion when Nick got scared, a nervous cough crept up his throat. The more anxious he got, the worse the cough became. Each time she missed something one of the doctors was saying, she wanted to scream. She rummaged in her bag. "Here," she handed him a lozenge as his cough grew louder.

To operate or not. That's what they were trying to decide. Two doctors said yes and two said no, with the anesthetist on the sideline, more grim-faced than the others. Peter, a junior in status, sat at the far end of the table. He had gone out of his way to act as an intermediary between them and the other doctors, patiently explaining all the medical jargon to them. At the same time, he managed to treat Natalie politely, although she avoided eye contact with him and sat glued to her side.

"Take your time," Dr. Viljoen said, standing up. "I'm going to get another cup of coffee."

Sofia glared after him. He was supposed to help them make a decision. Instead, he was taking a coffee break while Dimitri's life hung in the balance.

Except for Kingsley, the others also got up to stretch their legs. She sighed and looked around the space where they'd been sitting on backless stools for hours. They were sitting in a recovery room to have their discussion, and a steel operating table served as their makeshift desk. Quite bizarre, she thought. A morgue could not have been colder than this windowless dungeon. To operate or not. Back and forth, maybe this, maybe that. For hours, the doctors agreed and then disagreed. Her head was ready to burst. All she wanted was certainty, but she could not get a straight answer from these men.

Slowly, the coffee drinkers trickled back. Under the harsh fluorescent lights, they all looked stiff and starched, like their white coats. Nick was the worst of all, as white as the hospital walls behind him. And poor Natalie, who had come straight from the airport, looked like she had been in an armed robbery herself.

Someone had to take control of the situation. She took a deep breath and turned to Professor Kingsley while they waited for Dr. Viljoen to finish sipping his coffee.

"What would you do if this patient were your son, professor?"

He looked her squarely in the eye and didn't hesitate even for a second.

"I would do it. There's always a risk with surgery, but it's unlikely to happen on my watch. The downside of delay is too high a risk. I've performed similar operations with good outcomes."

Unlikely to happen on my watch. Sofia grasped at those words like manna from heaven. If anyone else had spoken this way, it would have sounded arrogant. Coming from him, it was a simple statement. It was not so much his kind manner that reassured her or the steadiness in his voice, but she had the distinct feeling he would not give up.

The other doctors avoided her eyes. Peter looked her straight in the eye and gave a tiny nod, barely perceptible. Except for the sound of Nick's cough, there was no other noise or movement in the room. She fiddled with her handbag clasp, snapping it open and closed, as she considered his opinion. Yes or no.

"What's that smell?" Professor Kingsley asked. "Basil?"

She sat up straighter. She reached inside her bag and touched the basil stem she had found in the church when Theo had prayed.

Was this the casting vote? The Hand of God?

The other doctors looked around blankly.

"I can't smell anything," Dr. Randall said.

"Yes," she said. "It's basil. I found it in the chapel."

Decision made. She wanted to go ahead. She looked at Nick.

"What would Dimitri want?" she said.

"We both know what he would want," Nick said. Dimitri would absolutely jump at even a one percent chance to live a full life.

She nodded. They were in agreement, thinking as one.

She stood up. "Professor Kingsley, we're going to place my son's life in your hands."

He bowed his head in an old-fashioned, humble kind of way, placing his hand over his heart, as if he were thanking her.

"My hands—*and* God's Hands," he said, before leaving the room. She stared after him. A man of science invoking the name of God. Wow. She wasn't expecting that. This was a good sign. A calmness began to settle over her. She walked slowly back to the ICU to check on Dimitri.

She leaned her forehead against the viewing glass, watching the machines breathe for her son. "I hope we're doing the right thing for you," she whispered.

Nick and Natalie came and stood on either side of her. The three of them remained like that until a deep male voice floated down the passage. She turned, recognizing the voice immediately. It was Andre. Elmarie and Annelize were with him.

"I'm so sorry, Sofia," Andre said.

She was not expecting him and could feel herself frowning as he engulfed her in a huge bear hug.

"Forgive me for what I said to Dimitri. I feel like I've contributed to this catastrophe. I wish to God I had encouraged him to get on a plane and leave the country. Maybe this would never have happened."

"No one is to blame," she heard herself saying.

"I want you to know," he said. "This surgeon, Professor Kingsley, is one of the best in the world. Probably *the* best. I phoned a buddy of mine in California, also a surgeon. He emigrated from South Africa a long time ago, but he knows Kingsley. They studied together. Kingsley is *the* top guy. We're lucky to have him. Everything's going to be alright. You'll see."

"Thank you, Andre," she said. For the first time, she stopped hearing an accent that was different to hers and instead heard the words of a kind man offering reassurance.

"I still can't believe this happened," Elmarie said, hugging her tightly. "Whatever we can do to help, Sofia, just let us know."

She was surprised at how much strength she drew from their presence. Even though she felt as if she were balancing on the edge of a cliff and that she might tumble over at any moment, she found their nearness comforting.

They sat and waited together outside the ICU. With each passing hour, the hush of the night became quieter and more still. Down the hall, a coffee maker gurgled and a clock ticked. Time was passing. But not for them.

SIXTEEN

The Beloved Country

Grace

Gates clanged. A grim-faced warden escorted Grace through a labyrinth of narrow corridors. When they reached the end, he told her to wait and pointed to a chair in a small airless room. Another sound, heavy and hard, like a steel door, echoed down the passage. She waited. More noise, an iron bolt releasing and grinding against iron. This was Isaac's life now. Lock and unlock. Suddenly, he stood in front of her, engulfed in orange overalls two sizes too big and looking absurdly bright and cheerful in the dark, depressing place. He had lost at least ten kilograms. "Why did you do this to me?" he said. She reached out to touch him, but he pushed her hand away. A roaring sound exploded in her head. Again, a loud thud.

When she opened her eyes, she saw that she was lying on the floor of her bedroom. Groaning, she rolled over slowly and got up rubbing her sore head. The bedside clock read three in the morning. She must have fallen out of her bed. Her blankets and sheets looked as if they'd wrestled a monster all night. *Isaac, where are you? What have you done?*

She paced around the room. She couldn't sleep, she couldn't sit, she couldn't stand still. She put on a dressing gown and walked down to the guardhouse, past the main house, barely able to look at it without reliving the robbery. Johannes sat by the guardhouse as still as a statue, clutching his rifle like one of those war heroes. As soon as he saw her, he waved her over.

"Grace, you can't sleep, right?" he said. "Come sit here with me."

She sat with him, their backs against the wall, letting the night seep into them like the dew on the ground. For a long time, neither of them said anything. He took out his pipe and lit it.

"It's a terrible thing that happened," he said, drawing a long puff from his pipe. "And those cops were ready to throw me in jail. They might still come after me if they don't find the real robbers."

After a while, he said, "I still don't understand how they got the code to the gate. I didn't give it to them."

She stared at him and wanted to smack her head against the wall. Too many lives were at stake here.

When the early morning sun began to push the darkness away, she got up.

"I have to go now."

"Where? To the hospital?"

She nodded, unable to tell him the truth.

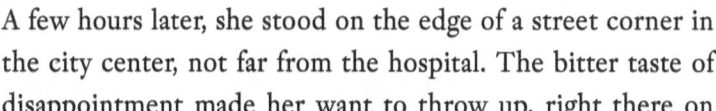

A few hours later, she stood on the edge of a street corner in the city center, not far from the hospital. The bitter taste of disappointment made her want to throw up, right there on the street corner. She had lived her life with a sense of expectation, not for herself, but for her son.

As she waited for the traffic lights to change, a funeral cortege drove by. It was a big funeral. Several cars crawled along. The passengers stared stonily ahead. She might as well join them, she thought.

When it was time to cross the road, she stepped back for a moment, looking at the road behind her, the one that led out of the city. She could easily take that road and walk away, never to return. Who would know? Who would care? At least Isaac would be free.

"Come on, make up your mind." Somebody gave her an impatient push, and she stepped forward with the other pedestrians, a mass of people going about their business.

~

Inside the police station, she waited her turn as a young police clerk with a thick moustache shouted at the person in front of the line: "What do you mean your son is missing since last night? It's not even twelve hours yet. Go away and stop wasting my time." The dismissed woman, still wearing a maid's uniform, stepped away wringing her hands.

"Next, please," he barked at Grace. "Can I help you?"

She moved forward. Vertical bars and a glass partition separated them, with only a small opening on the countertop for speaking. She bent down, bringing her mouth to the opening.

"I have an appointment with Captain van Rensburg. He's expecting me."

He looked at her skeptically and picked up a phone receiver. She couldn't hear what he said, but he hung up and told her to go to the sixth floor, room 612.

At the lifts in the corridor, the doors shut just as she got there. She quickly pressed the button and the doors swished open. Three white police officers grinned, barring her way, arms crossed, legs astride.

"Can't you see the lift is full?"

There was plenty of space, she wanted to say, but it wasn't as if they were going to move. Was she mad? To hand over her son to such people?

The doors slammed shut again, and she could hear their laughter through the steel doors. As she turned and walked to the stairway, again it crossed her mind to keep walking, straight out the building, and take that other road. Instead, she climbed the six flights of stairs. At the top, she stopped to catch her breath.

She hesitated outside his office. Her hand hovered by the door handle. Then she took a deep breath and knocked. A voice said, "*Kom binne*," and she entered the room. He was standing with his back to her, staring out the window for what felt like a very long time. She noticed how his shoulders stretched the cotton fabric of his khaki shirt at the seams.

"Captain van Rensburg?"

He turned, "Yes, Mrs. Molepe. Did you remember something after all?"

"Yes, sir. I did."

"Take a seat and tell me all about it."

"I recognized one of the robbers."

"I thought you said they were covered from top to toe?"

"That's correct. But there was something unusual about the shoes one of them wore."

"I see. And you are able to identify this person by his shoes?"

"Yes, sir, because I know the shoes. They are unusual shoes." She swallowed hard. "The shoes belong to my son."

He sat back and stared hard at her.

"Are you sure?"

"As sure as I am the woman who gave birth to him." She then told him everything, including where she thought they might be hiding in Alexandra.

He leaned his elbows on the desk and rested his chin on his hands, all the while staring at her with a mixture of horror and pity on his face. But there was something else. She saw respect in his eyes, and thought this was a very hard way to earn respect.

"I'm so very sorry," he said.

She heard a softness in his voice for the first time.

"Can you write down all the details? His name, his friends' names, the address where we can find them?"

He pushed a writing pad towards her.

She began to scribble down whatever she knew, alternating between writing information and wiping tears, which dripped onto the pad. He pushed a white handkerchief towards her, but she didn't take it. When she finished, she skimmed her eyes over what she had written. The letters didn't even look like her handwriting. It was as if another person had written this. What mother would do such a thing? She pushed the writing pad back to him.

He glanced at her notes and said, "Has he ever been in trouble with the police before? Any arrests?"

"Just once, in February. For damage to property. But the charges were dropped. Before that, nothing. He was a good boy. Then I sent him to university, and he got mixed up with the wrong crowd."

"Are you prepared to testify against him in court?"

"Oh," she shrank back in her chair. She hadn't thought of that. What kind of a mother would testify against her own son.

"Okay," he said. "I'll try to avoid that, if possible. Maybe affidavits will suffice, but I'm not sure. I don't want to give you false hope, but because he's young and hasn't been in trouble, maybe he will get a lighter sentence than the others. This is only if the Levantis boy doesn't die. If that boy dies, then your son will be an accomplice to murder."

"I understand," she said, and stood, unable to stop herself from shaking. She reached out a hand to steady herself and grasped at the bookshelf next to his desk. It was stuffed with thick files and a sparse collection of books. Even in her lightheadedness and through the blur of tears, one small book jumped out: *Cry, the Beloved Country* by Alan Paton.

He followed her gaze. "I had to read that one in school. For my matric year," he said. "I'm not much of a reader. But it was a story that stayed with me long after I had written the exam."

"I've read it, too," she said. "Many times."

"The story of our country's pain," he said.

And suddenly she didn't hate him anymore.

"Mrs. Molepe, my cousin is part of the criminal division who will go after these boys in the next couple of hours. I will ask him to keep me posted about your son. I'll let you know what is happening. I give you my word."

"Thank you, sir."

"What will you do now?"

"I'm going to the hospital to see the other boy, Dimitri."

"If you need anything, you have my number. Call me."

She thanked him and began to walk out quickly because she didn't want to start crying again in front of him. But at the door she stopped and looked back one more time. She'd betrayed her son to this man. She didn't even know him. He sat slumped behind his desk, holding his head with one hand, and dabbed his cheeks with the handkerchief he'd offered her.

Outside, Johannesburg was full of noise and laughter, as if people were under the illusion that life had returned to normal after Mandela's release. Dimitri had been right. Nothing was going to change. At the taxi ranks across the road, an older woman embraced a tall young man as he boarded a minibus. She hurried along but kept turning back, staring at the mother and son, filled with a terrible emptiness and a longing to embrace Isaac one more time.

SEVENTEEN

The Greek Birthday Song

Sofia

A different nurse had taken over the shift, and this one smiled as Sofia slipped quietly into the room. In the dim light, Sofia stroked Dimitri's hair. His face looked like that of a child again. Suddenly, she noticed a few wisps of gray. So young to be graying. Only twenty-six. Oh my God, tomorrow it will be Dimitri's birthday, she realized. They were going to operate on his birthday. *Please, God, give him life on his birthday*, she prayed. If He granted her this request, she would never ask for anything again.

She looked at the nurse.

"Do you think Dimitri can hear me?" she said.

Yes, the nurse nodded.

Softly, she began to sing in Greek:

> *Long may you live Dimitri*
> *And may you live many years*
> *May you grow old*
> *With gray hair*

> *May you spread the light*
> *of knowledge everywhere*
> *And may everybody say*
> *There, is a wise man.*

"That's beautiful," the nurse said. "Is that Greek?"

"Yes. It's the special Greek birthday song. I'm wishing him a long life." She stroked his temple. For one heart-stopping moment his eyelids fluttered.

"Look... Look... He's moving his eyelids. See? He can hear me." She touched the nurse's sleeve.

"Yes, the blessing of a mother is a good thing," the nurse said, and turned away.

"Everything's going to be alright," she whispered in his ear. "Tomorrow, they're going to operate. On your birthday. Can you believe that? The surgeon is brilliant. He's the best of the best. He even lectures in America. Dimitri, get better, and I'll dance at your wedding. I'll lead the dancing, okay? You can marry Annelize or whoever you want. And you can live wherever you want—America, Australia, Alaska. I don't care. I'll follow you to the ends of the earth and visit whenever you want me."

"Mrs. Levantis, why don't you try to rest now? Tomorrow will be a long day."

The nurse led her to the La-Z-Boy chair, and she sat there waiting for the hours to pass, staring at the nightstand. The icon of the Panagia with the Christ Child stared back at her. *Please, Panagia, ask your Son to look after my son. He'll listen to you. Sons always listen to their mothers.* And she began to cry again.

She was up before the sun, unrested and agitated. Twenty-six years ago, on this day, she had given birth to this boy. *Please, God, don't take him from me on his birthday.*

She tiptoed to the others in the waiting room. Nick had taken over one sofa and Natalie and Annelize another. They were all half dozing, half awake. Andre and Elmarie were nodding off in two bucket chairs, heads leaning against each other. No one spoke. She covered them with blankets the nurses had left, and then paced up and down waiting to catch glimpses of the staff. A nurse clattered past with a cart, rattling medical equipment and her nerves. An older couple followed, deep in conversation: "But he looked so well last night—what could possibly have happened in twelve hours?" Her heart lurched as she heard these words. Hospitals were horrible places.

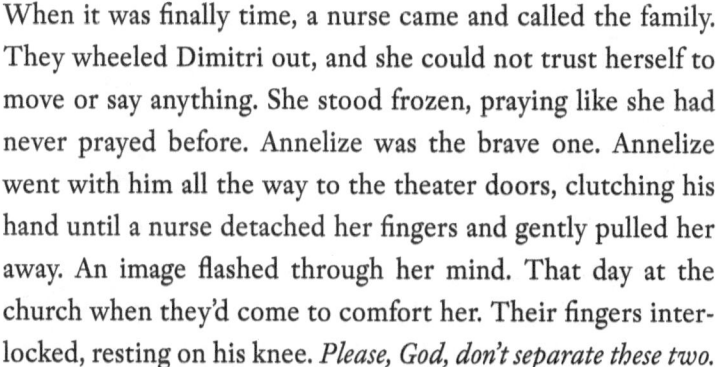

When it was finally time, a nurse came and called the family. They wheeled Dimitri out, and she could not trust herself to move or say anything. She stood frozen, praying like she had never prayed before. Annelize was the brave one. Annelize went with him all the way to the theater doors, clutching his hand until a nurse detached her fingers and gently pulled her away. An image flashed through her mind. That day at the church when they'd come to comfort her. Their fingers interlocked, resting on his knee. *Please, God, don't separate these two.*

She watched a little longer. Even when Nick said, "Come, let's go," she continued to stand there. The others left as she watched the theater's steel doors swing open and shut. One after another, the medical team filed past, their eyes staring straight ahead. The last one stopped. Masked and capped, he was barely distinguishable from the others except for his short stature and the intensity of his eyes. She'd recognize those eyes anywhere. Professor Kingsley paused and held her gaze.

"I'll be here the whole time," she said, pointing behind her. "In the waiting room. I'll be here. I'm not going anywhere. Please take good care of my boy."

He was in another zone now, detached, preparing for battle. But in his eyes, she read a silent promise: *I will do my best.* He gave a curt nod, and then the man who stood between her and death vanished behind the steel doors.

There was nothing else left to do. She turned and saw a tall dark-clad figure at the end of the corridor. Theo. His black rasa swept across the white floor tiles.

"I'm here, too," he said, greeting her with a hug.

"I'm so glad to see you. Dimitri is in the hands of the doctors now."

"And in the Hands of God."

A round-shouldered nurse shooed them away. "There's plenty of tea and coffee in the nearby lounge. Even some rusks—biscuits." The cheerful voice grated on Sofia's nerves. They were about to cut open her son and the woman sounded like she was inviting them to a tea party. She wanted to tell her to shut up, but she didn't. Theo's presence made her behave.

In the waiting area, the table lamps threw shadows around the cramped space. A television flickered on the wall and a coffee percolator chugged softly on the refreshment table. She checked her watch. Eight-thirty. The doctors had said the operation would last at least four or five hours, if not longer. She sank into a chair and wondered how she would get through these agonizing hours. *How many people before her had sat in this room waiting? How many had received bad news, and how many had received good news?*

Please, God, let it be good news. She repeated this over and over again, until the prayer sank into her heart, a continuous background chorus. Prayer had been wrung out of her in a way she would never have imagined, even in her worst nightmare.

Nick finished all the rusks on the plate and sat hunched in his chair, staring into space. Natalie and Annelize whispered quietly to each other. From Elmarie came the clickety-clack of knitting needles. "I must do something with my hands," she explained, looping a deep red yarn several times around her wrist. The only other sound in the room was a low murmur coming from Theo's lips. He sat alone in the corner with a prayer rope in his hands.

For the hundredth time, she checked the clock. The hands were moving but time was not. The hours stretched, growing longer and longer, like the scarf dangling beneath Elmarie's fingers.

And suddenly, as she stood up for the hundredth time to stretch her legs, Professor Kingsley appeared. He was capless and unmasked. She could see his face clearly and she scrutinized it. He looked flushed, like a runner after a marathon. She ran up to him, the others behind her. *Good news or bad news?*

His smile lit up the room. Relief washed over her like a wave, and her knees wobbled. She heard a soft sound and realized she had been holding her breath.

"He's going to be fine."

"Thank you, thank you, thank you!" She grasped his hands and barely restrained herself from smothering them with kisses.

"He's going to walk?"

"He's going to walk and dance the Zorba and do anything his heart desires. Not tomorrow, obviously, but in due course. I'll check on him again later. They'll call you shortly, one at a time. We've already removed the ventilator. He's a very strong young man."

As long as she lived, she would never be able to repay this man. Every Sunday, she decided, she would light a candle for him and his family for the rest of his life. *Thank you, God. Thank you, God.*

They sat in a hush of joy, until the nurses called her first and she rushed to the recovery room, trembling with gratitude and relief. She leaned over the bed bars and looked at his beautiful face. He was pale but breathing on his own, without those horrible tubes in his throat.

Suddenly, she was afraid. *Please, God, if this is a dream, don't wake me up.* She stood still, not daring to move, not wanting to lose the moment. Then he opened his eyes slowly and looked into her eyes.

"Mom," he said in a hoarse voice. "Is it my birthday today?"

She began to laugh and cry at the same time.

"Yes, Happy Birthday. *Chronia Polla. Na zisis.*"

In his eyes, the first spark of a smile.

"You sing nicely."

He closed his eyes again.

And then.

"Mom, are you going to dance at my wedding?"

"For you, I'll dance on the table."

"Mrs. Levantis, we mustn't tire him," a nurse said. "The others need to see him too."

She walked out slowly. *Thank you, God. Thank you.*

"He's going to be fine," she said to the others, watching her with anxious faces as she came out.

Nick rushed past her. She stood there, bursting with happiness, beyond grateful for God's mercy. *God never abandoned me.* She felt someone's eyes on her, and she turned to see Theo. She smiled at him. There was a reason why God had woven him back into her life. Theo had kept her sane at her darkest hour. Never again would she argue with God.

———

A quiet, familiar voice called her name, and she turned around.

"Grace, is that you?" Sofia almost didn't recognize her. Grace's eyes looked puffy and swollen, as if she'd been crying nonstop. She seemed to have aged overnight.

"Yes, it's me, Madam." Grace stood there shaking. Even her voice trembled. "How is Dimitri?"

"He's going to be fine, Grace. Thank God. He's going to be fine." She moved towards her, arms outstretched. "I'm so sorry. I forgot all about you with my worries for Dimitri."

And then she stopped. Something wasn't right. Grace wasn't reacting with the joy she expected. A strange sense of fear came over her. Grace seemed distressed, as if she was going to break in half.

"Grace, what's wrong?"

The others stopped speaking and waited.

"Madam, I've just come from the police station. Isaac was the one who brought the robbers to the house. I am so very sorry. I told Captain van Rensburg. The police are on their way to arrest him and his friends."

She felt a tightening across her chest and wondered if she were having a heart attack, right there in the middle of a hospital.

"I don't understand," she said in a hoarse whisper.

"I recognized Isaac from his shoes. You bought him those shoes." Grace's voice was dull and lifeless, as if all the life had been sucked out of her.

She stared at Grace. At first it was a faraway rumble, and then the truth hit her like an oncoming train. A roaring sound began to explode in her ears, and she thought she might keel over. She remembered. She had stared at those shoes during the robbery while she lay on the ground with someone's foot digging into her neck.

"Why would he do such a thing?"

"I'm sorry, Madam." Grace began to sob, shaking her head. Her voice sounded like a distant echo, as if it belonged to another person.

They reached out for each other, and she could feel Grace's tears on her cheeks as they held each other.

Theo put his arms around both of them, holding them together, and she wondered what it would be like to hide inside one of those black rasa the priests wore, cocooned inside a world of prayer and peace. She was dimly aware of Andre and Elmarie exchanging helpless looks, and she could hear Natalie and Annelize crying.

"What's going on here?" Nick said, as he walked out of the recovery room.

She looked up and watched his smile fade. A strange sound came from her throat. She took a deep breath and tried again.

"Nick, you were right. It was Isaac who let them in."

There was a long silence.

"You and Grace made me bail that bastard out of jail. Remember?" He was red in the face. "I should never have listened to you. I should have left him to rot in jail. Grace, you must leave. I don't want you in the house anymore."

"I understand," Grace said.

"No, Nick. Grace just came from the police station. She reported him to the police."

"Doesn't matter. I don't care. I would have handed him over myself," Nick said. "I didn't need *her* to do that."

He pushed his face up close to Grace. "You must pack your bags and leave. I want you off my property by the end of the day."

Sofia stepped between them, shocked by his cruelty and the savagery in his voice. "Nick, no! Grace is not going to leave. She's done nothing to deserve this."

She heard the sharp intake of his breath. He raised his arms in disbelief, and for a moment she thought he might strike someone. She touched his arm, but he pushed her away.

"Who else would give up their son?" she said.

He ignored her and walked away, then stopped and turned around, pointing a finger at her and Grace. "*You* almost lost *your* son. *My* son. Because of *her* idiot son."

"Two wrongs don't make a right," she said.

"Madam, it's better if I leave." Grace was twisting the straps of her bag round and round in her hands.

"No, Grace. He'll calm down. Go home with Father Theo. Stay with him for a few days. Everything will settle down."

Grace stood with a doubtful expression on her face.

"Go ahead, I'll be fine," Sofia said. "I need to go back to Dimitri. Please, Theo, take Grace and let her stay with you."

Even Theo looked flustered and undecided.

"Please," she said to both of them, "just do as I say and go."

As they walked away, she collapsed onto the bench behind her, afraid she might never be able to get up again. Natalie and Annelize sat down on either side, pressing close to her, keeping her upright.

"It's Dimitri's birthday," she said.

She watched as Natalie and Annelize scratched inside their bags, wondering what they were looking for. Annelize pulled out a packet of Kleenex tissues and handed them to her.

"I'm not crying," she said. "I'm happy. It's Dimitri's birthday, and the doctor said he's going to be fine." But she took the tissues and wiped the tears pouring down her cheeks.

EIGHTEEN
A Time to Heal
Sofia

After ten days of gloomy skies and rainy weather, a blue sky finally appeared over Johannesburg one morning. And when Professor Kingsley walked into Dimitri's private ward and said, "I think it's time for you to go home, young man," Sofia wanted to dance and cry at the same time.

Dimitri jumped up from the chair as if he'd never been shot and sent his crutches flying across the room. "I owe you my life," he said, and hugged Kingsley.

"Me too," Sofia said.

The doctor smiled and hugged them both. "Nothing will remain from the injury," the doctor promised. "Just a small scar from the incision, but you'll be as high functioning as ever. What you have to make sure is that you get over the psychological trauma up here," he said, while pointing to Dimitri's head.

"I'll be fine," Dimitri said. "And don't forget you promised to dance at my wedding."

"I wouldn't miss it for the world. Are you sure she's going to say 'Yes'?" he teased.

Dimitri laughed and Kingsley said, "Remember, when you kneel down on one knee, make sure you get up without falling, or else it's going to look like I didn't do my job properly."

This doctor has made up for all the others, Sofia thought, listening to their laughter.

"We're going home," she said, almost in disbelief. She couldn't wait to surprise Annelize. For the last three weeks, the girl had been by his side every day. There could not be a better outcome to this ordeal than a wedding.

They left the hospital with a stack of papers, instruction sheets, medicines, numbers to call, and well wishes from all the nurses who had fallen in love with Dimitri.

As they drove home, he turned to her and said, "Remember what you asked me once when we talked about Annelize?"

I said a lot of things, Sofia thought, squirming a little in the car seat. Some were not very nice. Oh God, don't let him be angry with me. Not now.

Dimitri answered for her. "You asked me once: Will she stand by you in your worst moment?"

"I think she passed that test with flying colors," she said. Her heart burst with love as he smiled and the dimple in his chin deepened.

―

When they pulled up the long driveway, everyone was there. Natalie had delayed her flight back to the US in honor of her big brother's homecoming, and Annelize could hardly contain her happiness as she rushed to greet him.

Nick stood on the side, and Sofia knew that he was trying to keep his emotions in check. "Welcome home, my boy," he said, as Theo engulfed them both in a big bear hug.

"Dimitri, I've censed this house from top to bottom," Theo said. "I went into every single room today and all around the outside. There's not a drop of evil floating around here."

"Thank you, Father Theo, and thank you for all your prayers," Dimitri said, kissing his hand. Holy hands. Sofia remembered what her father had once told her about why people kissed the hands of Orthodox priests: Those hands touch the Body and Blood of Christ at every liturgy when the priest prepares the bread and wine for communion.

As she watched Dimitri climb the front stairs without much help, Sofia was glad that Dimitri had kissed Theo's hand. This priest, who lived on earth and belonged to God, had an open line to heaven. Of that, she was now certain.

Grace hovered in the background and only came down once Nick was inside with the others. Grace had continued to clean, wash, iron, and cook for them, but when Nick entered a room, Grace withdrew into an uncomfortable silence, and Sofia had no idea what to do. A coldness had settled into the house, almost freezing them all.

Before the robbery, Grace had lived with them. Now she only occupies space, Sofia thought. She's marking time, waiting for Dimitri's return and Isaac's court case.

"I'm very happy that Dimitri is home," Grace said, pulling Dimitri's abandoned crutches from the back seat while lifting his overnight bag with her other hand.

"Me too," Sofia said.

And then.

"Madam, I promised I'd stay at least until Dimitri got home from the hospital. Now, it's time for me to move on."

"Grace, please, let's not talk about this today. You know I haven't had time to get over the trauma, let alone find a suitable replacement for you. And you're not easy to replace. Please. Just give us a little more time. Maybe things will change."

"Nothing will change," Grace assured her. "Every time Master Nick walks into the kitchen and sees me, he walks straight out the other door. Not that I blame him."

"Maybe now that Dimitri is home, he'll have a change of heart. Please, Grace, let's give it a chance."

Grace gave her a doubtful look and walked ahead.

"Grace, wait, listen to me. All those years under apartheid, the two of us were together. It would be silly for us to separate now as the country comes together. I know we can work through this. Master Nick will eventually realize that he's wrong. You'll see. Before you know it, we'll be voting together in the first democratic elections. You and I can't go into the new South Africa without each other."

Grace gave her a sad smile and carried on walking.

"Have you heard anything from Isaac?" Sofia called out.

"They don't let them phone much when they're in jail," Grace said.

"God, give me strength," Sofia muttered under her breath. Sarcasm was the last thing she needed today. She trudged upstairs to make sure Dimitri was comfortable.

Annelize had already unpacked Dimitri's clothes. He was lying comfortably on top of the bed with Annelize curled up on one side and Lola, now the only family pet, kept watch on his other side. Our miniature guard dog, Sofia thought. She patted Lola's head and felt a tightness in her throat as she remembered Rex.

"Come see what I found in one of Dimitri's books as a placeholder," Annelize said. Dimitri handed her the photograph he was studying.

She took it and had to look twice before recognizing the boys in the photo. Dimitri and Isaac. They were probably eight or nine years old, standing together after a soccer game, sweaty and happy, arms slung around each other's shoulders, squinting in the sun, and looking at a perfect world. Or so they thought, at the time.

"I still can't believe he brought those guys into the house," Dimitri said. "He nearly got us all killed, and yet—I feel bad for him. Either I'm a moron, or the trauma affected my head. And I feel even worse for Grace."

"Rest now," Sofia said. She had no words to soothe these conflicting thoughts but she knew exactly how he felt. "Do you mind if I keep this photo?"

"Go for it, Mom."

She watched Dimitri lie back and close his eyes. She crossed herself, thanking God for bringing him home, and slipped the photograph into her pocket. She thought about how the apartheid monster had robbed two boys of a beautiful friendship, and she feared it would do the same to her and Grace.

Before she went downstairs, she peeked her head into Natalie's bedroom. She had grown used to having Natalie around again, and hated the idea of her pending return to New York.

"Are you sure you won't change your mind?" she said, trying to keep her voice casual as she watched Natalie squeeze a few more coats and jackets into an already bulging suitcase.

"No, Mom. I'm not ready to come home yet." Natalie pounded two fists on the upper flap of the suitcase before straddling it with a determined expression on her face.

Sofia got down on her hands and knees and helped her pull the zippers closed, even though she wanted to unpack all her clothes.

"Everyone has forgotten about you and Peter. They're all talking about the robbery now." She had promised herself and God that she would never again interfere in her children's lives, yet here she was doing exactly that.

Natalie gave the zipper a final tug and got up. "Mom, it's not about Peter. We've been through this before. After what happened to you and Dimitri, you should be glad I wasn't here when it happened. Can you imagine what they might have done to me? And—"

"And what?" She could feel her nerves stretching to a breaking point.

Natalie smoothed her hands through a thick mass of silky hair and pulled an elastic tieback from her wrist. She twisted her hair into the loop with a determined tug. Sofia realized she was choosing her words carefully.

"I've always placed my life on hold, trying to please you, looking for your approval. I lost myself somehow in that effort. Now, on the other side of the world, I'm finding me again."

Sofia swallowed hard. She forced herself not to react. "Fine. But promise me that if you change your mind, you'll come home sooner."

"I promise. I'll be back for Dimitri's wedding anyway. And by the looks of those two, it's around the corner."

She consoled herself with this compromise and went downstairs again. By this time Nick had escaped to his comfort zone of work, and Theo had left.

She sat down in the armchair by the window in her study, filled with gratitude that her boy was home but exhausted by Grace's mood, and the thought of Natalie leaving again. She leaned her head against the headrest and closed her eyes, trying to forget about everything for a few minutes. But there it was again. Every time she closed her eyes, the whole scene replayed and she was powerless to stop the thoughts as she watched herself being pinned to the carpet. His large body straddled hers. Those evil eyes stared down at her. His fingers tightened the stocking around her neck. And just as she opened her mouth to scream, a knock at the door. She jerked her eyes open and sat up straight.

Grace stood at the door. She looked as if she'd seen a ghost.

"Grace, what's wrong?"

"Captain van Rensburg is here. He needs to speak with you."

Oh, dear God. What now? Something must have happened to Isaac. Terrible things happened in those jails. Grace was thinking the same thing. She could tell by the worried expression on her face.

"Okay, I'm coming," she said, and got up quickly.

In the living room, Van Rensburg perched on the edge of a chair. Grace had already served him coffee, but the captain sat stiff and rigid, staring into space as if he'd forgotten he had a mug in his hand. When he stood up to shake her hand, he almost dropped the mug.

"I'm sorry to barge in like this," he said.

"That's okay. It must be important." She motioned for him to sit and Grace to leave.

"I'll get straight to the point," Van Rensburg said. "There's a possibility that the state could lose this case."

"What?" A wild panic gripped her. "Grace handed the whole lot over to you. Including her son! And you're going to lose the case? What kind of incompetence is this?" She was screaming at him but she didn't care.

"Mrs. Levantis, please, if you'll just let me explain."

"Explain what? I could have lost my son. I cannot believe what I'm hearing. How will justice be served if you let them go?"

"We won't let that happen. There is a way. The problem is that we cannot identify five of the six. They wore face coverings. They left no fingerprints. Isaac is the only one we can positively identify. Because of the shoes he wore and his mother's testimony."

"So what are you saying?" She sprang to her feet and started pacing, convinced the police were idiots. "Only Isaac will go to jail? The least guilty one must take the hit for all the others? He didn't pull the trigger and he wasn't the one who tried to strangle me." Even she could hear the hysteria in her voice.

"Mrs. Levantis, I have a better proposal. If Isaac turns state witness, we can get all the others. He is the only one who can identify them."

"Then they will definitely go to jail?"

"Yes."

"So what's the problem?"

"Well, there are two problems. Or maybe only one, depending on how you look at it."

He was offering a solution but still frowning. She was losing patience quickly.

"In return for his testimony, Isaac could go completely free, or receive a very light sentence, depending on the prosecutor."

Was this good or bad? She wasn't sure. "And the second problem?"

"I've spoken with Isaac, and I'm convinced he had no evil intention," Van Rensburg said. "But he believes that he deserves to rot in jail for the rest of his life. He refuses to turn state witness."

"Hah! He's right about that." As she said these words, she looked up and locked eyes with Grace who stood in the doorway. A night from long ago jumped into her mind. Both boys were babies, and Isaac had been burning with fever. Had it not been for the doctor's intervention, they might have lost him. She felt all over again the fear she and Grace had shared that night. *A mother losing a child.*

What would be the point of throwing Isaac into jail now? Dimitri's life had hung by a thread. She stared at her friend who hovered at the edge of the room. She could not let Grace go through that again. Maybe Isaac deserved one more chance.

"Grace, come over here," she said. Grace hurried over, eyes wide with shock, and a glint of something else. "Grace, you heard everything that the captain just told me?"

"Yes, Madam."

"I want you to go with him now to the jail and convince your son to turn state witness."

Grace looked at her for a long time without saying anything. Then a sound came from her throat, barely a whisper.

"Madam, are you sure?"

"Yes."

"Thank you. I will speak to him. This is a second chance. Like we used to give the boys when they were little."

And then.

"But Madam, what about Dimitri? Will he be okay with this?"

"Yes."

"And Master Nick?"

"I can handle him."

"I called Mr. Levantis before I came here," Van Rensburg interrupted. "He said I should speak to Mrs. Levantis. He said it's her decision."

Grace's tears turned to loud wracking sobs, and Sofia held her. How much pain can a human being endure? Slowly, she extracted herself from Grace's arms.

"Grace, do you want me to come with you?"

Grace's shoulders trembled and she pressed a hand to her face, but the tears broke through anyway, pouring down her cheeks. "No, Madam. I'll be fine. Thank you. Dimitri has just come home from the hospital. You go to your boy, and I'll go to mine."

Van Rensburg stood nearby, shifting his weight from one foot to the other, head bowed the whole time. "I can take Grace to the jail and I'll bring her back," he said.

"Thank you, Madam. Thank you, Captain. I'll be ready in five minutes."

—

After they left, Sofia returned to her study and sat down again, unable to move. She kept hearing Grace's words in her head. *This is a second chance. Like we used to give the boys when they were little.* Suddenly, she recognized what she'd seen in Grace's eyes: hope. A tiny glimmer, but she'd seen it. It was the spark that kept Grace standing all those years under apartheid, and the same spark that had kept her going in the hospital, waiting to see if Dimitri would make it.

She pulled out the photograph in her pocket and stared at the faces of the two boys again. So young and innocent back then. She knew she'd done the right thing. *And yet.* Why did she feel so awful?

She picked up the phone and dialed a number. There was only one person who could answer this. "Theo, you'll never guess what happened." She told him about Van Rensburg's visit.

"This is good," he said.

"So why do I feel so bad?"

"It's normal. Isaac did a terrible thing. Deep down you want to punish him," he said.

"Yes, but I don't want his mother to be punished. I think I did it more for her. I don't know if I can forgive him," she said.

"Let me ask you this," he said. "Have you forgiven your mother? For what she did to us?"

For a moment, he caught her off guard. *Why was he going off topic?* After a long pause, she said, "Yes."

"Good," he said. "That's how forgiveness works. It's not automatic. It takes time. If the goodwill is there, after a while, the bad memories pack their bags and leave. Once you forget those, you wake up one day and all that's left is a small scar. That's when you have forgiveness."

"I hope so," she said.

After she hung up, she sat there for a long time, thinking about Theo's words. He was a good priest.

When Nick came home, he found her still sitting in the study and kissed her forehead. "What did you decide?" he said.

"I sent Grace with Van Rensburg to the jail. She's going to persuade him to turn state witness."

"I thought that's what you'd decide," he said.

"I'm surprised you didn't make the decision for me."

"I'm not sure what I would have done," he said. "I'm not the one who was almost strangled. But I know how much you care about her."

"They nearly killed our son," she said, and for the first time since the robbery, she began to cry for what might have happened.

"That's why the five must go to jail," he said. "You did the right thing. As for the sixth one, he gets one more chance—and hopefully, it will work out."

"I can't believe I'm still standing after everything that's happened."

"That's because you're a tough lady," he said. "Come here."

He held her for a long time, and when she finally stopped crying and looked at him, she noticed how his hair had thinned at the temples. She reached out and smoothed a stray hair, thinking that she had been married to this man for a long time.

He stroked her hair and said, "No more tears. All the bad things are over. Now you have another wedding to plan. Hopefully this one will happen."

"This time it's Elmarie's turn," she said. "I'm too worn down to plan a wedding and I'm thrilled that someone else will do it."

"Agreed," he said. "It's been a rough ride."

"It all began with Alex's funeral," she said. "Thank God we're ending with a wedding." She rested her head on his shoulder and thought life had a strange way of turning people's plans upside down.

NINETEEN

A Second Chance

Grace

By the time Grace arrived at John Vorster Square with Captain van Rensburg, she was a nervous wreck. Her fingers trembled as she opened the car door. The man had tried to make conversation during the car ride, but she just couldn't. Whatever he said barely registered. Her mind spun in circles as one thought collided with the next. The possibility that Isaac might get a second chance. The odds that he might refuse to listen. And if he did cooperate, what if the immunity thing didn't work. She was dizzy with fear and hope.

As she walked next to Van Rensburg through a maze of corridors, the security guards eyed her curiously, and she felt herself shaking under their scrutiny. She was with the captain and they couldn't do anything to her. But Isaac. What about him? He had been in detention for as long as Dimitri had been in the hospital. Almost a month now. Anything could have happened to him during this time.

As her mind raced with a hundred what-ifs, she lost her footing and stumbled on the smooth linoleum floor. Van

Rensburg caught her by the elbow just in time. He kept his hand on her arm till they reached the end of a dimly lit corridor.

"Wait here, Mrs. Molepe," he said, guiding her into a small room. "I'll get one of the officers to bring Isaac to the consultation room. It shouldn't take long. Can I get you some water or a Coke?"

"No, thank you, I'm fine." But as he turned to leave, she called out after him. "Captain, what if... what if he identifies the others but still ends up being sentenced and jailed with them? And then what if...." She couldn't say the words. *What if they kill him in jail?*

"I won't let that happen," he said, not allowing her to finish.

"Okay." What else could she say? She sat down heavily on one of the four plastic chairs tucked around a rickety square table. She tried to remember what Van Rensburg had said about immunity and wished she'd listened better. If it failed, Isaac's life would be over. And so would hers. She had already believed their life was over the day she had reported him at the police station. But now she could see a tiny ray of light. She then remembered Father Theo. The way he looked when he prayed. If this worked out, she would also pray to the invisible God.

She looked around. Van Rensburg had called the space a consultation room. Sofia's broom closet was bigger than this. And the walls. There was a strange smell that clung to the walls. Like the smell of disinfectant, or something worse. She hated the place, and this wasn't even where they kept the prisoners. As she waited, the room seemed to grow smaller by the minute. Beads of perspiration trickled down the sides of her face, and she took some tissues from her purse. Stop panicking, she told herself. But how terrible to be locked up in a prison cell, day in, day out, month after month, year after year.

When Van Rensburg knocked and walked in, she jumped up, startled, and the plastic chair toppled over.

"He's on his way," he said.

She picked up the chair and remained standing. A few minutes later, another knock. A police officer escorted Isaac into the room. She stared at her child, handcuffed at the wrists, shackled at the feet. He wore a wrinkled gray jumpsuit and could barely look her in the eye. She searched his face for cuts or bruises. On the outside, he looked okay. But she could see his shame in the slump of his shoulders and in the way he avoided her eyes. My boy. My poor boy.

Van Rensburg motioned to the officer to unlock the chains and wait outside. As Isaac slid his wrists out of the cuffs, he flexed his fingers several times. She noticed how the veins on his hands bulged and forked in different directions. So many little pathways.

"I'll leave you for a few minutes, and then I'll be back so we can talk," Van Rensburg said, and left the room.

"Mom..." Isaac said. "You shouldn't have come here."

"You're my son. If I don't come, then who will? Tell me what happened that night after I left you at the taxi rank?"

He closed his eyes briefly, then opened them and stared at the floor as he spoke. "The taxi didn't come. So I went back to my friends' house. They saw I had money on me. They said we should get more money from the Levantis family."

She knew she should have waited with him that night. His words landed like a blow, not for their truth but because of her guilt in leaving him alone.

"I didn't think they would try to kill anyone. I'm so sorry. I never thought it would end up the way it did." His voice cracked as he said this, dropping to a whisper, and a tear slid down his cheek.

"You didn't think, that's for sure." She tried to hold herself together, clenching her hands in her lap.

For a while they sat in silence. He hadn't even asked about Dimitri. She sighed and said, "Dimitri came home from the hospital today."

He flinched at the sound of Dimitri's name.

"Is he okay? I was afraid to ask. I deserve to rot in this place."

"He'll be okay. *Your friends* deserve to rot in this place. Has Captain van Rensburg told you about the problem? He can't put them away unless you identify them."

"Yes, but if I turn on them, they will come after me in jail."

"No, they won't. The way I understand immunity is that in return for your testimony, you will not get jail time. Maybe you will get a suspended sentence. They won't be able to get near you."

For a moment, she saw a flicker of hope in his eyes, but then he shook his head again. "I don't deserve a break. I've done a terrible thing."

"You're right. You don't deserve a break. But I do. Your mother deserves a break. I've sacrificed my whole life for you. If you won't do this for yourself, then do it for me."

He looked at her as she said this, his eyes full of regret, and then he looked down and traced his fingers over the cracks in the battered old table. Just then, Van Rensburg walked back into the room.

He broke the heavy silence by pulling up a chair. "We need to talk," he declared. His tall frame seemed even larger in the cramped space.

"Look at me, Isaac," Van Rensburg said. "And listen carefully. If I get you this plea deal with the prosecutor in return for your testimony, then you will not go to jail."

"But the others will know I'm the one who betrayed them."

"You will identify them in a closed setting. *You* will be able to see them in a lineup. They will not be able to see you. Maybe they'll realize it's you. Maybe they won't. You will sign an affidavit confirming who they are, but the document will remain sealed until a judge reviews it."

"So, I'll remain in jail till the judge reviews it?"

"I'm going to ask the prosecutor to expedite the process. My hope is that you will be released conditionally as soon as you identify your co-defendants, and even before the expedited review process."

Isaac gasped. She wanted to reach out to him, but she remained seated and watched him wringing his hands.

"What are you afraid of?" she said, losing patience. "You have nothing left to lose."

"I'm getting a second chance, but maybe it's wasted. I've messed up everything anyway. My degree. I blew it up. All those years of studying. Gone."

"Maybe not," Van Rensburg interrupted. "Given that your status is considered low risk, the high value of your testimony, and the fact that you are cooperating with law enforcement, the university might be willing to work with you and a local police station near the University of Fort Hare."

"You mean I could take classes again?" Isaac sat on the edge of his chair, disbelief in his voice. She had never seen him so animated about the thought of going back to university. She leaned forward. Please, God, help him understand this is his very last chance.

"It's possible," Van Rensburg said. "You'll have regular check-ins at the police station once or twice a week. Maybe there will be some restrictions on a few activities, but I don't see why they would prevent you from attending classes. We will do whatever we can to help you in return for your testimony."

She was also stunned. She had walked into this place with little hope, and now Van Rensburg was offering more than just an opportunity to get him out of jail. Could she dare to dream again? She looked at Isaac perched awkwardly on the small plastic chair and dared to dream once more. She let herself imagine a different ending. She saw him wearing a graduation cap and gown, holding a diploma in his hand.

"Isaac, you *must* do this," she said. "I will move there with you. I have money saved, and we can rent a small flat near the campus. I'll stay with you until you get your degree."

"Good," Van Rensburg said. "It's decided then. I'll take your mother home now, and I'll get moving with all the arrangements to get you out of here as soon as possible."

"Thank you, sir," he whispered in a shocked voice. He could barely get the words out of his mouth.

She stood up, wanting to hold him, but he pulled back. "Better not," he said. "I don't know what I might have picked up in this place."

She dug into her bag and pulled out a foil-wrapped sandwich she'd brought just in case. She turned to Van Rensburg. "May I give this to him?"

"Yes, but he had better eat it now," Van Rensburg said. "When the officer comes, he'll handcuff him again."

She handed him the double-layered beef, tomato, and cucumber sandwich, and he wolfed it down. For a moment he looked like a child again, the boy who had sat at the kitchen table with Dimitri, gobbling up whatever food she placed in front of them. When the other officer came back and shackled him, she stood with her back against the wall. She watched Isaac shuffle out of the room. At the doorway, he turned to look at her once more. His eyes brimmed with tears, and he blinked hard. He couldn't wipe the tears, not with shackled hands. He blinked some more and she wondered if the pain in her chest might cause her heart to break in half.

"Don't worry," Van Rensburg said. "We'll get him out of here."

They left as soon as Isaac left. This time, as Van Rensburg navigated her out of the building, she didn't trip over her feet and she ignored the security guards. She was no longer afraid of them. Soon, she would have her son out of this place.

When they got into Van Rensburg's police car, she said, "I don't know how to thank you, but I'm very grateful for what you are doing for Isaac."

He nodded and stared straight ahead. They drove in silence, and after a while she said, "Sir, why are you doing all this?"

He kept his eyes on the road. "Because I have the greatest respect for you. And because your son needs help. He's not a bad person. He got mixed up with the wrong crowd. And because those bastards must go to jail before they hurt anyone else."

He could have turned a blind eye, she thought. Instead, he chose to go out of his way to fix the mess. She tried to hold herself together, but loud wracking sobs welled up from somewhere deep inside her. Tears poured down her cheeks, and she could not stop crying. He pulled out a white handkerchief and offered it to her. This time, she took it.

TWENTY

The Dance of Isaiah

Sofia

Sofia stood on the steps of the church and looked into the distance. The city built on a reef of gold seemed small and vulnerable, like a miniature model of itself. Clouds raced across the heavens. A summer thunderstorm was on its way.

Her gaze moved past the skyline and past the trees to the courtyard filling with wedding guests. Screeches of laughter and giggles bounced across the square as huge droplets of water began to hit the ground. Everyone ran for cover beneath the church portico. The Afrikaans ladies wore colorful, flowery designs while the Greek ladies had chosen more subtle monochromatic colors. All around, Afrikaans and Greek words bypassed each other, not quite touching, while English and laughter served as the common exchange. Only one person was missing from the joyful crowd.

If only Grace could have been here, Sofia thought. Grace said she would do her best to attend but had made no promises. With Isaac attending classes and checking in twice a week at a local police station, Grace was nervous about leaving him alone in the Eastern Cape. Sofia understood Grace's anxiety but missed her so much. If the circumstances had been reversed, she knew she would have felt the same as Grace.

"Do you think it'll work?" Nick said, interrupting her thoughts. When she looked at him blankly, he said, "I'm talking about seating the Afrikaners and the Greeks together rather than at separate tables?"

Sofia smiled at Nick's nerves. Normally, she was the one who worried about the details, but this time she was carefree, and it was a wonderful feeling. It had been Elmarie's suggestion to combine the guests, and Sofia loved the idea. "Go for it," she said, encouraging Elmarie. "Once they're stuck with each other, they'll have to make it work."

As the skies broke open and the rain came down in gusts and blasts, the courtyard bubbled up in pools of water. Elmarie paced up and down talking to herself, "*Ag nee*. Oh no. This is terrible. The white dress and the rain. How is this going to work?"

"Don't worry," Theo said, resplendent in royal red vestments. "It's a blessing when it rains on a wedding. It's a sign that God is showering blessings on the couple."

After everything the couple had endured, they deserved all of God's blessings, Sofia thought. Only time would tell if Dimitri had made the right decision to postpone his emigration plans. He seemed happy, and that was all she cared about for now. She watched him huddle under the portico with his friends, cracking jokes and roaring with laughter, not a trace of the trauma he'd suffered. He caught her eye and gave her a thumbs-up. "Don't worry, Mom. *This* bride will arrive."

"He looks so happy." Nick squeezed her hand and echoed her thoughts.

Then he motioned toward the crowd. "Look who's here," he said. "This should set tongues wagging."

She followed his gaze and the murmur of the crowd as another guest ran up the steps, shaking water from a sodden umbrella.

Peter, her brave boy. Her other favorite boy.

"He's greeting Natalie quite fondly," Nick said, nudging her in the ribs, barely able to contain his excitement.

"Don't get your hopes up. She won't change her mind," Sofia said. Natalie placed two sisterly pecks on Peter's cheeks, one on each side.

"Never say never," Nick insisted.

She ignored his wishful thinking as she caught sight of Penny Apostolou marching up the steps holding a raincoat over a stiffly teased head of curls. In a moment of weakness, Sofia had invited her to the wedding. She now feared she would regret it. She's not over wanting Dimitri for her niece, Sofia realized, as Penny stood in front of her with a smug smile.

"To think we're losing a *leventi*, a good-looking boy, like Dimitri to an Afrikaans girl. Who would've believed it, Sofia? Nobody made more effort than you and Nick to keep the children Greek in a foreign country. And yet here we are. He's marrying a *xeni*."

"True love knows no boundaries," she said. "And you should hear Annelize speak Greek. Better than some of our Greek girls."

Penny looked astonished but offered Sofia her obviously insincere congratulations and walked away. Sofia took a deep breath and looked up at the mosaic icon embedded above the doorframe. The Christ of Sinai, with two deliberately different eyes, looked down at her. The stern eye of judgment and the loving eye of compassion. She focused on Christ's loving eye.

When the dark clouds rolled away as quickly as they'd appeared, the bridal entourage pulled up to the church entrance. All eyes turned to the white Mercedes. There was a unanimous gasp as Annelize unfolded her long, slim body from the leather seat of her father's car. A hum of compliments and comments erupted into the air. The strapless silk gown stunned in its simplicity and emphasized her tall frame. The white set off Annelize's golden tan to perfection, and her fine blonde hair was pulled back, half up, half down, with feathery wisps framing her high cheekbones.

"Mom, look at her neck," Natalie whispered. "She's wearing the diamond cross I gave her when we baptized her into the Orthodox faith." Natalie's gift, as the godmother, was the only accessory the bride wore.

"It's beautiful," Sofia said. But it was the bride's face, glowing with happiness, that crowned her beauty and had the Greeks whispering: her looks were the reason he had fallen for her. Sofia smiled as she caught snippets of speculation. She knew there was more to Annelize than met the eye.

As Andre led his daughter up the steps of the church, Dimitri gazed at Annelize with a smile that said he couldn't quite believe his luck. Annelize walked towards him as if the whole world had shrunk and disappeared, leaving only Dimitri and her in the church courtyard. The sun had broken through the remaining clouds and light slanted through the leaves of the trees, dancing on their cheeks. Sofia was close to tears.

Natalie squeezed her hand. "This is what I want, Mom. The real thing."

Sofia hugged her tightly and wanted that for her too.

"Well, you can hold out for that one great love, Natalie, but it doesn't happen to everyone. Remember, *before* you pick *the* one, make sure your eyes are wide open; *after* you're married, make sure to keep your eyes closed."

"Especially if you end up with someone like your father," Nick said.

Natalie laughed and they all took their places in the bridal procession behind Dimitri and Annelize. Theo beamed from ear to ear as he led them down the aisle toward the altar.

Everyone settled into the pews. A movement from the chanter's stand caught Sofia's eye. Michalis was standing there, not in his usual black attire, but once more in a freshly ironed, white shirt. He tilted his chin upwards and brushed a finger against his nose in an upward direction. Sofia followed his gaze. And there she was. She had come after all! Grace sat quietly in the overhanging choir balcony. *Thank. You. My. Friend.* Sofia mouthed these words. Grace smiled down at her.

"Grace is here," she whispered to Nick.

"I told you she'd come," he said.

"Thank you, Michalis," Sofia said. He stood in front of her, motioning wildly to the front pews then back up to the balcony. "I get it," Sofia said. He had told Grace to sit downstairs with the family, but she had chosen to sit upstairs. "That's okay," she said, patting his shoulder. Michaelis seemed appeased and scurried back to the chanter's stand, where he stood a little behind it. Always in the back, never in the front, Sofia thought, smiling at him.

She thought about all the people gathered beneath the sky-blue cupola of the church: Greeks and Afrikaners, Grace and Michalis, Natalie and Peter, Dimitri and Annelize, herself and Nick, Theo, all so different, and yet the same, with heartaches and troubles, fears and joys; each one struggling with their own cross, and then, in the blink of an eye, it was all over with only a few flashes of joy scattered here and there like the unpredictable summer rains.

Thank you, God, that we're here altogether in your church. She crossed herself and focused on the joy before her eyes as Theo began the ceremony with the joining of the hands and the blessing of the rings. Soon, they reached the highlight, and Dimitri's best man stepped behind the bridal couple, crossed his arms awkwardly, and switched the crowns joined by a ribbon, from one head to the other. Three times, over and back, in the name of the Father, the Son, and the Holy Spirit, he moved the crowns above the heads of the bride and groom. Somehow he managed not to tangle his sleeves and the ribbon too much. Natalie repeated the same ritual with more finesse.

Before long, they reached Sofia's favorite part: the Dance of Isaiah. Theo took the joined right hands of Dimitri and Annelize in his hand and led them three times around the table. Their first steps as man and wife, but in her mind's eye, Sofia saw Dimitri as a baby, taking his first steps into her waiting arms, and then six months ago, his first steps on crutches, walking toward Annelize.

With each completed circle, the photographer's camera clicked and the flash lit up the gold cross at the center of the table. The chanter's voice, a deep baritone, filled the church and her heart with the ancient words: "O Isaiah, dance your joy, for the Virgin was indeed with child; and brought to birth a Son, the Emmanuel, Who came as both God and man." Her heart overflowed with an indescribable joy. Whatever had been ripped from her heart long ago, on a hot summer evening in Cyprus, clicked back into place, filling the emptiness of that hole. Suddenly, she understood Isaiah's joy when the old prophet had foreseen that the Virgin would have a child, and the child would be Christ. The old prophet had known that Christ and the resurrection would overcome all the struggles of life. Isaiah's joy stretched across space and time and touched her, lifting her in that moment with the hymn's ancient words. She took it all in: Dimitri and Annelize laughing as they circled the table; Theo leading them; Natalie walking behind them, holding the white ribbon that joined the wedding crowns. "Dance, Isaiah, dance," she sang quietly to herself.

And then it was over. Nick squeezed her hand as Theo explained some of the rituals for the benefit of those unfamiliar with the customs and traditions.

"The crowns are the highlight of today's sacrament," Theo said. "Dimitri and Annelize were crowned with glory as the king and queen of their new home, but these crowns also remind us, and them, of the crowns of martyrdom for the sacrifices they will make for one another in their marriage."

"Like the sacrifices I make for you," Nick teased.

"And me for you," she said, not letting him get away with that.

Then Theo lifted the white ribbon joining the crowns. "This ribbon symbolizes not only their union as man and wife," he said. "But also the presence of Christ in their marriage. There are three in this marriage: Dimitri, Annelize, and Christ. The priest represents Christ as he leads them around the table. Whatever happens in their life together, Christ is with them through this holy sacrament of marriage."

She looked at Nick. By the grace of God, their marriage had survived all the cracks.

"The joy that the Church feels today is a double joy," Theo continued. "It's about the union of Dimitri and Annelize to each other, and it's also about their union with God. Just as a priest at his ordination is set apart to live a life in Christ, so this couple is set apart from the world by this holy sacrament to live a life in Christ together, and that's why we chant the same hymn, the beautiful Dance of Isaiah, at both weddings and ordinations." As he explained all this, she heard the exuberance and passion in his quickened voice. His enthusiasm rang through the words like a church bell pealing, and she remembered her mother's voice from long ago: "This man belongs to God."

"Did you know all that?" Nick said. "About the Dance of Isaiah being chanted at ordinations as well as weddings?"

"Now I do," she said, "It makes perfect sense."

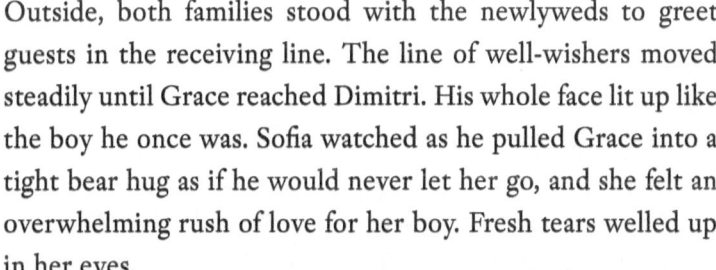

Outside, both families stood with the newlyweds to greet guests in the receiving line. The line of well-wishers moved steadily until Grace reached Dimitri. His whole face lit up like the boy he once was. Sofia watched as he pulled Grace into a tight bear hug as if he would never let her go, and she felt an overwhelming rush of love for her boy. Fresh tears welled up in her eyes.

"You're here," she said, as they clasped hands when Grace reached her. Grace's smile trembled, and a soft laugh escaped through her tears.

Grace shook her head in wonder, eyes bright with everything they didn't need to say. So many things had happened but nothing had changed between them.

"I told you I would try," Grace said. "I'm very happy for Dimitri."

"And Isaac? How is he?"

"The dean said he will pass with honors. Can you believe that? He will graduate this year for sure."

"Thank God," Sofia said.

"Yes, thank God," Grace said. "I lit a candle inside."

"We'll see you at the reception," Nick said, and gave Grace a hug. "You have made my wife's day."

When she and Nick headed to the car where the driver was waiting to take them to the reception, Sofia could still feel herself smiling. She and Grace had been through so much together. She wished she could stretch out the hours a little more. Everything was passing too quickly. That was the thing about joy-filled hours. They would not slow down.

As they were about to step into the car, the sound of running footsteps made them turn. Peter caught up with them, a little breathless. She stared at the young man standing in front of her, the one who had almost become her son-in-law. There was no hint of bitterness in his expression, but she could sense his loneliness, and her heart ached for the pain he had suffered.

"I wanted to congratulate you for Dimitri and Annelize. I'm so happy for them. Unfortunately, I can't make it to the reception." With an awkward smile, he pointed to a beeper jutting above his belt by way of explanation. But she knew it had nothing to do with being on call.

She hugged him tightly. "Thank you for coming, Peter. You're like my other son. I wish for you the same happiness as Dimitri one day."

"My boy, if it weren't for you, we might not even be standing here today," Nick said. Nick hugged him for a long time until Peter said he had to leave.

They sank into the back seat of the car and the driver pulled out of the parking bay. She could sense that Nick was a little deflated by Peter's appearance and the memories of what could have been.

"Man plans and God decides," she said. She took his hand and rested it on her knee.

―――

At the reception hall, the main table was slightly elevated, and she scanned her eyes across a sea of faces and tall white centerpieces. Laughter and joyful conversations filled the space. Elmarie's plan had worked well. None of the guests seemed to be experiencing communication problems.

By the time the speeches were over, and the band had begun strumming their instruments, she was tapping her feet under the table.

"Sofia, I have a surprise," Elmarie said. "When the dancing begins, instead of the bride and groom opening with a waltz, we're going to open up as a family with a Greek *kalamatiano* dance. *Oli mazi*, all of us together! Won't that be nice? Annelize and Dimitri will lead the circle, followed by you, Nick, and Natalie. Andre and I have been practicing."

"That's a wonderful idea," Sofia said. "Very traditional for a Greek wedding."

The familiar notes of the *kalamatiano* filtered through the banquet hall and the master of ceremonies announced that the two families would open up the dancing. She paused at the edge of the dance floor, soaking up the picture of Dimitri leading, healthy and full of life, clutching the hand of his wife, while Natalie danced next to them, gazing at her big brother with adoring eyes, and Nick smiling from ear to ear with an Afrikaans in-law on either side. But it was the two in-laws, Andre and Elmarie, who stole the show. They had picked up the rhythm of the Greek music as if they had been born

Greek. This was as close to paradise as she was ever going to be while still on earth, she thought, and tried to sear the image into her mind. Surely, it didn't get much better than this. Even Professor Kingsley joined the end of the circle with an enthusiasm that suggested he carried Greek genes.

A small movement from the sidelines caught her eye. Grace was standing in the shadows, also clapping her hands to the beat of the music. And again, Sofia's heart exploded with happiness. There were so many ways their path together could have ended. And yet, they had been spared.

"Why are you waiting, Sofia? Go dance before the song is over." Theo came up to her and gave her a gentle nudge. For a split second, a night from long ago flashed in front of her, when she had left the circle of a dance to follow him. He touched the cross at his chest and smiled at her.

"Mom, come on! You promised you'd dance at my wedding. Come lead us," Dimitri insisted, waving a white handkerchief at her. A second wind came over her.

She'd promised Dimitri she would dance on the table at his wedding. He would have to settle for her dancing up a storm on the dance floor. She lifted her long skirt and nudged off her heels. As the sound of the music pulsed through her, she grabbed Dimitri's handkerchief and led the way.

Nick beamed with pride as he spotted her bare feet and smiling face. The music transported her back to another time when she was young and free and innocent, moving to the rhythm of the island songs. On this night bursting with joy and second chances, being Greek felt large enough to embrace everyone.

When Nick spotted Grace and dragged her onto the dance floor and into the circle, Sofia's happiness was complete. She twirled across the floor and pulled Grace to the front.

They held hands and led. Three steps forward and one back. Together, they could do this.

Epilogue

Johannesburg, April 1994

On the eve of the elections, with the country's freedom a breath away, Grace was in a pensive mood inside the two-bedroom house she and Isaac had bought in Soweto. She stood in the small kitchen and gave the pot an absentminded stir before turning off the stove.

There was still time, she decided, and picked up the phone. She dialed Sofia's number.

"Madam, do you want me to pick you up tomorrow so we can drive together to the polling station?"

"I'd love that Grace. The family is going later in the day, but you know me. I'd rather go early."

They agreed to meet at eight o'clock, and Grace was glad she'd called. She missed Sofia all the time. They had been through so much together. She sat down to rest while she waited for Isaac. Now that he had his own office, he often worked till late at night. And for the hundredth time, she admired the two degrees and the attorney's certificate of admission lining the wall behind the sofa. She never tired of looking at these three pieces of paper.

"These are yours," he told her on the day he nailed the framed certificates to the wall. He kept the originals at the house and the copies at the office. "You earned them. No other mother would have done what you did."

She didn't think renting a room near the university campus for that last year was such a big a deal. In her mind, there had been no other alternative. He had tackled his studies the way he should have done in the first place. But the degree was now on the wall and that was all that mattered.

She turned on the small electric heater. Immediately, the heat warmed the whole house. She was still in a small space with four walls, but she had her books. And she admired the growing collection on the new bookshelf. The only item she'd splurged on was a larger bookshelf. That was the good thing about not working. She had more time to read.

When she heard the outside gate open and clap shut, she got up and began to lay the silverware on the small kitchen table. When Isaac walked in, she said, "I need a favor."

"For you, anything." He smiled, and she admired the width of his shoulders and the life in his muscular body.

"I need you to fetch my car from the neighbor's garage down the road, and bring it here first thing in the morning. I'm going to pick up Mrs. Sofia and we're going to vote together."

"Ahh, you want to show off your car and your driver's license. Sure, I'll get it for you. So you're abandoning me for Mrs. Sofia?"

"No, I just know that you'll be busy assisting officials to set up at the polling booths, and you'll forget about me. Besides, I want to vote with my Madam."

"You mean your *friend*," he gently scolded her.

"Yes, my friend," she said.

"I'm teasing you," he said.

She smiled. For some strange reason, the word *madam* always slipped from her lips without her even realizing it. But in her heart, Sofia was always Sofia, never mind what her lips said. She couldn't wait to show her that Isaac had finally matured into a responsible young man who had bought his mother a car. Their efforts and sacrifices had not been in vain after all.

"Listen," she said, cupping a hand over her ear as a chain of firecrackers exploded somewhere in the distance. "The celebrations have begun early." They both hurried to the window and peered into the night. The roofs of houses shone as remnants of flashes flew across the skies. One grand finale lit up the darkness with ribbons of fading silver sparks, and then it was over.

When they sat down to eat, she reminded him that it was time to start looking for a suitable wife.

"You sound like Mrs. Sofia now," he said.

"All mothers sound the same," she said, but she was glad that he had not objected to her suggestion.

After she cleaned up and Isaac sat down to work again, she went to bed and lay awake for hours, too excited to sleep. The long-awaited day of freedom was only a few hours away and she could barely contain the idea in her head. She thought of her father and how proud he'd be that she had managed, against all odds, to bring his grandson to this point. From her small bedroom window, she still caught glimpses of silver sparkles lighting up the sky every now and then.

She barely slept and got up early to wash and dress. Then she sat by the window in a daze, watching the pale rays of the sun christen the city in a new day. Slowly, lights flickered on inside other homes. She made herself a cup of tea and for the twentieth time rummaged in her bag. It would be embarrassing if she forgot something. Yes, her identity document and driver's license were in the middle pocket where she'd placed everything the previous evening.

When it was time to leave for Sofia's house, she climbed into the driver's seat of her car, which Isaac had dutifully parked outside. She stared at the empty ignition switch. The key. Where had she left it? Before she could think, Isaac knocked on the car window. He stood smiling, with the key dangling in one hand. In the other hand, he held a large envelope.

"Please, will you give this envelope to Mrs. Sofia?" he asked.

"What is it?"

"The university's graduation brochure with my picture in it."

"Good idea. She'll appreciate it." She took the key and the envelope and set off. As she gazed through the windshield, the sky was an uneven blue, bright in some spots and hazy in others.

~

"Grace, is that you?" Johannes ran up to her car as she pulled into Sofia's driveway.

"Yes, Isaac bought this for me," she beamed.

He gave a long, low whistle. "A Toyota is a very reliable car," he said, walking all the way around the car. He checked it out from top to bottom.

"When are you going to vote? Do you need a ride?" she said.

"No, I'm fine, thank you. Freddy has gone ahead. I'll drive later with Master Nick."

"You're afraid to drive with me," she said, and accelerated over the gate railing, making the gravel scatter.

When she pulled up to the circular driveway at the front of the house, Sofia was already halfway down the steps, clickety-clacking across the pavement in high heels. Grace rolled her eyes as she climbed out the car and watched her beautiful former boss. Those shoes. Some things never change. Did Sofia not realize they would be standing in long lines for hours?

"Grace, look at you! Getting a driver's license at your age! I'm so proud of you," Sofia said, beaming. "And this car, it's beautiful. I love the bright yellow color. It suits you."

"Isaac bought it for me."

"I'm proud of him, too," she said, and hugged her tightly before they jumped back into the car. From the corner of her eye, Grace could see Sofia buckling her seatbelt in the passenger seat. "How long have you had your license?" Sofia asked, pulling the strap a little tighter.

Grace tried not to laugh. "Madam, relax, I promise I'm a better driver than you. I don't drive nearly as fast as you do. And we're just going to be in the suburbs anyway. No highways for us."

She drove slowly, and Sofia suggested they might want to move a little faster, but Grace ignored her. She was in the driver's seat now.

The polling booths were less than ten minutes away and they chatted about the children. Sofia bemoaned the fact that as yet there were no grandchildren on the way, and that Natalie was not seriously dating anyone. "But at least she hasn't moved to America," Sofia said. "I still have them all here, and for that, I'm grateful."

Grace told her about Isaac's work progress and Sofia said, "I'm so happy for you both. But I miss you, Grace. If you ever want to come back, you know I'd love to have you. You don't even have to work. Your room will always be there for you."

"Don't be surprised if I call you one day," Grace said, and pulled into an empty parking space near the front of the polling station. "If Isaac gets married one day, I won't stay with him and his wife in the same house."

"Agreed," Sofia said. "You'll come back and live with me. Grace, you just parallel parked so perfectly! You're a better driver than I am."

Grace laughed and handed her the envelope.

"What's this?"

"It's for you from Isacc."

Sofia opened it and Grace saw a purple bookmark jutting from the pages. Sofia opened the brochure to the marked page. Isaac's face beamed up at her. Capped and gowned, he clutched the hard-earned diploma. She read aloud the inscription beneath his picture: *I'm forever grateful for the love and support of two extraordinary women, my mother, Grace Molepe, and her friend, Sofia Levantis.*

Sofia was quiet for a few seconds. Grace could tell that she was swallowing back a few tears. "Grace, please tell him thank you for this. I'm so proud of him. Let's go vote before we start crying."

Half laughing, half crying, they got out of the car. The path leading to the voting hall was lined with voters, and they stopped for a moment to take it all in. There were so many different people. From the wealthy northern and southern suburbs, from the townships and the informal settlements, they had all come to stand together in long lines: the elderly with canes and walkers, the young in gym clothes, maids and nannies in uniforms, gardeners in dirt-covered overalls, and painters in paint-splattered shirts. All around them people chatted and talked, swapping stories while teenagers from the townships offered Coca-Cola and water to the voters.

"Can you believe this, Madam? So many times I imagined this scene in my mind."

"It's a miracle," Sofia said, shaking her head with tears in her eyes.

Slowly they moved forward. Even with the holiday-like atmosphere, police guards with guns holstered to their belts roamed up and down, alert and serious, their eyes darting left and right.

"Are these the lines to vote?" Grace asked one of them, but he barely glanced at her and didn't answer. She stiffened her shoulders and ignored him back, a little offended. They went ahead and stood with the others. After an hour, they reached the front of the lines, much quicker than she had expected. Sofia took one booth and she took another.

Trembling, Grace unfolded her ballot paper, suddenly afraid of making a mistake. She looked for Mandela's face and found him easily. It seemed as if all the sorrow of Africa was furrowed into the deep lines on his face. Everyone carried the scars of political failures, but some had bled more than others. She picked her president and placed the ballot paper carefully into the box.

As she emerged from the booth, an official pointed her to the exit. It was a different door from the one she'd entered. A little disoriented and giddy from excitement, she stepped outside. The same policeman who had ignored her earlier beamed at her now, as if she had suddenly transformed. She stopped and stared at him. His friendliness confused her. Then it dawned on her. She had gone in as a Black person, and now she had come out as a member of the human race. She graciously returned his smile, pushed back her shoulders, and held her head higher.

As she waited for Sofia, she looked up and noticed the sky was crisp and blue everywhere, as far as the eye could see. When she spotted Sofia, she waved and called out, "Sofia, I'm over here."

For a moment, they stared at each other. She wasn't sure who was more surprised, her or Sofia. For the first time ever, she had called Sofia by her name. Sofia's smile stretched from ear to ear as she linked an arm through her friend's arm and pointed upwards. "Grace, look at the sky. It's so beautiful and clear now. Not a single cloud anywhere."

And from all their years together, Grace decided this was the moment she'd remember forever. Two mothers under an African sky.

Acknowledgments

Immigrants never forget their country of birth. As Odysseas Elytis wrote in *The Axion Esti*, "What I loved, I am still paying for. What I touched has left its mark on me." *Under an African Sky* is a tribute—to South Africa, the land of my birth; to immigrants who straddle continents and stretch their roots to a breaking point; and to those who feel like foreigners in their own countries.

After years of writing, revising, and remembering, this novel is finally born. While writing is a solitary act, publishing is a team effort. Many gifted, kind, and generous people have encouraged me along the way. This book would not exist without those who believed in the story and in me.

To my editors: Robin Smith, thank you for bringing enthusiasm to a manuscript in its rougher stages. Henriette Lazaridis, gifted editor, writer, and teacher, thank you for your editorial insight, encouragement, and ability to push a new writer toward deeper truth. Thank you also for your stamina. I'll always remember how you completed a final edit two nights before your wedding. Peter Selgin, writer and teacher extraordinaire, thank you for the sharp questions that helped me tighten those first pages. Paula Fitzgerald, my brilliant and eagle-eyed copy editor, thank you for your attention to detail, for catching what others missed and ensuring that every word landed just right. Your care went far beyond the page. And to David Aretha, thank you for teaching me that every novel needs a final pair of unforgiving eyes.

To Marianna King, the best tech consultant in the world, a miracle worker, and patient saint. Thank you for the remote rescue missions when you swooped in more than once to find lost chapters or tame unruly laptops with kindness, grace, and humor.

To Julia Glass, a teacher and author I've long admired. Thank you for the advice you gave me at the Yale Writers' Conference: "Perseverance matters more than talent." Your words stuck and kept me going.

To the communities of The Creativity Workshop of New York, the Yale Writers' Workshop, the Krouna Writing Workshop, and The Atlanta Writers Club—thank you for your wisdom, generosity, and shared love of the written word.

To Mel Berger, the legendary agent who gave his time to an unknown debut author. After all the rejections, one thing remained: The courage to carry on alone, fueled by the hope that if *you* had seen something in my work, then perhaps the others had simply missed it. Thank you for the effort.

To Chrysoula Argyros, the renowned Greek South African artist who said yes without a moment's hesitation for a book cover, and to Abe Mathabe, the gifted South African artist who collaborated with Chrysoula to capture the heart of the story for the stunning cover image. Your enthusiasm and commitment touched me deeply. And to the American graphic design team at AuthorImprints—thank you for honoring the spirit of the original South African artwork and ensuring that nothing was lost. To David Wogahn, founder of AuthorImprints, the quiet force behind it all—your commitment to writers allowed me to chase this dream. Thank you for the unwavering support.

To Jared and Julia Drake, I'm deeply grateful for your early enthusiasm, professionalism, and genuine care for this story. Your willingness to jump in wholeheartedly, even on weekends and vacations, speaks volumes, and I'm excited for all that lies ahead.

To Danielle Nix, thank you for your thoughtful feedback that made the story stronger. To Donald Templeman, fellow writer and friend, your insight and support means the world to me. To Johnnie Bernhard, fellow writer who saw the heart of the story before it had found its form, and whose encouragement over the years has stayed with me. To my early readers, Christine Sprouse and Andy and Maria Patterson, thank you for your enthusiasm that encouraged me during times of doubt. Also, thank you to Joan Swanepoel, an exceptional teacher who read the first story written by a seven-year-old girl in South Africa—and kept it safe for more than fifty years before returning it to the original owner in America. Thank you for your dedication to children and education. I hope you enjoy this story as much as that first one.

To all the lands that have shaped me—your presence lives in these pages. South Africa, thank you for showing the world what it means to reconcile, forgive, begin again, and imagine a future without division. Greece and Cyprus, my ancestral homes, whose long traditions of reflection, dialogue, and democracy have influenced the way I see the world. And America, thank you for opening your arms and giving my family and me the space to grow, work, and dream.

To my aunt, Alexandra Katrakilis, and my dear friend, Wendy Kraitzick, both gone from this world: Thank you for believing in this book before it even had a name. Your faith in me reaches across time and space.

To my sisters-in-law, Eva Catrakilis and Nikki Catrakilis-Wagner: Thank you for believing I'd finish this book even though I took so long!

To those who came before: my parents, Stylianos and Elpida Georgiou, and my in-laws, Nicolaos and Irini Catrakilis—immigrants who carried faith, hope, and tradition wherever they went. Your legacy lives on across continents. You now rest in your final homeland but remain forever in my heart. Memory eternal.

And finally, to the heart of it all: my children, Nicholas and Natasha. Thank you for being the joy of my life, my best chapters, and for never once wavering in your confidence that Mom would get the book done. Anna Maria, thank you for your quiet support of a mother-in-law who is always writing. And to my husband Harry, my steadfast champion and quiet strength, thank you for walking beside me, even when the road was long and the words came slowly. Your patience, humor, and belief in me made this possible.

And always, I thank God. My Orthodox faith is a constant anchor in a world that changes by the minute.

Book Club Questions

1. *Under an African Sky* tells the story of two women, Sofia and Grace, from alternating perspectives. In what ways are Sofia and Grace different from each other and in what ways are they alike? Did you identify with one more than the other, and if yes, why?
2. What wounds does each woman carry from her past? How do they each try to protect their children from mistakes they've made and challenges they've endured in their lives? Is this a good thing or a bad thing and is there such a thing as the perfect parent?
3. How does Sofia's emigration from Cyprus impact her life? She seems to identify with people who are outsiders in one way or another. Why do you think this is?
4. The Greek philosopher, Aristotle, identifies three levels of friendship: utility, pleasure, and virtue. Utility friendships are based on mutual benefit, pleasure friendships on shared enjoyment, and virtue friendships on a shared love of character and virtue. Which level of friendship applies to the relationship between Grace and Sofia?
5. What is Grace's greatest strength?

6. As a child growing up in a small village on the island of Cyprus, Sofia was aware of the dangers of gossip. How do you think this contributed to the formation of her character and her obsession to keep her children close?
7. The feelings that many immigrants experience, such as displacement and nostalgia, are recurrent themes in novels of the Greek diaspora and other immigrant stories. Why do people try to hold onto their roots, and if they don't succeed, does it matter?
8. Why is Grace obsessed with reading and learning? Is she correct in her belief that the only way to get inside another person's head is by reading their words?
9. In the story, both Grace and Sofia must deal with loyalty challenges within their family and also with respect to each other. What circumstances have shaped these characters and influenced the decisions they make?
10. What does Sofia finally understand when she listens to the Greek Orthodox hymn "The Dance of Isaiah" at her son's wedding?
11. What is the perfect homeland that everyone is seeking whether they realize it or not? Is it a physical place like the one Grace is hoping for in the new South Africa, or is it something more?
12. Why do Grace and her son, Isaac, feel like foreigners in their own country? Can parallels be drawn to other countries today?
13. South Africa manages to survive apartheid. In what ways does the story of South Africa provide hope for other countries suffering political upheaval?
14. Family loyalty and expectations affect many characters in this story. How do the children of both Sofia and Grace

wrestle with these pressures and do they make good choices?
15. Do you think faith and family play a role in influencing Sofia's decision to hold on to her marriage when her first love turns up, and if so, to what extent?
16. How does Father Theo's role as a calming presence during the storms of the story reveal deeper aspects of his character? Do you think the others rely on him out of respect for his role, or because of something more personal about who he is?

About the Author

Elene Catrakilis was born in South Africa to Greek-Cypriot parents. A former attorney turned writer, she now lives in Atlanta with her husband and is the mother of a son and a daughter. *Under an African Sky* is her debut novel. Her legal background and multicultural heritage continue to shape her understanding of human complexity and influence her work.

www.ingramcontent.com/pod-product-compliance
Lightning Source LLC
LaVergne TN
LVHW091712070526
838199LV00050B/2366